WRAP YOUR TROUBLES IN DREAMS

Corrigan Sisters - Book Three

JENNIFER LAMONT LEO

MOUNTAIN MAJESTY MEDIA

WRAP YOUR TROUBLES IN DREAMS

Published by Mountain Majesty Media, Inc.

PO Box 638, Cocolalla, Idaho 83813

ISBN: 978-1-7378741-6-4

Copyright © 2022 by Jennifer Lamont Leo

Cover design by Dee Dee Designs

For information on this book or author visit: www.jenniferlamontleo.com

This is a work of fiction. Names, characters, and incidents are all products of the author's imagination or are used for fictional purposes. Any mentioned brand names, places, and trademarks remain the property of their respective owners, bear no association with the author or the publisher, and are used for fictional purposes only.

Library of Congress Cataloging-in-Publication Data

Leo, Jennifer Lamont

Wrap Your Troubles in Dreams / Jennifer Lamont Leo 1st ed.

Printed in the United States of America

Books by Jennifer Lamont Leo

Corrigan Sisters
You're the Cream in My Coffee
Ain't Misbehavin'
Wrap Your Troubles in Dreams

Windy City Hearts
Moondrop Miracle
The Rose Keeper
Love's Grand, Sweet Song (coming 2023)

Novella Collections
Lumberjacks & Ladies
The Highlanders

Join Jennifer's Reader Community
https://JenniferLamontLeo.com

For all who work to uphold truth, beauty, and goodness in the media, and to shine a light in a dark world. The world needs more people like you.

"Having friends around for a pleasant evening is one of life's most cherished joys, as far as I am concerned. But when those with me are fellow believers, how much greater that joy is, for we know that it's rekindled, one day in eternity."
—Jimmy Stewart, 20th century movie actor

CHAPTER ONE

Kerryville, Illinois. July 1933

Helen Corrigan's lower lip trembled. With great drama she thrust forth her arm and gripped Nanette Johnson's hand. Hard.

"But you must help me. You're my only hope." Her voice quivered in anguish.

Nanette's elfin face contorted. "Your only hope?"

"Yes. There's no one else I can turn to."

Nanette blinked rapidly. "I'd do anything to help you."

Helen drew her friend's hand to her heart, jerking her closer. "You must tell no one. I'm going to marry Will!"

Nanette gasped and recoiled. "Marry! That rascal?"

"*Shh.*" Helen cast an anxious glance toward the door.

Nanette lowered her voice. "Don't your parents know?"

"No, Alice, and they mustn't find out. Not now. Not until Will and I are well on our way to Willa—I mean, Walla Walla—oh, shoot."

"Cut!"

At the director's sharp command, Helen bit back the rest of her impassioned plea and released Nanette's hand.

"Sorry." Her midsection contracted. Not only had she blown the line, but she'd displeased Chet Scarborough, the play's author and director and the one man whose opinion she most cared about. On multiple levels.

She lifted her arm—no easy task in her heavily corseted costume. Shading her eyes against the glare of the footlights, she squinted in the direction of his disembodied voice.

From the hollow darkness of the vacant auditorium, Chet barked, "Nanette, you're supposed to be excited and happy for your friend, not wincing as if you're in pain."

Nanette rubbed the offended appendage. "But I *am* in pain. She practically crushed my fingers. I've got a ring on, you know."

We all know. Helen bit back the snappish remark. Nanette's engagement to Ted Barber was recent enough that she talked virtually of nothing else whenever cast and crew took a break in rehearsal. Even so, Helen was happy for her friend, and if she were honest, more than a little envious. Nanette had landed her Prince Charming, while Helen didn't have the foggiest notion where she stood with hers. Chet's mercurial moods shifted between being warm and loving one minute, cool and detached the next, keeping Helen perpetually off balance.

At present her prince was experiencing a cool-and-detached moment, his creative-genius mind focused entirely on the production. As hers should be, she reminded herself, during the second-to-the-last dress rehearsal before opening night.

"Sorry about your hand," she murmured to Nanette. "I guess I got a little carried away."

"I'll say." Nanette caressed her beloved ring.

"All right, ladies." A note of weariness laced the director's deep baritone voice. "Let's go back a few lines. Perhaps we can do without all the stuttering this time, Helen."

Her face heated at his sarcastic remark. It wasn't *her* fault she'd stuttered. She hesitated a moment, then spoke into the darkness.

"I'm sorry, Chet. It's the line."

Beside her, Nanette inhaled sharply. Actors rarely contradicted the director, who in this case happened to be the playwright as well.

"The line?" Though she couldn't make out Chet's face in the dimness, Helen imagined his steely gray eyes fixed in her direction. She pressed on.

"Don't misunderstand. It's a good line, a necessary line, but it's difficult to say." Helen picked up a dog-eared script from a nearby table and flipped to a page. "'Will and I are well on our way to Walla Walla.' It's... it's awkward."

"Awkward." The ensuing silence was unnerving.

She took a step toward the footlights. "With all due respect, Chet, it sounds like a joke. Like the opening of a limerick or something. I don't believe it's something Susannah would say. Not in the middle of a serious scene like this one. Can't we rephrase it?"

His reply was firm. "We will not be rewriting the script at this point, Helen."

"I didn't say to rewrite the script," Helen protested. "Just this one line. That's all."

"That one line makes deliberate and effective use of alliteration." Chet's tone was crisp and professional. "It will remain as is."

Helen sealed her lips, reminding herself he was a renowned theatrical wizard. A genius, many said. Critically acclaimed. She was just an untrained actress from the sticks. And even if she were better qualified to argue her point, contradicting him was futile. *His way or the highway*, as Helen's brother, Charlie, would say.

It didn't make it any easier that she was in love with the man. Absolutely head-over-heels loony-tunes about him. She couldn't help herself. What girl could? In the eight weeks or so they'd been working on the play, she'd fallen under his spell.

And he was falling for her, too. She was sure of it. Oh, he hadn't said as much. Not in so many words. But his lingering glances, the way he brushed his fingers against her hair or her cheek and remarked on her beauty—those gestures told Helen everything she needed to know.

Even so, his remark stung. He needn't have snapped at her in front of everyone. She was only trying to help.

After a seemingly interminable pause, he spoke again. "You two wait there."

Helen and Nanette exchanged a glance.

"Where does he think we're going to go?" Nanette muttered under her breath.

Helen smiled in grim camaraderie. She rubbed her forehead as a headache formed at the edges of her skull. The Kerryville Players' production of *Under the Flaming Oak* was opening in less than forty-eight hours. Chet only wanted the play to be a smash hit, as they all did. They were all feeling wrung out, from the fastidious director on down to the high-school boys pasting flowery Victorian wallpaper onto the scenery flats.

She smoothed her hair as Chet's lean frame emerged from beyond the footlights, his long legs taking the stairs two at a time. In spite of her headache, she couldn't help but feel a thrill, thinking how much he reminded her of Gary Cooper. Tall and good-looking in a rugged sort of way. Even the faint lines visible around his eyes and mouth, the touch of silver in his dark hair, gave him a wise, authoritative look.

He strode across the stage and stood before her and Nanette. "The show opens this weekend," he said with strained patience. As if they needed reminding.

He reached out, grasped Helen's shoulders, and shifted her position. A thrill coursed through her at his gentle touch and Brylcreem-scented nearness. Drawing a deep breath, she forced herself to focus on his words.

"Now, honey, when you deliver that line, turn your shoulders like this, so the light captures your elegant profile." He touched her chin and lifted it. As he did so, she couldn't help glancing at his mouth. At his strong, well-shaped lips. She wondered what it would be like to kiss those lips.

Darn it all. She forced herself to look away. He could be such a demanding director—to the point of rudeness at times—and yet something about his commanding presence never failed to reduce her to a star-struck schoolgirl. Maybe that quality was what her favorite dime novels meant by "charisma." That ability to charm your way back into people's good graces, no matter how shabbily you'd treated them just moments before.

"Hold it. That's it. Nanette, you stay right where you are. Perfect." Chet took a step back and surveyed the scene with a critical eye.

Helen felt a fleeting disappointment when he let go of her shoulders. She gave herself a sharp internal pinch. *Get a grip on yourself, girl.*

Of course he knew best. He was the professional. Who was she to question the way he'd written the line?

"Take the scene from the top, please." Chet returned to his seat in the darkened auditorium. They repeated the scene three more times in all, during which Helen managed to utter the tongue-twisting line without a single stutter. Then they moved on through the rest of Act Three to the finale.

Just when Helen thought she could not endure one more minute of rehearsal, "That's it for tonight," Chet called. Murmurs of relief sounded all across the stage as actors and crew milled around, shutting down equipment and gathering their belongings. "See you all back here tomorrow, seven sharp, in full costume, ready to go." He stood. "Helen, can you hold up a moment? I'd like to speak with you."

Helen's tummy fluttered. She was unable to read his tone. Was he going to pay her the sorts of compliments he'd been doling out all summer—about her skilled acting, her flaxen hair, or her cornflower-blue eyes? Or, in the extreme other direction, would he read her the riot act for questioning his playwriting ability in front of the others? She never knew with Chet. That was part of what made him so exciting.

She was never bored when he was around.

Nanette gave her shoulder a playful nudge. "Good luck," she whispered. She knew all about Helen's not-so-secret crush on the dashing director, had listened to her praise him to the skies over the long, hot weeks of rehearsal.

"He's as hard on himself as he is on us," Helen had insisted on more than one occasion. "He's a perfectionist, that's all. He insists on the best. All the great directors do."

"How do you know what the great directors do?" Nanette had teased.

Helen's face had heated. "I just know."

True, Helen hadn't come across many directors in her sheltered life. As theatrical venues went, the Orpheum was only one modest step up from the Kerryville High School auditorium. Neverthe-less, she faithfully pored over every issue of *Photoplay* and *The-atre*, so she knew the score. Genius directors were perfectionists, and Chet Scarborough was a genius. She needed to take his crit-ical comments to heart—no matter how difficult they might be to hear— if she was going to make professional acting her career. Even though Chet directed plays, not movies, she knew his advice was invaluable.

Acting had been her deepest hope since she was ten years old, watching her first motion picture on the Orpheum screen. She'd planned to head for Hollywood as soon as she finished high school. Then the stock-market crash had forced her to put her dream on hold to help keep her family's store in business. But the dream hadn't died. Not ever.

Now here she was, twenty-one years old and not getting any younger, still acting in scruffy little small-town productions instead of on the silver screen. Her dissatisfaction with the direction her life was going had been building for some time.

Feeling conspicuous even though no one was paying attention, she walked with forced casualness from the stage to where Chet stood stuffing papers into a brown leather briefcase.

"You did well tonight, Helen," he said with hearty cheer, loud enough for the others to overhear. "I just had a few thoughts about your entrance in the third act."

"Oh?" Her stomach clenched as it always did in the face of criticism. "Am I doing something wrong?"

"You're doing fine." He busied himself with his papers until most of the others had cleared out. Then he turned to her with that intense look in his gray eyes—the look he gave her whenever she did something that pleased him. She'd come to love that look, to yearn for it and do whatever it took to get it. She practically melted in relief that he wasn't annoyed with her.

He lowered his voice. "I'd just like to talk some things over with you. Matters of some importance. Come back with me to my hotel."

An electric shock jolted her to her core. She took an involuntary step back. "I—I can't do that." Maybe the city girls he was used to could freely visit men at their hotels, but she wasn't a city girl, and Kerryville sure as heck wasn't the city.

His handsome face broke into a lopsided grin. "You should see the look on your face. Don't worry, I'm not trying to seduce you. What kind of a cad do you think I am?"

She didn't know which was more embarrassing. To be propositioned, or to assume you were being propositioned when you weren't.

"It's just that I'd like to talk to you in private," he continued, "and the hotel lobby is the only place where we can scare up a cold drink at this hour."

Her shoulders relaxed. He was right. Downtown Kerryville, such as it was, did shut down early, especially on a weeknight. Even the Tick Tock Café was closed. The Excelsior Hotel—opened with great optimism in 1929 just one month before the stock-market crash—offered the only nightspot to speak of. But tempting as the offer was, she couldn't do it. *Wouldn't* do it. Even though perfectly innocent, all they'd need is for some biddy hen like Eugenia Wardlow to spot them entering the hotel together and soon the whole town would have the wrong idea about their... their... well, whatever this was.

She lifted her chin. "I have to work early in the morning. I need my beauty sleep." Even to her own ears, the excuse sounded straitlaced and stuffy.

He chuckled, his face etched with the smile lines she found so appealing. "Whatever you say, honey. At least let me walk you home."

"All right." The likes of Eugenia Wardlow could find nothing objectionable about a girl accepting a walk home this late at night. Safety first, and all that. Even Helen's brother-in-law, Peter, a police officer, would approve.

"Meet you out front as soon as I'm done here," Chet murmured. Then he raised his voice, once again all business. "John, may I speak to you for a moment before you go? I have a few notes."

The warm, sultry air enveloped Helen as she stepped onto the sidewalk. In the bright electric light from the marquee, she reviewed the promotional poster mounted on the brick wall. *Under the Flaming Oak*, it proclaimed in flowing script. *July 23, 24, and 25, 1933*. Her own image smiled back at her from beneath the costume bonnet she wore in the role of nineteenth-century belle Susannah McCabe. Beside her in the photo stood John Morton, Kerryville's balding postmaster-turned-romantic lead, along with Nanette Johnson in the role of Alice and Bob Green as Susannah's father.

Her gaze trailed down the poster to the words, "Written and directed by Chester Scarborough, distinguished Chicago impresario." *Distinguished impresario*. She shivered deliciously. The Kerryville Players were unbelievably lucky to have him, even if the arrangement was only temporary, part of some government project to bring culture to the hinterlands. He'd be leaving soon—gut-wrenchingly soon—to return to Chicago's glittering theater scene. And equally glittering actresses, no doubt.

An unexpected arrow of jealousy pierced her midsection.

All through the long weeks of rehearsal for the summer-stock production, she'd done her best to make a good impression on the eminent director, to prove that a Kerryville actress could be just as polished and professional as those in Chicago. And along the way, she'd fallen in love. Chet Scarborough was older, sophisticated, intelligent, and experienced—just the sort of man who could have a life-changing impact on Helen's longed-for acting career, as well as her heart, if that intense look in his eyes meant what she dreamed it did. That she was special. That she had a shot at being his leading lady not only on the stage, but in real life.

The theater-industry rags occasionally linked Chet to this or that actress but made no mention of a serious girlfriend. That role, it seemed, remained open. Now he wanted to meet with her in private! This walk home might be her tryout, her audition for the coveted role of Mrs. Chester Scarborough.

The heavy glass door opened, and she glanced up in eager expectation. But instead of Chet, Nanette's sprite-like form appeared.

"You still here?" She looped her arm through Helen's and drew her toward a dilapidated Ford idling at the curb. "Come on. Ted will give us both a lift home, and you can tell me what Chet said to you just now."

Helen stood her ground. "No, thanks. I—I'm waiting for him."

Nanette lifted one penciled eyebrow. "For Chet?"

Helen forced a little shrug, as if to say *no big deal*. "He's offered to walk me home, that's all. Says he wants to talk to me about something."

She should have known better than to try to get anything past Nanette, whose dark eyes sparkled at the prospect of romance. "That's good, isn't it? Isn't that what you've been waiting for?"

"I suppose so." For a quick moment Helen regretted confiding in Nanette about her crush. The two had been lounging around on the Corrigans' wide porch one hot evening after rehearsal, marveling over their good fortune to have landed such a swoon-worthy director. Helen had been candid about her hope that he'd ask her out. But now that her idle daydream was perhaps becoming real, Helen felt awkward about sharing her feelings with her friend. However, they might as well have been written across her face, because Nanette's next words were, "Has he asked you on an actual date?"

"No. Not in so many words," Helen admitted. Not unless being walked home counted as a date.

"Maybe tonight's the night!" Nanette winked. "Well, behave yourself. I'll see you tomorrow." She lifted her hand and slid into the Ford's passenger seat. As the sedan pulled away from the curb, she called back through the open window, "You should introduce him to your sister as soon as possible. If he's going to be walking you home, she's going to insist on meeting him."

She'll flip her lid, more likely, came the unnerving thought.

Why, oh why, hadn't Helen made sure her family met Chet before things had progressed this far—particularly her overprotective big sister, Marjorie? After all, she'd had all summer to orchestrate a meeting, to warm them up to the idea that Chet was somebody special in Helen's life. That Helen would likely be leaving Kerryville soon.

It was a rhetorical question. She knew why. She'd intuited Marjorie's disapproval in advance. *He's too old for you*, she'd say. *Does he go to church? What's his family like? What do you really know about him?*

In spite of her misgivings, Helen had no time to ponder her sister's probable interference in her love life, because Chet appeared in the doorway. As he turned the key in the lock and gave Helen a winning smile, any further thoughts of Marjorie flew straight out of her head.

CHAPTER TWO

HOLLYWOOD, CALIFORNIA. JULY 1933

Rusty Noble tugged at the snug collar of his white cotton shirt. Only two scenes into the first read-through of his latest screenplay, and already the perspiration was seeping through under his arms. The screenplay was a rollicking Western. One of his best, he thought. One he'd toiled over and had been feeling particularly proud of.

Until now.

As the actors droned on, Rusty watched their faces, desperate for some sign that at least a few of them liked his script. Thought it had potential. Appreciated the occasional elegant turn of phrase or subtle bit of humor. Most faces were passive. A few were frowning, or worse yet, yawning.

At the far end of the conference table, studio president Stanley Cooperman clutched in his massive paws the precious pages covered in Rusty's blood, sweat, and tears. As he turned a page, a dagger of sunlight from a high window glinted off his signet ring. His jowled face was expressionless, impossible to read from Rusty's vantage point.

Lined up between Cooperman and Rusty—like vultures on a tree limb—sat members of the film's cast and crew, faces registering varying states of ennui. Only Debbie Fagan, the fresh-faced seventeen-year-old reading the part of the gunslinger's daughter, showed the least hint of enthusiasm for the lines Rusty had so painstakingly crafted.

"Howdy, ma'am," drawled Mark St. Ives, the romantic lead, peering at the script through thick reading glasses with all the sex appeal of an inquisitive owl. Like Clark Gable's dentures, Mark St.

Ives's spectacles would have startled the adoring fans who only knew his eyes to be dark and mysterious, not severely farsighted. "You're lookin' right fetchin' today."

Silence followed this declaration.

"Cynthia. It's your line," Rusty prompted.

"I *know* it's my line." The platinum blonde slapped the script to the table. Her kohl-fringed eyes looked Rusty square in the face. "Honestly. How can I be expected to play such a simpering idiot?"

"Annabel Brewster is not a simpering idiot," Rusty protested. "She's a sweet, innocent schoolmarm from back East who has just arrived in Dust Valley on the stagecoach and—"

"I don't want to play a sweet schoolmarm. That doesn't sound fun at all." Cynthia rubbed her temples. Probably another headache. She always had headaches, and always at the most inopportune times, particularly when asked to do something she didn't want to do.

Cynthia's look of disdain melted into a beguiling smile. "Can't we spice her up just a little?" She knew how to turn on the charm to get what she wanted. Fortunately, over the space of six years and twice as many pictures at Cooperman Studios, Rusty had grown impervious to the actress's manipulative allure.

"Believe me, Annabel Brewster is no ordinary schoolmarm," Rusty assured her. "No, siree. Under that calico sunbonnet, she's got a brilliant mind. She's one smart cookie. You'll see."

Cynthia stuck out her lower lip. "She doesn't seem very smart to me."

Rusty did his best to keep his tone patient and upbeat. "She's only just arrived in Dust Valley. Give her character some time to develop. Let's read on, shall we?"

"And she doesn't exactly ooze sex appeal," Cynthia continued as though she hadn't heard him.

What could he say to that? "Um, she's a schoolteacher. She's not supposed to ooze sex appeal."

"Of course she needs sex appeal," Cooperman thundered from the end of the table, releasing a choice expletive. "Audiences always want sex appeal. We need a strong box-office draw. That's why we cast Cynthia in the lead. The Cynthia Starling brand *means* sex appeal. That's why she's America's darling."

"Cynthia Starling, America's darling. Hey, boss, that's a pretty clever slogan," Mark St. Ives said.

Toady. Rusty rolled his eyes with no small degree of resentment. *Cooperman,* you *were the one who cast Cynthia in the lead. I knew she was all wrong for the part.*

Out loud he said, "I didn't mean she'd have *zero* sex appeal, Mr. Cooperman." He backtracked fast. "I just meant that, as a schoolteacher, she'd be a little more buttoned up than, say, the proprietress of the Lazy R Saloon."

"You mean Trixie Belmont?" At the mention of her soiled-dove character, Gilda Miller sat up a little straighter, clearly energized at the prospect of exhibiting greater sex appeal than Cynthia Starling.

As the story threatened to slip out of his grasp, Rusty said, "We have to keep a lid on some of that stuff if we don't want to have a tough time with the Hays office."

"Zee time, she flies," interjected Jean-Luc Renard, the film's mercurial French director, tapping his wristwatch. "Zee show, she must go on."

Cynthia stared daggers at Rusty. "I can't continue. I simply *can't.* We have to fix this *now.*" As she turned her lovely head toward Mr. Cooperman, her expression melted from ice to liquid. "Coopie, tell him."

Coopie?

Disgust rose in Rusty's throat. He shot an exasperated glance heavenward, breathed a silent prayer for patience, and reached across the table for the water pitcher.

"Now, Cynthia," Cooperman said in a soothing, conciliatory tone rarely heard on the backlots of Cooperman Studios. "Let's try to keep an open mind. Noble here has worked hard on this script. Let's give it a chance. Perhaps it gets better later on."

But Cynthia could not be appeased.

The rest of the read-through lumbered on in fits and starts as Cynthia and Cooperman kept changing her lines, taking her character in a languid, seductive direction Rusty had never intended it to go.

"What this thing needs is a good old-fashioned *scandal,*" Cooperman declared in his trademark foghorn blast, midway through Act Three. "That's what audiences are looking for these days. Scandal. Without a scandal, it's just another lousy love story."

Rusty gave an inward groan. As one of Cooperman Studios' leading scriptwriters, he was accustomed to receiving criticism of his work and taking it well. No screenwriter worth his typewriter ribbon could afford to be fragile about his words. Even when someone called them *lousy*. He knew it was nothing personal. After all, it was in everyone's best interest to make the best film possible, no matter what it took.

But *The Courage of Annabel Brewster* was different. This was the story closest to Rusty's heart, the one he'd been longing to write for years. Six weeks earlier, when Cooperman had assigned him to write a pioneer love story, he'd jumped at the chance. At the core of it was the real-life story of Rusty's own great-grandmother and her adventures on the Nebraska prairie—embellished, of course, with romance and intrigue and a Hollywood-style happily-ever-after ending. But Annabel Brewster, the heroine, was supposed to be courageous, determined, and undaunted by the grueling hardships of the frontier. Not... sexy. Certainly not scandalous.

At long last, the painful read-through stuttered to a close and the members of the company stood, stretched, and began decamping to their next appointments. No one said anything to Rusty, who sat dejected, surrounded by the pages that represented weeks of his toil, now littering the table for the custodian to throw in the trash.

"Rewrite the script, Noble," Cooperman boomed as he left the room. Then he stopped, turned back, and eyed Rusty for a long moment as if evaluating him. Then he gruffed, "My office, Noble. Four thirty this afternoon."

Rusty gulped. "You want it done today, sir?"

"Isn't that what I just said?"

"Well, look, chief," he began.

"I know I'm rushing you, but I get rushed all the time and still get my work done," Cooperman roared. "Why can't you?"

Rusty resigned himself to his fate. "Yes, sir."

He sighed. Writers often found themselves as scapegoats for power struggles. He would have expected to have gotten used to it by now, but he hadn't.

When as a novice screenwriter he'd dreamed of making his mark on Hollywood, this wasn't the sort of situation he had in mind at all.

CHAPTER THREE

As Chet and Helen strolled down the empty Kerryville side-walk side by side, leaving the lights of the Orpheum behind, she stole a glance at his profile, marveling at the firm set of his jaw. He caught her looking and grinned. Holding his leather briefcase in one hand, he grasped her hand with the other and swung it lightly between them.

"Ah, little Helen Corrigan." His voice sounded husky and intimate as they meandered under the moonlight. "You've got too much talent, too much natural stage presence, to stay hidden away in Kerryville all your life. You know that, don't you? What are your plans?"

"My plans?" The giddy sensation of her hand tucked securely in his nearly prevented coherent thought.

"For your future. How old are you now? Eighteen? Nineteen?"

"Twenty-one."

"Ah. Just the right age."

"Do you really think so?" Relief poured through her veins. She'd been worried he'd think her too young, would find the nearly two-decade age gap between them an insurmountable obstacle to a romantic relationship. Apparently not.

"Sure thing," he said. "And with legs like yours..." He gave a low whistle that made her blush. Then his expression turned serious. "But believe me, honey, auditions are filled with plenty of girls even younger than you. You don't want to waste any more time."

With a whisper of disappointment, she realized he was talking about her future in the theater—not with him. Of course. Why wouldn't he talk about the theater? *Focus, Helen.*

Quickly she regrouped. "The—the competition for good roles must be fierce."

"It is. But you'd have an edge. Blondes are in hot demand on the stage these days. With your looks and talent, and a lot of hard work, you could write your own ticket. Make it big in Chicago, maybe even New York, eventually."

Her heart fluttered. "Do you really think so?"

He nodded. "I do. You have the sort of sweet, unspoiled, girl-next-door quality that's always in demand."

"You flatter me." As wildly inappropriate as it was, Helen wished he would return to his earlier assessment of her legs. No boy in Kerryville had ever said anything complimentary about her legs, other than perhaps noting how fast they carried her around a baseball diamond.

"You might think it's silly," she continued, "but my daydream has always been to try my luck in Hollywood. In motion pictures."

"Motion pictures!" He spat the words with all the passion of Pastor Rooney railing from the pulpit against blasphemy and the lake of fire. "You're kidding, right? No actress worth her salt would choose motion pictures over the legitimate stage."

A wave of shame washed through Helen. "But I *love* going to the movies," she confessed, deflated by his scornful attitude. "Why, my sister Marjorie and I are practically the first in line whenever a new picture arrives in town."

"That's because there are no alternatives in this hick town. No exposure to higher culture."

Helen flinched inside. Kerryville might have been a hick town, but it was *her* hick town. Even so, she couldn't argue about the lack of artistic venues. The Kerryville Players represented virtually the only attempt at raising the town's cultural profile a notch or two, unless you counted the hospital auxiliary's annual fund-raising talent show, which Helen decidedly didn't. Eugenia Wardlow swathed in a toga and reciting Sappho hardly constituted high art.

"In any case, you won't achieve anything staying in Kerryville. Believe me, honey, I know what I'm talking about."

"I know you do." She loved when he called her *honey*. At first she'd assumed he tossed the endearment around freely whenever he couldn't remember an actress's name. But now she knew by the way he said it that, in her case, he really meant it. She was his honey. "Sometimes I feel like if I stay in Kerryville, I'll simply shrivel up and perish. But I don't have much choice at the moment. If my sister has her way, I'm afraid I won't be going much further than Normal for the foreseeable future."

His brow creased. "Normal?"

"Normal, Illinois. That's where the state teachers' college is."

"I see." He cocked an eyebrow. "There's a real place called Normal?"

She laughed.

"Don't tell me that, with all your talent, you're planning to become a teacher," he continued in a serious tone.

"Well, *I'm* not planning it, but my sister is. She wants me to train for a practical career. You know, like secretary, nurse, teacher. The trouble is, business bores me, and I get squeamish at the sight of blood. So that leaves teaching. Not that there's anything wrong with teaching. I just have my own ideas about things." Since teaching was a favored career for so many people, it was hard to explain why she'd find it suffocating. She simply knew it in her bones.

"Not acting?"

"No. Never acting. Even though it's what I've wanted to do my entire life, whenever I bring it up, Marjorie thinks I'm being. .. flighty. Overly romantic. Not serious enough about life. She doesn't realize I'm dead serious about making it as an actress."

"Why do you care so much what your sister thinks?"

Helen groped for an explanation that would make sense to Chet. "She's always been an authority figure to me. I've always wanted to please her. She practically raised me after our mother died, you see."

"Hmm." They walked in silence for a few moments, then Chet said, "So, let me guess. You landed the female lead in all your high-school plays. And I'll bet you pretended to be Juliet in front of your bedroom mirror."

She stared at him in amazement. "How did you know?"

He laughed. "I have a sixth sense about these things." He squeezed her hand. "And that, honey, is what I want to talk to you about. You've heard of the Goodman Theater in Chicago?"

"Of course." Helen had heard of the prestigious theater, but only because she'd spotted the name in *Theatre* magazine. She'd never actually been there.

"I've just received word that the Goodman wants to produce *Under the Flaming Oak* this fall, and they want me to direct it."

"They do? Chet, that's wonderful news!"

"It sure is. It represents a golden opportunity for me. A real honor. And that's why I have a very special proposal for *you*."

"You do?" Helen fought to keep her voice steady, but her legs nearly gave out beneath her.

"I want you to share this experience with me. I want you to come with me to Chicago," Chet pronounced with an air of finality.

"What?" A strange tingling feeling warmed her stomach. She searched his face for signs he was joking, but he wasn't smiling.

He stopped and turned her to face him. "Come with me. The sooner the better. I want you to be my Susannah."

She gasped. Did he mean what she thought he meant?

He searched her face. "What's wrong? You have thought about it, haven't you?" He continued walking, and she followed. "I mean, I can't be the first person to have suggested you leave Kerryville to pursue your career."

"Actually, you are," she admitted when she finally found her tongue. "My sister acts mortally wounded if I ever broach the subject of leaving home. As for my brother, Charlie, he thinks I'm too silly and irresponsible to be out on my own."

Chet's mouth quirked. "He said that?"

"Not in so many words. But I can tell what he's thinking."

"You need to come to the Windy City with me," he repeated. "You play the role of Susannah as if it were written for you. You've made it yours."

Helen was speechless. To be invited to reprise her starring role at a major big-city theater would indeed be a career-launching move. But if she were honest, she wasn't thinking about the *career* part at the moment. She was thinking about the *come with me* part.

"I can't believe you were thinking about Hollywood," Chet scoffed into the silence. "Why would you want to degrade your art on motion pictures? Such a cheap, worthless form of entertainment."

It's not worthless, she wanted to protest, feeling stung. But her indignation soon washed away in the warmth of his smile. When she thought about making a choice between chasing her dream in Hollywood all on her own, or in Chicago with Chet, the decision became very clear.

"A talent like yours belongs in the legitimate theater, not in the movies," he continued in a gentler tone. "Chicago's the place for you." He gave her hand another squeeze. "Just tell me you'll think about it."

"I will."

When they reached her house, she stopped. "This is it."

He surveyed the large white Victorian with its wrap-around porch. "Kind of big for you, isn't it?"

She laughed. "It isn't only me. Marjorie lives here too, and her husband, Peter, and Charlie and Dot, and their twins, Bobby and Barbara. My father and stepmother lived here too, before they moved to Arizona."

His brows lifted. "That's quite a houseful."

"Yes, it is." A sudden pang of nostalgia sliced through her. "It will be hard to leave my family."

"It's not like you'd never come back and visit. Besides, you can't let your family hold you back."

"But they wouldn't want to hold me back. Not on purpose, anyway."

"What about your sister?"

He had a point there.

"She... she just wants what's best for me."

"So do I."

Standing on the sidewalk, he turned her to face him. Beneath the porch light, his luminous gray eyes sought hers.

"I can tell you this much, Helen Corrigan. You're not cut out to be a teacher."

"How do you know?"

"You have star quality. Your talent is wasted in a backwater place like Kerryville."

Her heart pounded as she rolled his words over in her mind. *Star quality*.

"You can make it as an actress. A real actress. None of this flaky silver-screen stuff. Your place is among true professionals. If you want to make it in this business, you have to be serious."

I'll be serious, she thought. In that moment, she'd be anything he wanted her to be.

He took a step closer. Her breath caught in her lungs.

"I'll be heading back home after the final performance." His voice was low and husky.

A sinking feeling squeezed her chest. "I know."

He bent and set his briefcase on the sidewalk, then grasped both her hands in his.

"Come with me. I'll set you up with auditions, ensure you make connections, meet all the right people. You'll be my little *protegée*."

Protegée. What does that mean, exactly? she longed to ask. *Does it include love? Marriage? A home?* But her mouth remained glued shut. The desire for him to like her—to love her—was so strong, she could scarcely form a coherent thought.

He lowered his head as if he were going to kiss her. She lifted her face in eager expectation, at the same time with the desperate hope that no one was peeking through the curtains. But he only gave her a light, brotherly peck on the forehead. Disappointment blended with relief that he'd been enough of a gentleman not to give her a real kiss out in public.

Clearly, he was the most thoughtful, generous, brilliant man on the planet. And now he wanted her to go to Chicago. With him. She felt dizzy with the sense of being special. Of being chosen. Of being *his*.

He chucked her under the chin. "See you at rehearsal tomorrow. Think about what I've said."

He seemed reluctant to leave, but nonetheless turned and strode down the sidewalk, tall and confident.

"I will," she whispered to his departing back.

As if thinking of anything else were even possible.

Thoughts swirling, she entered the front door, latched it behind her, and leaned against it.

Chicago. Chet Scarborough. Her name in lights on a theater marquee. "Starring Helen Corrigan."

Or maybe... *starring Helen Scarborough?*

Marjorie's silver tabby cat, Mr. Whisker, rubbed himself against her shin. She picked him up and kissed the top of his furry head.

"What do you think, Mr. Whisker?" she whispered, then held him close. A delicious shiver tickled her spine as she carried him up the stairs.

Her brilliant future lay tantalizingly within reach.

If Marjorie didn't kill her first.

CHAPTER FOUR

I n the stark, white-walled writers' bungalow located off a remote backlot at Cooperman Studios, Rusty sweated over his typewriter, trying to salvage *The Courage of Annabel Brewster*—the script that was growing dumber by the minute under the inane suggestions of Cynthia Starling and Stanley Cooperman.

"Cynthia's got to be a sympathetic character," Cooperman had insisted. "The dame in the script is not sympathetic enough. We've got to make the American public warm up to her after that embarrassing Errol Flynn business."

"I get what you mean, chief. I get it," Rusty had promised. But who in the heck could turn out an Academy winner in a day?

"They're going to ruin it," he said out loud to no one in particular. "What were they thinking, casting that hellcat as Annabel?"

Across the room, Rusty's friend and fellow writer Maxwell Smith, known to all as Smitty, cast a sympathetic smile in Rusty's direction.

"Cynthia can't act her way out of a paper bag," he said. "But she's photogenic. She's been blessed with good bones, the kind of face and figure that the camera loves."

"And so does Cooperman, apparently," added Jim Ingersoll from his desk next to Smitty's. "He's vulnerable to long-legged blondes."

"Yep. She crooks her little finger and he comes running. Whatever she wants, she gets." Rusty sighed. He leaned back in his chair, drew a pencil from behind his ear, and threw it at the keyboard. "I can't wait until I get my own studio going. Then I won't have to put up with this nonsense anymore."

"Still chasing after that pipe dream, are ya?" Smitty quipped. "Better not let Cooperman get wind of your plans."

Rusty knew very well that his contract with Cooperman prohibited moonlighting. "That's why I've only told you two," he said. "I can trust it will go no further."

"My lips are sealed." Smitty pantomimed closing a button over his lips. But the button didn't hold, because immediately he added, "Running your own studio takes a whole lot of things you don't have, buddy. Like money. And time. And star power." He shook his prematurely balding head with a world-weary air.

"Golly. Thanks for your support." Rusty's words oozed sarcasm.

Jim Ingersoll didn't smirk. Instead he said, "I think you should do it, Rusty. You've got the brains and the talent. If anyone could pull it off, you could."

"Thanks, Jim. I refuse to give up," Rusty replied in a firm voice. "I want to make films I can be proud of. To keep creative control over my projects. Not have them blown to smithereens by the likes of Cynthia Starling."

"But what about funding?" Smitty said. "Where do you think you're gonna come up with that kind of dough?"

Rusty exhaled. "I have no idea."

"Well, lotsa luck," Smitty said.

"In the meantime, try not to take it too hard," Jim said. "You're the best writer we've got—with the exception of myself, of course—and deep down Cooperman knows it. If anybody can pull it off, you can."

"Thanks. I hope you're right." Rusty stared at his typewriter for a moment. Then he picked up his much-gnawed pencil—more of a lucky talisman than a writing instrument—shoved it behind his ear, and resumed pounding the keyboard.

At four thirty sharp, he arrived panting at Mr. Cooperman's outer office.

"Hi, Midge. Is the chief in?"

He leaned against the secretary's desk in an attempt to look nonchalant, half hoping she'd say no. Behind her, the door to Cooperman's private office was slightly ajar, giving support to Rusty's hunch that the boss had forgotten all about their meeting and had left for the day.

Clutched in Rusty's fist was an envelope containing a typewritten manuscript—the latest revision of *The Courage of Annabel Brewster*. After typing furiously all afternoon, desperate to meet Cooperman's unrealistic deadline, he'd ripped the last page out of the typewriter mere minutes earlier. Now he hoped he could leave the envelope with Midge and not have to endure some big discussion about it.

The middle-aged secretary stopped typing and smiled at Rusty, her blue eyes enormous through black-rimmed cat's-eye glasses. "Well, howdy do, Rusty. He should be back any minute, if you'd care to wait."

Rusty didn't care to wait. Not at all. But the decision was made for him, because just then the great man himself cycloned into the office.

"Midge, get me New York on the telephone," Cooperman ordered. Then he stopped short and glared at Rusty. "What do you want?"

Rusty swallowed his anxiety and held forth the envelope. "Here you go, chief. It's the rewrite of *Annabel*, right on time, as promised. I think you'll be pleased."

Cooperman grunted. He took the envelope from Rusty with a look of distaste, as though it smelled of rotting mackerel. "This had better be good!" he thundered as he disappeared into his office. "Midge! New York." The door slammed behind him.

Buoyant with relief, Rusty thanked Midge and turned to leave when the door flew open again.

"Noble!" Cooperman barked. "In here."

Midge threw Rusty a sympathetic glance as he entered the office with trepidation. Cooperman shut the door and headed for his enormous desk. He motioned toward a club chair and Rusty took a seat. A stuffed cougar glowered at him from a corner, teeth bared. One of the more unnerving of Cooperman's many hunting trophies.

The big man regarded him across the desk. "Well done, Noble."

Rusty's face grew warm. "Thank you, sir. I think you'll like it."

"Like what?"

"Er... the script, sir. The script for *Annabel*." Was the boss's memory failing? After all, the old man must have been fifty years old, at least. Practically ancient. "The one you asked me to rewrite." *In great haste, I might add.* "I'm sure that once you've had a chance to look it over—"

"Oh, that." Cooperman made a dismissive motion with his hand. "Don't bother with a rewrite. The script is fine as is."

Rusty wasn't sure he heard correctly. "It's—it's *fine*, sir?" A bolt of anger flashed through his solar plexus. Why had he just wasted an entire day slaving over a rewrite, with his brain on fire and his fingers practically bleeding on the keys, if the script was fine?

His protest was preempted by Midge's voice floating over the intercom. "New York on the line, sir."

Cooperman picked up the handset, pressed a button, and boomed. "Louie. How are ya, you old son-of-a-gun?"

Rusty stood to leave, but Cooperman motioned him to stay. He slumped back into his chair, stewing in resentment over the unnecessary rewrite. But by the time Cooperman finished his lengthy conversation, Rusty's temper had cooled to the point where he could address his boss in a calmer tone.

"Now, where were we?" the chief said as he replaced the handset in the cradle.

"Sir, I don't understand why you requested a rewrite if you thought the script was fine."

"Oh, I just said that to placate Cynthia," Cooperman replied with a wink. "You know how unreasonable she can get."

Rusty's anger returned to a slow boil. "Yes, I know, sir, but—"

Cooperman waved his hand. "Never mind that. Rewrite it, don't rewrite it, I don't care. I trust you. You have an uncanny sense of what makes for a good story. I called you in to talk about something else." He threw a sly smile at Rusty. "Young man, how would you like a shot at being second assistant director?"

Rusty couldn't believe he'd heard correctly. "Sir?"

"Just temporarily, of course." His beefy finger tapped the envelope Rusty had given him minutes earlier. "I'd like to try you out on this one picture as second assistant director."

As quickly as it had flared, Rusty's anger turned to astonishment. "Really, sir?"

"What I'd *really* like is for you to go on location with the crew and help oversee the filming of *Annabel*. I'm putting you on as second assistant director on this film, just to see how you make out."

Rusty pointed toward himself. "Me?"

Second assistant director! A slurry of flattery mixed with gratification coursed through Rusty's veins. To be sent on location was in itself a feather in his cap. To be promoted to second assistant director was a significant step up from scriptwriting. Best of all, it would include a raise in salary that would help him save money to start his own studio.

"Just on this one picture, mind you. If you do all right, I'll consider making it permanent. You'll be paid at the higher rate, of course." Cooperman stood and turned toward the large window overlooking Sunset Boulevard. "I like you, Noble. You're a straight shooter. Honest. I know I can always count on you to give me the straight dope."

"Well, I try."

"After all, we're practically family, aren't we? You and me?"

"If you say so, sir." In Rusty's experience, the "practically family" line was something Mr. Cooperman trotted out whenever he wanted something. Even so, Rusty couldn't believe he was getting promoted, even on a temporary basis.

"Gosh. Second assistant director!" There had to be a catch.

"Don't look so astonished, Noble, or you'll make me question my judgment," Cooperman snapped. He returned to his desk, the moment of warm camaraderie over. "As you know, the picture will be shot in Arizona, at a location not far from Tucson. You'll leave with the crew next week and stay as long as it takes to get the job done. Midge will arrange all the details, train ticket and lodging and so on."

"Yes, sir." Rusty practically saluted. "Thank you, sir." No catch? He stood uncertainly, waiting to hear further instructions.

Cooperman looked at him. "That will be all."

Rusty turned toward the door.

"Oh, and Noble. One more thing."

Rusty turned back. "Yes, sir?"

Cooperman lowered his usual foghorn blast to a rumble. "While you're out there, keep an eye on Cynthia for me, will you?"

Confusion fogged Rusty's brain. "Sir?"

"Just keep tabs on what she does, where she goes, and who she goes there with. Make sure there's no hanky-panky going on between her and St. Ives."

Ah. There it was. The catch.

Rusty swallowed his rising apprehension. "Hanky-panky, sir?"

Cooperman waved a dismissive hand. "You weren't born yesterday, Noble. You know what I mean. Cynthia can be—flirtatious. I trust her, but I don't trust him. Just make a note if you see him acting overly familiar with her, or if anything else seems off about the way they're behaving around one another, and report back to me."

Rusty questioned his hearing. Was his boss really asking him to spy on his girlfriend *du jour*? "Uh, sir, I don't think—"

"That's all, Noble. And congratulations on your temporary promotion."

His promotion. That put a new spin on things. Clearly the position of second assistant director required certain duties that were new to Rusty. Duties like babysitting the head honcho's girlfriend, distasteful as it seemed. He should have known the promotion would come with a string attached.

A long, filthy string.

As he walked back to the writers' bungalow, he weighed the pros and cons of the situation. By the time he reached his typewriter, he'd made his decision. He'd go to Arizona, make sure Cynthia said her lines the way they were intended to be said, and be the best second assistant director Cooperman Studios had ever had. In whatever time was left over, he'd heave buckets of cold water on any flicker of flirtation that happened to pass between Cynthia and Mark St. Ives, so he could return and give Cooperman a clean report. Then the promotion would be his, and he'd gain a higher level of experience that would stand him in good stead when he left to start his own studio.

What could possibly go wrong?

CHAPTER FIVE

H elen and Nanette huddled over coffee and pancakes at the Tick Tock Café and discussed Chet's invitation from the night before.

"Are you seriously thinking of going away with him?" Nanette's dark eyes rounded to match their saucers.

"Why not?" Helen replied. "Not only are we crazy about each other, but he can give me a real shot at success as an actress. At the Goodman, for pity's sake! Why wouldn't I want to go with him?"

"Because he hasn't made any kind of real commitment. He hasn't asked you to marry him." Nanette might as well have flung her glass of ice water all over Helen's hopes and dreams.

"Of course we'll be married," she snapped. "Eventually. That goes without saying."

"Well, it *needs* to be said." Ever-practical Nanette reached for the syrup jug. "Preferably by him, in the form of an actual proposal."

Helen shifted in her seat. "He'll get around to it, I'm sure."

Nanette tilted her head. "Because without that ring on your finger..."

"I *know*, Nanette. Quit harping."

"Who's harping?" Nanette lifted a shoulder. "I'm simply being realistic."

"Why can't you be happy for me?"

Nanette speared a forkful of pancakes. "I *am* happy for you. About the Goodman, I mean. I just want to make sure you're not diving off the deep end here. What has Marjorie said about all this?"

"I haven't told her yet." At Nanette's shocked expression, Helen added, "I'm waiting for the right moment."

"Well, the right moment had better come soon. Chet's leaving town as soon as we're done."

"Yes, I know," Helen muttered. Did Nanette continually have to state the obvious? "I only wish Marjorie weren't so stubborn about teacher's college. She has my whole future planned out. I'm supposed to earn my certificate and then come back home to teach and live in Kerryville, forever and ever, amen." She stirred her coffee. "It all makes me feel so... so *smothered*. It's like she doesn't want me to grow up or something."

"Can you blame her? She practically raised you. She's more like a mother to you than a sister."

"I realize that. And I'm eternally grateful for everything she's done for me. But, golly, does that mean I have to give up leading my own life?"

Nanette looked thoughtful as she chewed and swallowed. Then she pointed her fork at Helen. "The key is to have Chet and Marjorie meet and get to know one another. I'm sure that once Marjorie meets him and understands his honorable intentions, as well as his glowing assessment of your acting skills. she will give you her blessing to do what you want to do."

"I sure hope so." Deep inside, Helen wasn't so sure. Even if Chet were an absolute saint, getting Marjorie's approval would be a tough sell. But he was hardly a saint. She didn't even know if he ever went to church, a red flag that Marjorie was sure to point out. And then there was the age difference. He was significantly older than Helen.

"Why don't you convince Marjorie to invite him to a family dinner before the show tomorrow night? That way Chet can meet everybody, and she will feel more comfortable about the situation."

"Good idea. I'll think about it." Helen promised.

"Well, don't think too long," Nanette warned. "He'll be—"

"Leaving town soon," Helen answered for her. "I know." She shoved aside her empty plate with impatience, along with her worries about Chet and Marjorie getting along. Then she leaned forward and rested her elbows on the table, eager to change the subject. "And now, dear one, let's talk about something *really* important—your wedding. Have you decided what to do about the bridesmaids' gowns?"

"Not yet," Nanette admitted.

"Well." Helen motioned to the waitress for more coffee. "As one of those bridesmaids, I have a vested interest in having something pretty to wear. You're getting married in December, right?"

"Right."

"Okay, then." Helen cast her warmest smile at her friend. "Have you given any thought to velveteen?"

Thirty minutes later, the bell hanging over the front door of Corrigan's Dry Goods and Sundries gave a merry jangle as Helen waltzed in, feeling refreshed and energized after her breakfast with Nanette.

"I'm here," she caroled.

Her brother and sister glanced up from some ledger sheets they'd been examining at the cutting table. "Where've you been?" Charlie said with a glance at the wall clock. "You're late."

Helen stashed her purse under the counter. "I was having breakfast with Nanette."

He opened his mouth, but Marjorie interjected quickly before he could object. "I told her she could come in a little late today. It's not like we're busy." She swept her arm around the store's empty aisles. In normal times, industrious Kerryville housewives would have come bustling in to stock up on cotton thread and rickrack trim. But these were not normal times—not with banks and businesses closing and people losing their jobs at an alarming rate.

Charlie grunted and turned back to the ledger sheets.

"I must say, that dress is a great color on you." Marjorie smiled at Helen. "Who knew you'd grow up to be a beauty? You were such a tomboy in the old days."

"Thank you—I think." Helen glanced down at her mint-colored linen frock. She'd chosen the fabric especially to flatter her blond hair and blue eyes and was glad it was having its intended effect. Maybe she should consider mint green for her own bridesmaids when she and Chet got married. Speaking of which—

"Have you got a minute, Marjie?" Helen tugged off her short white gloves. "There's something I want to talk to you about."

"Sure. What's up?"

"Well, you know this play I've been doing. As it turns out, the director—"

"I hate to interrupt you two," Charlie said with a touch of sarcasm, "but if you don't mind, can we get back to what we were doing?"

Helen stopped short at the look on her brother's face. "Well, for heaven's sake, if you aren't a gloomy Gus. What's the matter?"

"Oh, the usual," Marjorie broke in, "trying to balance the books and pull a rabbit out of a hat."

Helen rolled her eyes. "Oh, that."

"*That*, missy, is what pays the bills around here, not to mention your paycheck," Charlie grumbled. "Oh, what's the use?" He swept up the papers and headed for the tiny office at the back of the shop.

Helen watched his retreating back. "What's eating him?"

Marjorie's forehead creased. "He's worried about making payroll. Again."

Helen bit her lower lip. "Oh, dear. And I just bought a new hat at Meyer's."

"Helen, you didn't!" Marjorie looked as if she wanted to slap Helen, if she were the slapping kind, which she wasn't. "Oh, *honestly*. From Meyer's, of all places? Our stiffest competition?"

Taken aback by her sister's outburst, Helen tried to explain. "I've been simply desperate for a new hat. I don't have a single one that's still fit to wear. Besides, we don't sell hats here at Corrigan's, so it's not exactly like we're competing. Not over hats, anyway. You'd have to go to Meyer's, too, if you wanted to buy one. Which, by the way, you might want to think about." She shifted her gaze to Marjorie's worn yellow cloche, hanging forlornly on the coat rack just inside the front door. For some reason Marjie absolutely loved that ratty old thing and refused to part with it. For the life of her, Helen didn't know why.

Marjorie heaved a sigh. "What's wrong with freshening up the trim on an old one? We have all this lovely ribbon just sitting here on the notions counter."

Helen didn't reply, but pressed her lips together in distaste.

"Well, I hope you didn't buy it on account," Marjorie continued. "You know how I feel about credit. We've just been going over Charlie's lengthy list of overdue accounts. If even just a few customers would make good on their bills, maybe the store wouldn't be in this mess. Everyone in town is feeling the pinch, but I must confess, my feelings of generosity and goodwill are growing more threadbare by the minute."

"Now, Marjie, don't get in a lather," Helen soothed. "I paid for it upfront."

"With what?"

She slid her sister a sidelong glance. "A teensy bit of my nest egg."

Marjorie rubbed her temples as if they ached. "Helen, that money is for college."

"Yes, it is." Helen lifted her chin. "And at *college*, a girl needs a decent *hat*."

Marjorie looked as if she were about to say something, then changed her mind. "I'm sorry. What were you starting to say about your play?"

"Never mind. It's not important." Now was not the moment to ask Marjorie to invite Chet over for dinner, much less announce she was moving to Chicago. She'd wait for a more opportune time, when her sister was in a better mood.

Marjorie sighed. "Well, in that case, you might as well make yourself useful. The front window display needs freshening up."

"Won't have time." Helen reached under the counter, pulled a compact out of her purse, and flipped it open.

Marjorie placed her hands on her hips. "Why ever not? It's not as if we're overrun with customers."

"We *will* be, quite soon." Helen dabbed a powder puff over her nose, smiled at the image in the mirror, snapped the compact shut, and returned it to her handbag. "That's what I was trying to tell you, before you started rambling on about hats. You know that Nanette is getting married."

"Yes, I know."

"To that jellybean Ted Barber. Can you imagine? Anyway, I talked her into coming here this very morning to shop for material for her bridesmaids' dresses."

"Bridesmaids?" Marjorie's face brightened.

"Yes. All nine of them."

"*Nine?*" Marjorie's mouth formed an O. "Why, that's—"

" —wonderful, that's what that is. And at least two of them are quite plump."

"Helen."

"I'm not being unkind. I'm simply saying, plump girls require extra yardage. *And* I plan to suggest floor-length skirts with lots of draping, like the kind Norma Shearer wore in *The Divorcée.*"

Marjorie looked askance. "I don't know if a movie called *The Divorcée* is a particularly appropriate source of inspiration for a wedding party." Then her expression shifted. "On the other hand, lots of draping means lots of fabric."

"Indeed it does," Helen said. "It's not that hard to persuade people. You just have to give them what they want. And if they don't know what they want, you help them figure it out." She patted her hair as the doorbell gave a merry tinkle. "So you see, dear sister," she called over her shoulder as she went to greet her friend, "I'm not entirely useless, after all."

CHAPTER SIX

Tucson, Arizona

S weating in the baking heat, Rusty sat in a folding chair next to a half-finished set that would become the interior of an adobe shack and watched the nightmare of a rehearsal unfold before his eyes.

Cynthia Starling crossed the creaking floorboards with an expression of doom worthy of Lady Macbeth. Holding a script in one hand and sweeping the other above her head, she enunciated her lines in an overly dramatic fashion.

"I shan't give you one red cent, you filthy louse!" she bellowed, shaking her raised fist at a bewildered-looking Mark St. Ives.

"Uh..." The leading man dropped character and squinted as he paged through his script in a desperate attempt to find his cue.

Rusty groaned and dropped his head into his hands. He didn't know how much more of this he could take. He lifted his head and called out with as much patience as he could muster,

"Cynthia, the line is 'I can't get any money until the bank opens,'" he called. "Not a word in there about red cents or louses."

Beneath her calico bonnet, the actress pouted. "But my way is so much better."

"Your way is ruining the entire scene." He rubbed his forehead. "Annabel is supposed to be a proper lady from back East, not a screeching harridan."

"I don't have to listen to you," Cynthia retorted, nose in the air. "I only have to listen to the director."

Rick Carter, the actor playing Dust Valley's crooked mayor, sat next to Rusty and nudged his shoulder. "Hey, Rus, she's right. You'd better say your piece to the director and let him tell it to us actors," he grumbled. "Otherwise we'll be stuck here all day and half the night. *Again.* We're already behind schedule, and if word gets back to Cooperman, he'll blow his stack and fire the lot of us."

Rusty doubted that would happen. Cooperman had already sunk too much money into *The Courage of Annabel Brewster* to scratch the whole project. But why take a chance?

He knew very well the protocol for working on set, understood the chain of authority for giving direction to the actors, but in his opinion, Jean-Luc Renard was being far too lenient with Cynthia. She needed a firm hand, lest she ruin the entire picture with her grandiose attitude.

With a heavy sigh he stood and approached the notoriously temperamental Frenchman.

"This is not supposed to be *The Perils of Pauline,*" Rusty hissed to Jean-Luc, frustration lacing his words. "She's ruining the whole scene by inventing her own lines and doing all those crazy exaggerated arm movements. She looks like a windmill gone haywire. Can't you do something?"

Jean-Luc drew himself to his full height, which only reached Rusty's eye level. "Meester Rusty, you will calm yourself, no? Zee actress, she does her best." He turned back to "zee actress" and said in a conciliatory tone, "Ceenthia. You will now say the line Rusty has written for you, yes?"

Cynthia planted her fists on her hips. "No. It's a stupid line."

"There are no stupid lines. Only stupid actresses," Rusty blurted before he could stop himself.

To his horror, Cynthia's lower lip quivered and her eyes grew watery. "Why are you always picking on me?"

Oh, brother. Once an actress, always an actress.

"I'm not picking on you." Rusty fought to keep his voice level. "I'm just trying to get you to say the lines as they are written." He punched his finger at the script for emphasis. "Is that too much to ask?"

Cynthia crossed her arms and scowled.

Jean-Luc wrung his hands. "Meester Rusty, I must in-*seest* you leave zee actors to *moi.*" He spread his hands in a pleading gesture. "Ceenthia, *ma cherie*, you will say zee line, no?"

"I'll tell you what I'll do." Cynthia flung her script to the floorboards. "I'll tell Mr. Cooperman you're both making my life miserable. Absolutely *miserable*." Enormous tears rolled down her cheeks, forming rivulets of black eye makeup that gave her the appearance of a mournful Pierrot doll. A make-up artist rushed onto the set with a tackle box filled with potions and pencils. She dabbed at Cynthia's face with a damp towel and a powder puff, but apparently the wreckage was too extensive to fix with a simple swish-and-swipe.

"I'll have to take her back to the make-up trailer and start over completely." The make-up artist cast a resentment-filled side-eye in Rusty's direction. "It will take at least half an hour to repair the damage."

"Why? What difference does it make?" Rusty complained. "This is just a blocking and lighting rehearsal. We aren't filming yet."

But his complaint fell on deaf ears as the make-up artist hustled Cynthia off to repair her war paint. He might as well be shouting into the wind. Jean-Luc lifted a megaphone to his lips. "All right, everyone. We break for *le déjeuner*. Be back here at two-thirty sharp to resume zee rehearsal. *Vite, vite*." He made a shooing motion with his hand.

Cast and crew murmured among themselves and scattered, most in the direction of the food tent erected at one end of the lot. Jean-Luc turned to Rusty and said in a snide tone, "You see what you have done? You have made *mademoiselle* cry. You are happy now, yes?" Before Rusty could reply, the director scurried off in the direction of the lighting supervisor, calling "Meester Bill, *un moment, s'il vous plaît*."

Thus dismissed, Rusty sighed and sank down in his chair. He had no appetite for lunch. Instead, he pulled a yellow pencil from behind his ear and scribbled some notes onto the script, searching in vain for some new combination of words that would appease Cynthia without ruining the scene.

A good thirty minutes elapsed before Jean-Luc approached Rusty.

"You must go to Ceenthia now and tell her you are sorry."

Rusty jerked his head up. "I must what now?"

The director spread his arms. "Zee *actrice*, she is inconsolable. She refuses to return to zee set until she receives an apology from you."

Rusty muttered something unsuitable for a Christian man to say. The director remained unmoved.

"Pleez, *monsieur* Rusty, I beg of you. Go to zee *trailair* of *mademoiselle* and tell her you are *très desolé*, so we can get back to zee rehearsal."

"I'm not *desolé* about a darn thing. Oh, for Pete's sake." At the look on Jean-Luc's face, Rusty stood, flung his script on a table, and stomped off in the direction of Cynthia's trailer.

It was going to be a long day.

CHAPTER SEVEN

Helen scuttled through the backstage hallway of the Orpheum as quickly as her cumbersome petticoats would allow. Earlier that day, the costuming of Nanette's nine bridesmaids in umpteen yards of dark green velveteen had turned the tide on the store's sales for that week, probably even the whole month. This triumph had put a smile on Charlie's face, and Marjorie's as well. By the time she'd turned the sign in the window from Open to Closed, Helen knew the time was ripe to ask Marjorie if she could invite Chet to dinner. As predicted, Marjorie said yes.

So now all that remained was inviting Chet.

Helen finally spotted him talking to the head technician in charge of the lighting. She waited for them to finish their conversation and for the technician to walk out of earshot, then approached Chet. He was staring intently at a chart clipped to a board. When he didn't acknowledge her presence, she tapped him on the shoulder.

"Hi, there," she said meekly, suffering a sudden attack of shyness.

His stern expression softened a little when he saw her—but only a little.

"Hello." He frowned as he studied her appearance. "Where are your necklace and earrings?"

"I haven't quite finished getting ready yet. I wanted to talk to you."

In the ensuing pause, he obviously was expecting her to say something more. Maybe this wasn't the best time to invite him to dinner after all, but here she was, so she got right to the point.

"My-my sister would like you to come over for dinner."

"Dinner?" Instead of the big smile she'd expected, his brow creased, as if partaking of the evening meal was an unfamiliar custom.

"Yes. To our house. Tomorrow night, before the performance. Or, really, any night you're free." She heard herself rambling.

He glanced around, distracted. "I'm afraid that's not possible, honey. I'm tied up every minute, and then I'm gone."

Gone. "Oh, well, sure," she stammered. "It's just that she hasn't met you, and she's never going to approve of my going off to Chicago with someone she's never met."

"Helen, how old did you say you were?" His voice was sharp, his words clipped.

The unexpected question took her aback. "Twenty-one."

"Time to grow up, honey. Your sister is no longer your guardian. Surely you don't need her approval, or anyone else's, to pursue your career in Chicago."

"Well, no. Not officially. But—" Confusion clouded her brain. She couldn't seem to find the words she wanted. Where was the gentle, kind man who'd spoken so sweetly to her just last night? And how could she make him understand why gaining Marjorie's confidence and keeping her trust felt so important to her?

He bent his head and softened his voice, but his eyes held no warmth. "Look, honey, I'm sorry I can't fit in dinner with your family. It will all work out. You do understand, don't you?"

"I suppose, but—"

"We'll talk about this later. Right now we have a play to rehearse." He lifted his head. "Places, everyone!"

Numbed by his curt attitude, Helen walked toward the stage with the other actors, aching with disappointment. It *wasn't* all right. She *didn't* understand. If she and Chet were to be a team, a real couple, if he planned for her to join him in Chicago where he'd take her under his wing, he had to meet her family first.

He simply *had* to.

Over the course of the dress rehearsal, Chet remained standoffish and businesslike. But Helen's frustration softened as she got caught up in portraying her character and concentrating on the intricacies of the play. When she wasn't on stage, she observed him directing, ordering, calling the shots, and she felt proud of him. He was a busy, important man, with many responsibilities riding on his shoulders. How silly of her to expect him to take time out of his packed schedule just to meet her family. If it wasn't possible, it wasn't possible, that was all. She would simply have to understand.

And so would Marjorie.

If red velvet seats and gold-flocked wallpaper were any indication, the Orpheum Theater had once aspired to be a great temple to the dramatic arts. Built during the glory days of vaudeville, its bill of fare had long since shifted to moving pictures—first the silents, then the talkies, and now the lively, upbeat musicals that helped people forget their troubles for an hour or two. But for special occasions such as the opening night of the Kerryville Players' summer production, the screen was rolled up, unveiling the grand stage behind it.

Grand by Kerryville standards, at least.

Two dusty backstage rooms, used mainly for storage, had been once again pressed into service as dressing areas, one for the men and another for the women. The cramped confines of the ladies' dressing room smelled of pancake makeup, face powder, drugstore perfume, and nervous perspiration. Someone had opened the windows, but the air remained warm and stagnant.

After elbowing her way through the crowd of actresses to find space at a cracked mirror hanging precariously over a dusty, makeup-strewn table, Helen peered into its hazy depths and carefully applied her lipstick. While her character, a genteel Victorian lady, would never have worn lipstick, it was a cruel fact that floodlights washed the actors out, turning their faces ghostly and featureless. Helen had no intention of being washed out.

A knock at the door and a muffled male voice called, "Flower delivery for Miss Helen Corrigan." Like a huge flock of birds, a sudden flurry of twittering and rustling rose from actresses in various stages of undress. Helen turned from the mirror as the door cracked open slightly and a long white box was thrust through the opening. Eugenia Wardlow, who in the play portrayed a nosy neighbor remarkably consistent with her real-life self, set down her hairbrush, accepted the box from the anonymous arm, and carried it over to Helen.

Helen swept bottles and jars aside to make room for the offering on the cluttered makeup table. "Roses!" she breathed as she lifted the lid and spied a dozen crimson roses tucked amid white tissue paper. "How gorgeous."

"Are they from your family?" Eugenia pried.

"I don't know. I suppose so." But she doubted it. Who among the Corrigans could afford to spring for a dozen roses?

"Maybe you have an ardent admirer, Helen," Mabel Meyer teased as she brought over an empty Mason jar to serve as a makeshift vase. "Anyone we know?"

Helen sure hoped so. She arranged the roses in the jar. Then, with a flicker of anticipation, she found the small white envelope and slid it open, elated to find the classically engraved calling card of one Chester D. Scarborough within. Sometime she must ask him what the D stood for. He'd scratched a line through the name and scrawled in blue ink, "To my leading lady, with fondest regards, Chet."

His leading lady. Her heart took flight, and her hand trembled slightly as she propped the card against the jar and picked up her lipstick. The fact that she would have preferred "love always" over "fondest regards" barely dimmed her joy, mixed with a substantial measure of relief that Chet still cared for her.

The previous night, when he hadn't responded to her clumsy attempts to attract his attention, her worry had escalated. In mere days he'd be leaving Kerryville forever, and they hadn't yet discussed the logistics of getting her to Chicago, much less about their budding romance and what it might mean for both their futures.

But now it was opening night. And here, at last, was proof of his feelings, tucked among a boxful of blooms, written in his own illustrious hand. *His leading lady.* Suddenly frantic to seek him out and thank him personally—hopefully in some private spot where they wouldn't be observed by the likes of curious stagehands—she hurriedly dashed a powder puff over her nose.

"So, Helen, don't keep us in suspense," Mabel called. "Who are they from?"

"From Chet." Helen smiled and tried to sound casual, but it was nearly impossible. She hoped the other ladies wouldn't be jealous. Well, maybe a little jealousy would be in order. But just a wee bit.

Before her thoughts could travel further down that road, another rap sounded at the door. "Flowers for Miss Nanette Johnson." More twittering and rustling, another box thrust through the door. Nanette squealed and hurried to accept it.

"Are they from Ted?" Helen teased. Then she stopped powdering, mid-puff.

Nanette's bouquet looked exactly the same as hers. Red roses wrapped in white tissue paper. Goodness, did the local florist have nothing else in stock?

Nanette read the card and her brows rose. "They're not from Ted. They're from Chet."

From across the room, Helen shot Nanette a broad smile and told herself everything was fine. How thoughtful of Chet. Nanette deserved flowers, too. Of course she did.

More knocks. More bouquets. "Flowers for Mabel Meyer." "Flowers for Diantha Davis."

Before long it became apparent that Chet had sent flowers to every woman in the cast.

Every last one. Even the walk-ons.

With every new delivery, Helen's own joy tarnished just a little. She wasn't so special, after all. It wasn't that she begrudged the other actresses their flowers, exactly. And wasn't Chet a thoughtful dear to have sent them to the entire cast? What did the men get? Anything? It was just that... well, was it so very selfish to want to be special in Chet's eyes? To hold a unique place in his heart? Was that too much to ask?

She sighed and finished powdering her nose, chiding herself to look on the bright side. The roses *were* stunning, even if not as exclusive to her as she had first thought.

But only her card bore the words *my leading lady*. She took some small comfort in that fact.

"Ten minutes to curtain. Everyone backstage." The stage manager's voice reverberated from the hall. As the cast and crew hurried to gather in the wings, Helen had no time to seek Chet out for a private conversation. Her blood stirred as he stood before them, tall and handsome in a dinner jacket, his silvery brown hair slicked back from his noble forehead.

Beside her, Nanette's poor hand, chilled with nervousness and excitement, crept into Helen's. She rubbed it in an attempt to warm it up, careful to steer clear of The Ring.

Chet addressed the whole group. "You're going to do great tonight. I'm so very proud of each and every one of you." He gave them a few more words of encouragement and a couple of last-minute instructions. Helen wished he'd pray for them. She could use a prayer or two about then. But he wasn't the praying type. So as the assembly broke up, she and Nanette quickly prayed together by themselves instead.

Then Helen hurried after Chet and touched his arm. "I just wanted to thank you for the roses," she whispered, suddenly feeling shy. "They're splendid."

He gazed down at her warmly, grasping her hands in his. "You're very welcome, Helen. I know you'll bring down the house tonight." He released her hands and touched the side of her cheek. "Such an extraordinary face," he said, as if he were seeing it for the first time.

For a split second everything and everyone melted away, leaving just the two of them gazing at one another.

"Places, everyone. Places!" called the stage manager.

Chet leaned down and gave her a peck on the forehead, just as he had the night he'd walked her home. "It's showtime," he whispered. He squeezed her hands again, then released them and strode over to say something to the props manager.

As the small orchestra struck up the overture, Helen tiptoed onto the dark stage, her mind whirling in confusion. What did he really think of her? Did he feel about her the way she felt about him? Was she truly his leading lady? Or merely the lead actress in his latest play, soon to be left behind as he moved on to other productions, other actresses? Had he been *serious* about taking her with him to Chicago?

Her thoughts continued to swirl as she took her place behind the heavy maroon curtain and draped her corset-clad form across the velvet settee as the graceful belle, Susannah. They kept on swirling as Bob Green, who played her bewhiskered father, settled his portly frame on a chair next to her, and as Nanette in her crisp pinafore and cap picked up her feather duster.

But as the orchestra swelled and the curtain rose, her mind stilled. This was no longer Kerryville. She was no longer Helen Corrigan. She was Susannah McCabe, seated in the elegant front parlor of the house situated under the flaming oak tree.

All worries and concerns about Chet Scarborough would have to wait.

Before she knew it, they'd come to the end of Act Three. In her role as the ill-fated Susannah, Helen gazed out into the middle distance, over the heads of the audience, as if looking into her uncertain future. Placing her hand over her heart, she declared in determined tones, "Never shall I see another sunrise like this one."

The stage lights darkened, and for a moment all was still. Then the theater broke into thunderous applause.

Temporarily blinded by the sudden blackness, Helen picked her way offstage. A strong pair of arms wrapped around her and lifted her up off the ground.

"Honey! We did it!" With a jubilant cry Chet swung her around, leaving her breathless. "We're gonna knock 'em dead in Chicago, you and I." Then he set her down, leaned over, and covered her mouth with his.

Her legs turned to jelly. She clung to him as if to a life raft, even after he broke the kiss.

"Curtain call," someone cried out.

She wanted to stay in his arms forever. But he turned her back toward the stage and gave her a gentle push.

"This is your moment, honey. Enjoy it."

Mechanically she glided in front of the footlights. Applause rang in her ears as she joined the cast in a deep bow. But she barely heard any of it.

Chet had kissed her. On the mouth. And nothing would ever be the same again.

CHAPTER EIGHT

"C ut!"

The director's order and the sharp snap of the clapperboard jerked Rusty out of his daydream—a disturbing daydream that involved placing his hands around Cynthia Starling's pale, slender throat and squeezing hard. He wasn't a violent man, not in the least. But her constant whining, complaining, and brutal disregard toward the lines he'd written for her sparked some primitive rage lurking deep inside his chest. His nerves were shot, and this was only the first day of filming. He could hardly wait to reach the end of his second-assistant-directorship and return to the relative peace and sanity of the writing room.

Feeling claustrophobic, unable to tolerate one more minute of Cynthia's terrible acting in the barroom scene, he rejoiced inwardly when Jean-Luc called for a break. He threw his script onto a table and burst through the swinging doors of the Lazy R Saloon. He strode across the porch and rested his forearms on the wooden railing. Clasping his hands loosely, he began to pray. Under the relentless heat of the afternoon sun, his last morsel of patience melting away, he buried his head in his hands.

Lord, help me. Help me finish this picture without losing my mind.

After several moments. he lifted his head. Prayer always helped him feel calmer. So did the soothing buzz of the cicadas, mixed with the distant hammering and sawing as the crew labored to finish the rest of Dust Valley before the filming of the big gunfight scene took place.

He wiped his forehead with his shirt sleeve and squinted across the dusty road toward the façade of the supply store. The construction crew had done an extraordinary job.

On seventy acres in the desert outside Tucson, Cooperman Studios' work crews, aided by local craftsmen, had erected a Western town in a matter of weeks, so authentic-looking that if it weren't for the cameras and filming equipment, passersby might mistake it for the real thing.

There were few passersby, however. Beyond the boundaries of the makeshift town, the desert stretched in all directions, an endless sea of gold, coral, beige, and brown. A hot wind whistled through the dry brush, carrying the scents of sagebrush and sand and the promise of relief as the sun set.

In spite of Rusty's general dislike of Arizona's relentless heat and dust, he was grateful for the opportunity to work on location. And as much as he preferred working in a soundstage where light and sound could be controlled, he had to admit, the Arizona desert had its own weird sort of beauty.

But having to work closely with Cynthia, let alone having to spy on her for Cooperman, made him more miserable than the climate. He hated being her babysitter. Keeping her in line was like trying to capture one of the rattlesnakes that were a constant threat on the set. Yet he suspected Cooperman would find some way to hold Rusty responsible if even a hint of a romance blossomed between Cynthia and Mark St. Ives, or anybody else.

The rumbling of the huge fans running outside the saloon to blow through water filters and cool the interior caught his attention. But even the relative coolness of being indoors couldn't entice Rusty to enter. Weary, he took a seat on the top step to wait until Jean-Luc ordered him back inside.

Behind him, the saloon doors swung open. Rick Carter emerged, folded his thin frame onto the step beside Rusty, and handed him an icy, uncapped bottle of root beer taken from an electric cooler hidden underneath the bar. Rusty thanked him, took a deep swig of the sweet, bubbly liquid, then held the cold, dripping bottle against his aching forehead.

They were alone on the porch. Everyone else had apparently decided to spend the break inside the relative shade and coolness of the saloon.

Rick cleared his throat. "Your patience is fading."

Rusty nodded. "Yes, it is."

"Mine, too." Rick squinted. "Cynthia's not a great actress."

Rusty snorted at the understatement.

"And yet, she's Cooperman's girlfriend." Rick seemed hell-bent on stating the obvious. "She's not going anywhere. We must think of a way to help Jean-Luc drag a good performance out of her." He turned to face Rusty. "What do you propose we do?"

Rusty gave a listless shrug. His imagination felt as barren as the landscape.

"You could start by being kinder to her." Rick's request landed somewhere between a plea and a command. "You could try not to lose your temper."

"I will try," Rusty promised. But he didn't hold out much hope for success.

Rick talked him into going back inside. Compared to the rough morning, the rest of the day's filming went relatively smoothly, thanks to the fact that Cynthia finished her part and retired to her trailer for a rest.

They were almost finished for the day when a scream ripped through the hot air from the direction of Cynthia's trailer. Cast and crew alike charged toward it.

Cynthia stood on the step of her trailer, wild-eyed, pointing mutely at the ground where a rattlesnake lay coiled.

Rusty leaped into action. Though he'd never encountered a rattlesnake, a boyhood spent fighting off assorted vermin made him bold.

He started toward the snake, then stopped short. The reptile lay rigid, its head lifted as though ready to strike. It was a good three feet long. Without thinking, Rusty grabbed a nearby shovel that the construction crew had been using.

The snake reared back its head.

Rusty raised the shovel.

The snake slithered into a dense shrub and made a furious rattling noise.

Rusty hacked into the shrub and dragged the reptile out with its back broken. He hacked once more. The creature stopped moving. Another poke with the shovel assured it was dead.

For a long moment no one moved. Adrenaline pumped through Rusty's veins, and a cold sweat drenched his shirt. With the shovel, he picked up the dead snake and carried it several hundred feet away from the set, tossing it into the sagebrush. When he returned, a shaky-voiced Jean-Luc declared work was done for the day.

Cynthia ran to Rusty and threw her arms around his neck. "Oh, Rusty, you're my hero! You saved my life." She planted a sloppy kiss on his cheek.

Gently he extricated himself from her embrace, resisting the urge to wipe his face. But on the chartered bus ride into Tucson for dinner and sleep, he continued to shake off praise from the cast and crew for his alleged heroic act.

"Aw, I was just the nearest guy to the shovel," he said. "Anyone else would have done the same." Although it was clear no one had.

He glanced over at Cynthia, who was blinking at him with grateful doe eyes from across the aisle—overly dramatic as usual. He turned away in disgust. For Cooperman's sake, and his own, he was relieved she wasn't snuggled next to Mark St. Ives. In fact, the actor was sitting way up at the front of the bus, behind the driver. Maybe he'd had enough of Cynthia too. Rusty hoped so. It made his job easier if he didn't have to watch those two all the time.

Turning his gaze out the bus window, he had to admit that the slanted rays of sunset revealed the full beauty of God's creation, even out there in the desert. A cool shower in his private bathroom at the Santa Rita Hotel and a change of clothes lifted his spirits even further. By the time he joined various members of the cast and crew at a local restaurant, he felt invigorated, his good humor restored.

They ate a hearty meal. During dessert, a small orchestra played dance music. To Rusty's discomfort, Cynthia asked him to dance. Reluctantly he followed her to the dance floor and held her at arm's length, hoping they wouldn't have to talk about the snake. Hoping they wouldn't have to talk to each other at all.

No such luck.

"I don't think Jean-Luc likes me," Cynthia said with her trademark pout.

Rusty sensed he needed to tread carefully. "What makes you say that?"

"He's always complaining about my performance. And he says my hair is too blond. As if that's my fault."

"I'm sure any man would find you attractive," Rusty said with diplomacy.

"Do you?"

"Well... sure."

"Because you don't seem to like me, either," she said. "You're always picking on me."

"I don't pick on you."

"Yes, you do."

Rusty chose his words with care. "I mean, I'd like it a whole lot better if you'd say your lines the way they're written. And if you'd stop arguing with Jean-Luc and me about every little thing."

"I'm so glad to hear you say that," she breathed.

He looked at her, surprised. "You are?"

"I only do that because I want your attention." She drew closer and laid her cheek against his lapel. "Thank you for saving me from that mean old rattlesnake."

Sweat that had nothing to do with the desert climate broke out on Rusty's back. The reality of what was going on landed in his gut with a cold thud.

Cooperman needn't have worried. If Cynthia Starling had ever batted her famous eyelashes at Mark St. Ives, she no longer was.

She was batting them at Rusty.

Maybe he shouldn't have killed that rattlesnake, after all.

CHAPTER NINE

As Helen took her final bow amid thunderous applause, she glanced toward the section where her family was seated. Marjorie and Dot had risen to their feet and were clapping enthusiastically with the rest of the crowd in a standing ovation. When the fervor died down and the house lights came up, she and the rest of the cast returned to the dressing rooms. Helen changed into her street clothes but skipped removing her stage make-up. She was eager to see her family and didn't want to keep them waiting too long. She collected her belongings and made her way to the crowded lobby. They were milling around, greeting people they knew which, this being Kerryville, was practically everyone. A pang to the heart reminded Helen that there were certain aspects of small-town life she'd miss when she moved to Chicago. But those aspects weren't enough to keep her here.

"Helen!" Mrs. Varney, Helen's former Sunday school teacher, practically catapulted herself across the crowd. "You played your part so beautifully," she breathed.

"Yes, she did," Marjorie admitted, coming up beside Mrs. Varney and giving Helen a kiss on the cheek. "Well done, baby sister."

"Such splendid acting," Mrs. Varney continued, wringing her plump hands. "I cried so hard at the end. Who knew you had such talent?"

"I did." Peter approached the group, smiling. "I always said Helen had a flair for the dramatic." He gave Helen an affectionate chuck under her chin.

Marjorie put an arm around Helen's shoulders and pulled her close. "You were magnificent," she gushed. "I couldn't be more proud."

"Thanks." A rush of pleasure at her sister's praise was tempered by guilt over her plan to leave town. Surely now Marjorie would see that she was serious about an acting career.

The back of Chet's tall, lanky form appeared as he greeted a nearby group of well-wishers.

"Chet! Over here." As he approached, Helen reached for his arm and drew him forward. "Marjorie, I'd like you to meet Mr. Chester Scarborough. Chet, this is my sister, Marjorie Bachmann, and my sister-in-law, Dot Corrigan."

"How do you do, Mr. Scarborough?" Marjorie shook his hand. "I'm so glad to meet you. The play was excellent."

"It's a pleasure to meet you, Mrs. Bachmann. Helen has told me so much about you." Chet directed a polite nod to Marjorie, then inclined his head toward Dot. "And you, Mrs. Corrigan." His gaze lingered, to Helen's mind, a bit longer than necessary. Apparently, Dot thought so too, because she returned a tight, polite smile in place of her usual full-wattage grin. Even though it was not unusual for Dot's good looks to draw that sort of attention, a wave of jealousy caught Helen by surprise. Thank goodness Dot was already married to Charlie, who was the next person in line to be introduced, followed by Peter.

"Really enjoyed it." Peter shook Chet's hand.

"Chet wrote the play, of course, and I think that his direction really makes the story come alive." Helen turned her dimpled smile to Chet. "I do hope you'll join us for cake and ice cream at our house. The whole cast is invited."

"Please do join us, Mr. Scarborough," Marjorie said. "Ice cream on the porch—a Corrigan family tradition after Helen's opening-night performances. Our house is just a few blocks from here."

"Yes, I know." He grinned. "And a fine porch it is."

At Marjorie's quizzical look, Helen rushed to explain. "He walked me home from rehearsal the other night."

Marjorie raised her eyebrows. "Oh?"

While she digested that morsel of information, Chet said, "I'm disappointed, but I'm afraid I must decline your kind invitation. Perhaps we'll have a chance to meet again sometime." He gently disengaged Helen's hand from his arm. "And I'll see *you* here tomorrow night, honey. Be ready to go. And between now and then, try to get some rest."

"I will." Helen couldn't keep the note of disappointment from her voice. Her cheeks burned as she glanced sideways at Marjorie. Surely her sister's perfect hearing had caught the word *honey*, not to mention *be ready to go*. She'd have so many questions. Didn't Chet realize how important it was for him to spend time with her family and vice versa?

If Marjorie noticed anything, she didn't let on. As Chet moved off to greet other well-wishers, she wedged herself between Helen and Dot and linked her arms through theirs. "What do you say we go and have ourselves some ice cream?"

Two more days. Just two more days and I'll be leaving for Chicago.

Her gut gave a sudden, anxious twist. Whether from elation at going with Chet or despair at leaving her family, she didn't know.

The Saturday performance went as well as the first. However, by Sunday, Helen was nearly blind with panic. The play was closing with Sunday's matinee, and Chet hadn't said anything more about her going to Chicago with him. She'd packed a bag anyway and stashed it in the dressing room so she'd be ready at a moment's notice. She wouldn't need much in the way of clothes and possessions, at least not at first. She would send word to Marjorie of their elopement just as soon as they were safely married.

It broke her heart a little that they would have to be married by a justice of the peace instead of in the church she'd grown up in. There was simply no time to plan a wedding, even a small one. And it troubled her deeply to not have Marjorie and the rest of her family present. But that couldn't be helped. Chet was a busy and important man, and Helen would need to adjust to that.

Pacing the dressing room before the final performance, she was frantic to find him and find out what was going on.

Hoisting her heavy skirt, she located the stage manager taking a smoking break in the alley behind the theater. "Hi, Steve. Have you seen Chet?"

Steve dropped the cigarette and smashed it under his heel. "I saw him talking to someone backstage a little while ago."

"Who was it?"

Steve gave her a curious look. "Don't know. Never seen her before."

Her?

She found Chet in a corner of the dim backstage, talking to a smartly dressed woman Helen didn't recognize. Who was it? A member of the audience? A fan from Chicago?

Chet leaned down to say something to the woman. Helen felt an unreasonable pang of jealousy, then chided herself for jumping to conclusions. After all, she could be anyone. A longtime platonic friend of Chet's. A theater colleague from Chicago. For heaven's sake, she could be his sister!

She put her smile in place, walked up to the couple, and prepared to introduce herself.

"There you are, Chet," she said in a light tone, subduing her panic. "I've been looking all over for you."

His head jerked up at her approach. The backstage light cast an eerie blue glow over his features. He lifted a forefinger. "Just a minute, Helen. I'll be with you in a moment."

The woman he was conversing with turned to face Helen. She was well dressed in a smart ensemble and had eyes like a cat's, slanted and rimmed in black pencil. She, too, had an otherworldly air in the blue light.

"So you're the famous Helen," she purred, sweeping Helen with an appraising gaze. "I don't believe we've met. Chet has told me so much about you."

"Has he?" *He hasn't told me anything about you.*

Helen glanced at Chet. His eyes didn't meet hers.

The woman extended her black-gloved hand. "Where are my manners? How do you do. I'm Denise."

"How do you do." Helen accepted her hand. She looked back at Chet, confused.

He coughed. His Adam's-apple moved in his throat. And suddenly she knew, even before he said the words. The room tilted a little.

"Denise," he said, "I'd like you to meet Helen Corrigan. Helen, this is Denise." He swallowed again. "Denise Scarborough. My wife."

His wife.

Though somehow remaining outwardly calm, inwardly Helen spun into free-fall, her blood erupting hot and cold through her veins. Slowly, slowly, as if underwater, she somehow managed to shake Denise Scarborough's hand and murmur the polite, automatic "How do you do" that had been bred into her from childhood. She forced her lips to curve upward in something approximating a smile. Above all, she avoided looking at Chet, knowing one glance at his face would cause her careful façade to crumble.

"So you're Helen Corrigan. The leading lady." Denise's dark eyes glittered. "Congratulations. I understand you've been quite triumphant in this play. I can hardly wait to see your performance."

I can hardly wait to be anywhere but here. "Nice to meet you," Helen breathed. Her lungs weren't quite working. "If—if you'll excuse me, I'm needed in the dressing room."

"Of course."

She turned and walked on leaden legs, sensing Denise's penetrating gaze on her back. She forced her legs to carry her down the hallway. Behind her, Chet hissed something to his wife—his *wife*—and she hissed something back, both of them tense and angry. Helen rounded the corner, pushed her way into the ladies' restroom, locked herself into a stall and slumped against the wooden door, willing the walls to stop turning.

Married! How could he be married? After all the things he'd said to her? After the plans they'd talked about? After he'd *kissed* her?

Over the rushing in her ears, she vaguely became aware of the outer door opening. She stood up straight and swiped her fingers over her face.

"Helen? Are you in here?" Nanette's voice sounded concerned.

Helen cleared her throat. "Yes."

"Are you all right? You sound funny."

"Yes. Perfectly fine," she caroled, her voice unnaturally bright to her own ears.

"All right. Ten minutes to curtain."

"I'll be right out. Thank you." She flushed the toilet for effect, then bowed her head and prayed. *Lord, give me strength to make it through this performance. We can untangle the rest of this mess later, but please, please, get me through this day. I can't do it under my own strength.*

When the outer door thudded to a close on its vacuum catch, she emerged from the stall, turned on the faucet, dampened a towel, and rubbed cool water on her wrists and the back of her neck. By some miracle she hadn't collapsed in a flood of tears or ruined her stage makeup, as there would be no time to fix it even if she had. Feeling like a robot in an H. G. Wells novel, steely and numb, she walked to the back of the stage, head held high. She nodded to the stage manager—if Chet was back there, she didn't see him—and took her place on the loveseat.

"Here we go, one last time," murmured Bob Green, her on-stage father. With a stab to her heart, she wished her real father were handy, not a zillion miles away in Arizona. His quiet strength and stability had always comforted her in times of emotional upheaval.

"The very last time," she whispered back. As the heavy curtain rose, she left Helen Corrigan behind and slipped into Susannah McCabe once again. Her heart was shattered, but for the sake of everything she believed in, the show must go on.

CHAPTER TEN

Since the filming of the big gunfight scene didn't require Cynthia's presence, Rusty breathed a little easier. Under ordinary circumstances, she never paid the slightest attention to any scene in which she was not the main attraction. He expected her to remain sequestered in her trailer, chanting spells or sticking pins into a doll crafted in Rusty's image, or whatever else she did in there.

But ever since the rattlesnake incident, "ordinary" had packed its bags and left on the first stagecoach out of town.

Cynthia emerged from her trailer wearing high-heeled sandals, a form-fitting pair of shorts, and a cotton shirt tied to reveal her tanned midriff. She planted her folding chair right next to Rusty's.

"I hope you don't mind if I sit here," she cooed. "I feel safer when you're around."

"Suit yourself." Rusty frowned as he concentrated on the script. The shootout was an action scene without a lot of dialogue. Those few spoken lines needed to carry their weight.

"What if that big, bad rattlesnake's family comes looking for him?" Cynthia whimpered, plucking at Rusty's sleeve.

He refused to make eye contact. "Then you'd better change out of those fancy shoes, or you'll break your ankle when you're running away."

Cynthia giggled. "Oh, Rusty. You're so funny." She patted his shoulder in a playful manner. When he jerked away, she rested her forearm on his armrest and kept it there. He leaned as far away from her as he could without tipping his chair clean over. At last he stood and shoved the chair several feet away, hoping she'd take the hint. Moments later, she followed, sticking to him like a burr on a coyote.

Even Rick Carter noticed. "What's with you and Cynthia?" he asked during a break. "You seem pretty cozy. You two finally patch things up?"

"There is no 'me and Cynthia,'" Rusty snapped. "If she's being nice to me, it's because she wants something."

He dreaded to think *what* she wanted. No jackrabbit ever stood on such high alert, frozen in the unblinking stare of a cougar.

Worse, if people like Rick were starting to notice Cynthia's flirtatious behavior, that could only spell trouble. The last thing Rusty needed was for rumors to fly straight back to Cooperman that he and Cynthia were becoming, in Rick's word, "cozy."

If it did, the next pelt displayed on Cooperman's wall would be Rusty's.

Light filtered through the closed curtains in Helen's upstairs bedroom. Sitting in her worn wooden rocking chair, she looked around the room, letting her eyes fall on the familiar objects without really seeing them. Her childhood bedroom. But she was no longer a child. Her supposed great romance was over before it began. Up in smoke, burned to ashes on a pile of lies.

Not lies, she reminded herself. He'd never told her he was a free man. She'd never asked, only assumed. He'd never told her he wanted anything more than a good performance from her in the role of Susannah. All the rest of their "relationship" had been a product of her imagination, conjured out of thin air.

She turned her head toward the untouched lunch tray that Dot had brought to her room at some point. A newspaper also lay on the tray, folded to show an article. "*Under the Flaming Oak* a resounding success," read the headline. She picked it up. In the muted light her eyes, sandy with sleeplessness, skimmed the words.

"Miss Helen Corrigan of Kerryville took the Orpheum audience by storm in *Under the Flaming Oak* this weekend. Capacity audiences for all three performances just couldn't get enough of

Miss Corrigan's stunning dramatic ability and heartfelt delivery." Further down the column was praise for the illustrious playwright and director. *And husband to Denise.* Don't forget *husband to Denise.*

Listlessly setting the paper aside, she waited for the contentment, the deep feeling of satisfaction such glowing words regarding her performance should have brought. Instead, she felt nothing.

Nothing but the certainty she was the world's biggest fool.

She shifted her gaze out the window, dry-eyed. Already the leaves on the gnarly old maple were beginning to droop. Summer would soon melt into fall. A sense of time's fleeting nature, of her very life slipping past, weighted her spirit.

Her memories of the previous day were a blur. Somehow she'd sublimated the humiliation and rage of Chet's deception through the character of Susannah McCabe, turning in her most powerful performance. That was what a professional did. After the final curtain, she'd pasted on a smile that lasted all the way through forty white-knuckled minutes of the cast party before pleading a headache. Then she'd walked home alone, tissued off her make-up, crawled into her bed, and hadn't emerged from her room since.

Faintly through the closed door, she heard muffled voices downstairs. Dot speaking to the children. And Marjorie and Charlie. If they were all home, it must have been after the store had closed for the day. After six. She should go down. But what was the point?

Bits of conversation floated up to her room.

"...exhausted..."

"...feeling all right?..."

"...hasn't eaten..."

"...I'll go check..."

Soft footfall on the stairs. A gentle knock on the door. Marjorie's quiet voice.

"Helen? Sweetie? Are you awake?"

The door creaked open. Helen turned her head as her sister tiptoed into the room.

"Dinner will be ready soon. You should eat something."

"Not hungry, thanks."

"I'm glad you're awake. Dot told me you've been sleeping all day. Aren't you feeling well?" Her sister's hand on her forehead felt cool and soft.

"I'm all right."

Marjorie walked to the desk and switched on a lamp. "Too much excitement."

"Yes."

Helen didn't have to look at Marjorie to know her sister was scrutinizing her face.

"You seem more than tired, sweetie. You seem... I don't know. What's going on? Did something happen?"

"I don't want to talk about it."

"I hear the matinee was a sensation. Did something happen afterward, at the cast party, to make you..."

Helen stiffened and withdrew her hand. "Marjorie, please. I said I don't want to talk about it."

Her sister's mouth tightened. "All right. But if you change your mind, you know you can always come to me."

Helen swallowed past the lump in her throat. "I know."

How could Marjorie possibly understand? Helen hadn't even confided in Marjorie how she felt about Chet... although her sister might have guessed. How could she now tell her that she'd fallen for a married man?

My wife. Those two innocent-sounding words had taken on so much freight over the past twenty-four hours.

How could she have been so blind as to not realize Chet was married?

Marjorie stood. "All right. You rest. Peter's working, and the rest of us are about to have dinner. We're here if you need anything." She paused at the doorway. "You really should eat something. Dot made a chicken casserole using Frances's recipe. You've always liked that." Gently she closed the door behind her, and Helen heard her soft footsteps going down the stairs, then more hushed conversation.

"...looks pale..."

"...say anything to you?..."

"...better soon..."

Helen sighed. Marjorie's mention of Frances brought to mind her father and stepmother, now living far away in Arizona. They had no idea of the heartbreak she'd just endured, much less her disgracefully poor judgment in falling for a married man. If only Pop were here to offer her his wise guidance, his unconditional love. If only she could slip into his arms for a hug, the way she used to when she was a little girl. Somehow he always made everything seem all right. How she longed now for his reassurance.

She lay on her bed for another quarter hour, an idea forming dimly through her fogged-over brain. At last she sat up, changed into fresh clothes, and appeared downstairs with washed face and combed hair.

"There she is." Dot placed a steaming casserole dish on the table.

"Oh, good." Marjorie was pouring ice water into glasses.

"You okay, kid?" Charlie clapped her on the shoulder. Helen nodded.

"You sure knocked 'em out this weekend," her brother continued. "It was all over Main Street today that you carried the show."

She forced a smile. "Thanks. It was a group effort."

They took their seats around the table. Over dinner, she poked at her food and let the talk swirl around her, until at last she spoke.

"I'd like to go visit the folks. Who knows when I'll get to see them again?"

Marjorie set down her fork. "In Arizona?"

"That's where they live, isn't it?" she snapped, then softened her tone. "Just for a week or two. I have enough saved up for the train fare, and you don't need me at the store, right?"

Marjorie and Charlie exchanged a glance.

Helen looked at her brother. "Things are slow there, anyway, right? Might as well save having to pay my wages for a week or two."

After a pause, Marjorie said, "I don't see why not. They'd be thrilled to see you, I'm sure. Likely Pop will even reimburse you for your ticket." She reached over and touched Helen's hand. "And you'll be home in plenty of time for the start of the fall semester at college."

Arguing would take too much energy. Maybe a teaching career was the best option for her, after all.

After dinner, a long-distance call was placed. Soon a flurry of details was arranged, and within a week Helen boarded a train bound for Tucson, Arizona.

CHAPTER ELEVEN

Rusty sat in his room at the Santa Rita Hotel and replayed the events of the past week in his head. He would not—could not—let Cynthia think he had any feelings for her other than platonic at best, and even that was a stretch. He ought to have put an end to it that first night, right then and there on the dance floor, but surprise made him lose his power of speech. Instead he'd made some hasty excuse and gone to his room, pleading exhaustion. And now, even though several days had passed—days in which he'd been as cool toward her as possible—she'd somehow gotten it into her vacuous head that he was her protector, her knight in shining armor.

This had to be stopped.

He made his way to the dining room where the cast and crew were having breakfast. He motioned to Cynthia to join him at a table for two near the window, far enough away from the rest of the bunch that their conversation wouldn't be overheard.

After they'd given the waitress their order, Rusty leaned forward on his elbows.

"Look, Cynthia. I don't know what game you're playing, but we need to nip it in the bud before it's gone too far."

"Before what's gone too far?"

"You. And me. It can't happen."

She stared at him. Her face turned crimson.

"I'm sorry," he added.

"But we're so good together."

He stared at her in shock. "We're terrible together."

She shot to her feet, practically carrying the tablecloth with her. "You'd better believe you're sorry," she spat. "Wait until I tell Mr. Cooperman what you've done. How you've hurt my feelings.

How you strung me along, pretending to care about me, and then treated me horribly." She stormed out of the dining room.

Crew members' eyes turned to Rusty, no doubt hoping for some dramatic reaction. These were movie people, after all, always ready to witness a good conflict. But this was real life, not some Saturday matinee.

"Now look what you have done," Jean-Luc exclaimed as he ran after her. "Ceenthia, *mon petit chou*, do not distress yourself!"

Rusty slumped into his chair. He'd thought it would be impossible to make things any worse between himself and Cynthia. But somehow he'd managed it.

The final days of filming wore on. For the most part, Cynthia ignored him completely, which was a relief. If she was forced to speak to him, she did so with cold contempt. Rusty vowed that, as soon as his part of the filming was over, he'd waste no time packing his things and hightailing it back to California. He wouldn't wait to ride back in the Cooperman Studios train with the rest of the cast and crew. He had to get back before anyone else did and repair whatever damage he could with Cooperman, even though it might be too late already. Besides, he needed time alone to think, to make plans, and he'd never have a moment's peace if he were on the same train as Cynthia.

As he checked and rechecked the train timetable, he practiced what he'd say to his boss if rumors had gotten back to him about Cynthia's flirtatious behavior—or worse, if Cynthia accused Rusty of being the instigator. He figured his job was toast anyway. For sure he could forget about any promotion.

The time to open his own studio was approaching faster than he'd thought.

Helen sat on the back patio of her parents' small adobe house, sheltered by a deep overhang of the red-tiled roof, and gazed eastward at the reddish-brown Sangre de Cristo Mountains in the distance. Happily, Pop and Frances had let her sleep late, and now it was nearly noon.

In place of her usual morning coffee, which seemed too hot to contemplate, she sipped a glass of cool tea. The sun had already started to burn its trail across the blazing blue sky. Heat shimmered off the Arizona landscape, beautiful in its own way in spite of the muted colors. The word *restful* came to her mind. And the penetrating aridity was a welcome change from the sticky humidity of Illinois.

If only her memories of Chet could be burned off as easily as the morning mist.

Behind her, the sliding glass door slipped quietly in its track. Pop came out and sat beside her, his knobby knees visible under plaid golf shorts. He handed her a wide-brimmed sunhat.

"Here. Frances wants you to put this on when you're outside. Can't be too careful in this strong sun."

"Thanks." She placed the hat on her lap and fiddled with the strings.

"Did you sleep well?"

"I did," she said, and it was true. Something about the clean desert air after days on the train had lulled her into a deeper sleep than she'd had since that terrible moment at the Orpheum.

Pop pointed. "So, what do you think of the lawn?"

She favored him with a grin. Not a blade of grass could be seen. Instead, the so-called lawn was liberally strewn with a variety of rocks, punctuated here and there with a cactus or orange tree or sagebrush.

"I think it's lovely," she said. "Such a clever use of space. And nothing to mow."

"Frances has brunch ready. Shall we go in?"

She set the hat on a side table and followed him through the door.

Inside, the living room seemed pleasantly dim after the brilliant glare outside. High beamed ceilings, cool tiled floors, and creamy white walls framed simple wood furniture strewn with brightly patterned Navajo blankets. Rough-hewn pottery jars and vases adorned the tables. This Indian-inspired décor was quite a departure from the Early American pieces they'd previously favored. When Pop and Frances had relocated to Arizona for Pop's health, they'd had to decorate completely from scratch, having left most of their former furnishings in the rambling Kerryville house where the rest of the family still lived.

Kerryville. The only home Helen had ever known. And only she knew she wasn't planning to go back. Not for a long time, anyway. Unless she lost her nerve.

At the long wooden table, Frances refilled a tall pitcher with iced tea, then passed a plate of flat round bread.

"These are called tortillas," she explained. "They're made of corn. Have one. They're kind of like thin pancakes or crepes, but not at all sweet." She thrust the plate toward Helen. Her deeply suntanned wrist bore a stack of beautiful turquoise and silver bangles that jingled as she moved. The melodious sound reminded Helen of the little bell over the door at Corrigan's Dry Goods. She felt a pang of regret. Had she done the right thing in leaving?

"Frances has been learning Mexican cooking," Pop explained with a note of pride in his voice. "It's delicious stuff, as long as she goes light on the spices." He winked at his wife.

Following her parents' example, Helen wrapped the tortilla around a tasty mixture of meat, cheese, and vegetables.

So many sights and sounds were new to Helen. Sombreros. Serapes. Wide-brimmed sunhats. Black-haired Navajo dolls, and the rich, vibrant colors of Navajo rugs and blankets.

Both Frances and Pop were tanned and had lost weight, the picture of health. Pop played golf. Frances socialized at women's clubs just as she had back in Illinois. They'd found a good church to attend. They'd managed to carve out a new life in Arizona and seemed happy. Why couldn't Helen carve out a new life for herself as well?

Over the week she'd been in Arizona, she'd let the story leak out of her, usually at moments when she and Pop were alone. She told him all about the play, and about what had happened with Chet.

"Marjorie doesn't know the whole story, and I don't want her to," Helen said. "I don't want her to be ashamed of me."

Her father looked at her with kindly eyes. "She could never be ashamed of you, sweetie. Nor could I."

Helen's throat thickened. "I contradicted her at every point. And it turned out she was right all along."

"I think you give your sister less credit than she deserves. I think she'd be a lot more understanding than you realize."

Helen turned to her father. "What should I do now, Pop? I don't want to go to college and become a teacher. I simply don't."

"What do you want to do?"

"I want to go to Hollywood and pursue an acting career. Like I've planned since childhood. But Marjorie thinks that's a foolish idea. She thinks I can have more security by becoming a teacher."

"At first blush, that would appear to be true," Pop said. "But if your heart's not in it, it's unlikely that God is calling you to teach. Those who are drawn to be dedicated teachers surely have a gift for it."

"But what if God's calling me to be an actress?"

"Foolishness," Frances interjected, startling Helen, who'd been so absorbed in the conversation, she hadn't heard her stepmother return from shopping and join them on the patio. "I'm inclined to agree with Marjorie. You can better serve God in an upstanding career like teaching than by going to Hollywood, of all the dens of iniquity."

"Respectfully, Frances, I disagree," Pop said. "Hollywood needs Christians, too. It's just as much a mission field as the Congo."

Frances looked shocked. "How can you say such a thing, Melvin?"

He spread his hands. "It's true. Hollywood is having a huge impact on the world. I predict that impact will grow. People of conviction and courage should go there and try to make a difference."

"If you'll both excuse me, I'm going to bed," Helen said. "I have a lot to think about."

And think she did. Lying in her comfortable bed at night, listening to the nighttime chirpings and rustlings outside her window. Walking along the dusty road. Helping Frances in the kitchen. She thought, and prayed, and thought some more.

On the last evening of her visit, she sought out her father. She curled up next to him on the sofa and said, "I'm going to go to Hollywood. I don't think I'll ever forgive myself if I don't try."

"I know you'll do the right thing, sweetheart," he replied. "I believe in the power of God, and I believe in you."

She plucked at the sleeve of his cotton madras shirt. "Marjorie will kill me."

"I'll handle your sister. On the condition that you write to her yourself the moment you get settled. I don't want this issue to come between you girls."

She put her arms around Pop and hugged him. "Thanks for everything. You're the best."

He patted her shoulder. "You're a smart young woman, Helen. Trust the Lord to help you make the right decision, and keep right on trusting Him to see you through."

The next morning, Pop drove her to the train. He pulled up to the curb and applied the parking brake.

"Are you sure you don't want me to wait with you?" he said.

"I'm sure," Helen replied. "I can do this on my own."

"By the way, I put through the call to Marjorie last night," he said as casually as if announcing the weather. "She knows not to expect you back in Kerryville anytime soon."

Helen winced. "How did she take it?"

Pop patted her knee. "She'll adjust. By the time your train pulls into Los Angeles, she'll have gotten used to the idea. But remember to write her immediately, even if it's just a postcard."

"I will."

After a weepy goodbye, Pop drove off, and Helen took a seat in the waiting room. She stared unseeing at the travel posters on the wall, still waffling over the wisdom of her decision in spite of Pop's support.

Should she stay? Should she go? For one wild moment she thought she might not go anywhere, might stay right there in Arizona. She could get a job selling turquoise jewelry in a gift shop, or giving tours at the local mission. She nearly called Pop from the station telephone to beg him to come get her, but fought the urge. Almost immediately, she knew how impractical that was. She couldn't escape her problems by living with her parents forever. The answer she sought was not in Arizona.

She fought the urge to telephone Marjorie collect, long-distance, to confess all, even though Pop had already explained on her behalf. What good would that do? Marjorie would only throw a fit and give her all kinds of reasons to doubt herself.

The waiting room grew claustrophobic. She went outside the station, carrying her suitcase, and she paced and stewed and waited. She had never felt such heat. It rose off the dusty brick pavement in waves. As the merciless sun beat down, she remembered the sunglasses she'd bought while shopping with Frances, and put them on.

Before her train arrived, she returned to the waiting room and walked up to the ticket counter.

"I have a return ticket to Illinois, but I'd like to exchange it."

"Where to instead?" the clerk asked.

"Los Angeles, California," she said with more confidence than she felt. He stamped the ticket and handed it to her. She hefted her suitcase to the waiting area and took a seat on a wooden bench. She still had more time to wait. Time to change her mind. Time to sit and think and stew about her decision.

What was she doing? Was she crazy?

But when the Southern Pacific's *California Limited* finally rattled and clanged its way out of the Tucson station, headed westbound to Los Angeles, the new, independent Helen Corrigan was on it.

Boarding the train in Tucson, Rusty spotted a familiar slim blonde wearing a headscarf and sunglasses. A cold sweat ran down his back, in spite of the heat. What the devil was Cynthia doing here? Had she followed him to the train?

Shocked that Cynthia would be on his train, minus her whole entourage, he knew something was up. Maybe she'd come to apologize—but that seemed totally out of character for the self-centered actress.

More likely she wanted to give any nearby photographers the impression she and Rusty were traveling together, so the "news" would make the gossip rags. Any hope he had of unlinking his name from hers would be ruined.

On impulse, anger rising in his chest, he decided to seize the opportunity to give the difficult actress a piece of his mind. He was going to lose his job one way or another, so he had nothing to lose but his dignity.

CHAPTER TWELVE

On board the *California Limited*, Helen located her seat, delighted to find it was next to a window. She settled in, fully expecting a seatmate to join her before too many miles had passed, but was startled when a man with hair the color of a bright new penny, looking not much older than herself, plunked himself gracelessly in the empty seat next to hers. Without even saying hello, he spoke to her in a sharp voice.

"What are you doing on this train?" he demanded.

She drew back. "I beg your pardon?"

"You're not supposed to be here."

She stared at him, speechless. How did he know?

"I mean it," he snarled. "What are you doing here?"

What kind of a question was that? An edge of anger pushed away her surprise. "Why, I-I bought a ticket, just like everybody else."

His voice rose. "Of all the nerve. Where do you get off taking *my* train instead of the one you're supposed to be on?"

Hot indignation burned in her chest, overtaking her alarm. She'd heard the old wives' tale that red-haired people could be prone to short-temperedness, but this was ridiculous. "What business is it of yours which train I'm supposed to be on? And where in blazes did you get the idea that this is *your* train?"

"You're supposed to come home on Thursday with everybody else."

"Look, mister, I think you're mistaken," she said. "I don't know you. I've never seen you before."

"Don't play coy with me, Cynthia."

"Cynthia? Who's Cynthia?" She whipped off her sunglasses and reached toward the bell rope to ring for the porter. Clearly the man was unhinged, possibly dangerous, a menace to society.

The man stared at her. Then his face turned redder than his hair. "I—I'm sorry, miss." He sounded truly contrite. "I—I mistook you for Cynthia Starling."

"Oh, sure," she snarked. "And you're the spitting image of Leslie Howard." She kept her hand on the rope, but in the ensuing pause, her alarm shifted to astonishment. "You mean it? You thought I was Cynthia Starling? *The* Cynthia Starling? Really?"

His demeanor changed completely. "Why, sure. Blond hair, similar hairstyle, same build, same..." His face turned even redder, if that were possible. He lifted his hands in a pleading gesture. "Look, miss, I'm terribly sorry. It was an honest mistake."

A concerned porter appeared in the aisle.

"Is everything all right, miss? Is this man bothering you?"

She realized she was still holding the bell rope and lowered her hand. Flattered that the lunatic had mistaken her for the famous movie star, her anger toward him dissipated.

"Thank you, no," she said to the porter. "There appears to have been a simple misunderstanding."

"Are you sure, miss?"

Helen became aware of the curious gazes of the other passengers. "Yes, I'm sure. Sorry for the trouble."

"Yes, I'm sorry, too," the red-haired man echoed. The porter cast him a cool glance and left.

"I really am sorry," he repeated. "It's uncanny how much you look like Cynthia Starling. You must hear that all the time."

"Actually, no one's ever said that to me. I'm glad you think so." She gave the man a bashful smile. As it turned out, her brash assessment that he looked like Leslie Howard wasn't too far off, after all. "She and I have something else in common. We're both actresses." It thrilled her to say it in so many words. She was an actress. A real live actress, on her way to California to—

"Let me guess," the man said with a knowing smile. "You're going to make it big in pictures."

"How did you know?"

"Just a lucky guess." He looked at her for a long moment. "May I ask what your name is?"

She told him. He gave a thoughtful nod.

"That's not too bad. They might even let you keep it. They made my friend change hers to Gilda Miller. Before that, she was Hilda Schwartzenmuller. Her name didn't stand a chance." Before she could respond, he added, "So tell me, Helen Corrigan. What do you think being in the pictures will be like?"

"I expect to work very hard," she said. "I've been honing my stagecraft for years and years. All through high school, and in community productions, too."

"That's good." He gave her an encouraging smile. "Too many girls—fellows, too, for that matter—go out there expecting to make it on their beautiful faces alone. An enchanting face might give you a leg up on the competition, but that's about it."

"Oh, I'm very serious about acting." She frowned a little to show him how serious she was.

"It's a dog-eat-dog world out there. Are you sure you're ready for it?"

"I'll try my best."

"That's all anybody can ask. Listen, kid. Let me give you a tip." He shifted in his seat to look at her. "You gotta have an inner desire, a real love for the process of making films if you want to work in this industry." He kept his eyes on hers. "You should be saying, 'I *gotta* do this.' You can't say, 'Well, I'll just try this and see what happens.' You gotta really want it."

"I do want it." The man's certainty made a new idea creep into Helen's mind. "You seem to know an awful lot about it. Do you work in the industry?"

"In a manner of speaking."

Her breath caught in her throat. "Are you an actor?" He was certainly good-looking enough to be. She scanned his features more closely to see if she recognized him.

"I'm a screenwriter at Cooperman Studios." His tone was matter-of-fact, as if it were no big deal. But it *was* a big deal.

"Cooperman Studios! Why, that's one of the biggest studios around," she said, impressed. "You must be very good at your job."

He tilted his head. "Depends on who you ask, I suppose. Cynthia Starling doesn't seem to think so, for one."

"Do you know her personally?"

"Know her! I work with her practically every day." He didn't look too happy about it.

"Golly," Helen breathed. "Working at Cooperman Studios, you must know a lot of important movie people."

He shrugged. "They're just people."

Helen couldn't believe her good fortune. She'd asked God for some confirmation that she was doing the right thing by going to Hollywood. And now, just minutes into the trip, here she was, sitting right next to a real, live Hollywood screenwriter.

She began to draw up a mental list of all sorts of questions to ask him about working in Hollywood. But minutes after the train pulled out of Tucson, a plump, bespectacled woman came through from another car and approached them.

"Excuse me," she said, shifting her gaze between the red-haired man and the ticket in her hand. "I believe you're in my seat."

The man apologized and stood. He turned to Helen. "It was nice to meet you, Miss Corrigan. Good luck."

"Same to you. I was hoping we could talk some more. I have so many questions. Another time, maybe."

"Maybe." His tone held no promise. He left for his own seat in another car, leaving Helen in a pleasant glow of stardust and daydreams.

Only much later did she realize she'd forgotten to ask his name.

Rusty located his seat, weak-kneed with embarrassment over his mistake. The young woman's resemblance to Cynthia was uncanny. And yet, in the space of only a few minutes' conversation—if one could call it a conversation—he knew the two women could not be more different in personality and temperament.

Cynthia was moody and manipulative, while Miss Corrigan was... well, the complete opposite. She'd been gracious and kind, readily forgiving Rusty's unseemly outburst. The fact that she was beautiful almost went without saying. But she seemed a little naïve, like so many other young hopefuls headed for Hollywood with stars in their eyes. Miss Corrigan seemed like a nice kid... the kind of kid the studio system tended to chew up and spit out. Aspiring actresses, especially the sweet ones, seldom lasted longer than six months in Tinseltown.

Almost before he realized what he was doing, Rusty leaned his head against the window, closed his eyes, and muttered a quick prayer for Helen Corrigan's safety and protection. Then he added a petition of his own.

Lord, thank You for sparing me the agonizing situation of giving the real Cynthia a piece of my mind. It would only have made her mad as a hornet. Word of my insolence would have gotten back to Cooperman at lightning speed and possibly cost me my job. I need more time and a cool head to plan my next move.

He concluded his prayer and stared out the window at the passing desert landscape. *My next move.* He stood and reached overhead to the rack where his leather briefcase sat. He clicked open the fasteners and lifted the lid. From its inner pocket he produced a notebook and fountain pen. Then, using the briefcase on his lap as a makeshift desk, he turned to a fresh page in the notebook. He uncapped the pen and scrawled across the top of the page, *New Movie Studio, Inc.*

He paused and stared at the blank sheet, considering the stupidity of the name. Well, it would do for now. He'd think of a better name later. Then he gazed unseeing out the window and tapped the end of the pen against his chin, thinking.

At last he turned back to the page, tightened his grip on the pen, and began jotting notes at a furious pace. Working on his dream was more productive than arguing with a ditzy actress.

Or worrying about some naive kid who didn't know what she was getting herself into.

CHAPTER THIRTEEN

As the train clickety-clacked over the rails on the overnight trip from Tucson to Los Angeles, Helen tried her best to sleep, but found it nearly impossible. She dozed a little, always jerking awake as the train pulled to a stop, or the whistle blew, or lights from a passing depot shone in her eyes. She shifted in her seat, trying to make herself as comfortable as possible and avoid disturbing her seatmate, the plump older woman with a kindly demeanor who'd displaced the copper-haired fellow. When Helen had offered her the window seat, the woman had declined.

"I've taken this trip many times," she explained. "I don't need to look at the scenery."

Not that there was any scenery to see for most of the journey, it being the middle of the night. Nonetheless, Helen had been relieved to sit beside such a motherly-type presence.

On the Chicago-to-Tucson leg of the trip, the train car had been heavily populated by traveling salesmen. She'd had to ignore their interested glances and fend off the occasional unwelcome remark.

Now the presence of this stalwart older woman, solidly positioned between Helen and the rest of the car, acted as a deterrent against any fellow traveler who might get a notion to speak to her.

There was only one passenger she would have preferred sitting next to, who could have told her all about life at Cooperman Studios, but she'd lost track of him when he left the car.

As the *California Limited* thundered through the black night, the two women hadn't shared much conversation beyond that initial greeting. But now, just as the first rays of the sun were slanting across the fields and orchards, Helen reluctantly tapped her sleeping seatmate gently on the shoulder.

"Sorry to disturb you," she murmured. "I need to powder my nose."

"That's quite all right, dear." The woman roused herself, removed eyeglasses from the seat pocket and slid them onto her face. For the first time Helen took a good look at her. Her thick eyeglasses, neat yet no-nonsense tweed suit, and graying marcelled waves gave her the appearance of a schoolteacher.

With an apologetic smile, Helen sidled past her and made her way to the restroom, trying to keep her balance as the train rocked and swayed. When she returned, the woman was fully awake.

"Did you manage to get some rest?" she asked as she made room for Helen to slide into her seat.

"As good as to be expected, I suppose. And you?"

"The same."

Helen checked her wristwatch. With a stab of regret, she thought of Marjorie, who'd given her the watch for high school graduation, and who would be hopping mad when Pop told her what Helen had done. Helen would have to write to her immediately upon arrival in L.A. and explain herself more fully.

"Are we almost there?" she asked her seatmate.

"Not quite. Another hour or so, I should think."

Helen glanced out the window, then did a double-take. The pink dawn revealed that the soil on either side of the train tracks, which had been dull, sandy brown in Arizona, was now covered with abundant wildflowers. Brilliant bands of yellows and oranges bloomed alongside the tracks, like beacons of light guiding the train to the Promised Land. After miles and miles of dry brush and reddish-brown earth, the ribbons of color were a welcome sight indeed, and they made Helen feel welcome.

"Aren't they lovely," she breathed. "Thank you, Jesus."

Her seatmate followed her glance. "What do you see?"

"The flowers," Helen pointed, her cheeks warm, not realizing she'd spoken aloud.

"Ah, yes. Aren't they lovely?" The woman leaned back in her seat. "We have the railroad workers to thank for that."

Helen cocked her head. "What do you mean?"

"The conductors have a little tradition. Many of them carry wildflower seeds in their pockets, which they then toss out of the train as it approaches California. Over the years their thoughtfulness has paid off with beds of flowers along the tracks."

"What a delightful idea." Helen sat up straighter. "That must mean we're getting close." She began to speculate in earnest on what Hollywood would be like.

"Almost. We've still got a ways to go."

Helen relaxed against her seat. "So you've taken this trip before?"

"Oh, yes. Many times. My home is in Los Angeles, but I travel frequently for work."

"What do you do?"

"I'm a teacher."

Bingo. Helen's first impression had been spot on. If a movie studio's casting department needed a teacher-type, they'd do well to cast Mrs.—Mrs.—

"I don't believe I've introduced myself." Helen extended her hand. "I'm Helen Corrigan."

"Lovely to meet you, Miss Corrigan. I'm Henrietta Mears."

"How do you do, Mrs. Mears."

"It's 'Miss.'" The woman's eyes twinkled. "And I'm assuming you're a 'miss,' too?"

"Yes, ma'am."

The woman smiled. "I was just speaking to a conference of young people about your age at Arizona State University. Are you in college?"

Helen shook her head. "No. Well, I was going to be, but then I had a change of plans." Guilt stabbed her as she thought of Marjorie sitting at home, wrestling with the idea that Helen would not be coming back in time for the fall semester. "I was just visiting my parents in Tucson. They retired there from Illinois, which is where we're all from. They moved there for my father's health. He owned a dry-goods store and now my brother and sister run it. I worked there too, selling fabric and buttons and things." She heard herself talking on and on and didn't know why she was sharing so much personal information with this stranger, other than the woman seemed interested and her face was kind and Helen was feeling dreadfully lonely.

"So you're a woman of business, then," Miss Mears said.

"Oh, no," Helen said quickly, though secretly pleased that this stranger thought she looked the part of a serious, responsible businesswoman. Marjorie and Charlie would chuckle if they heard that. Her heart gave another twang at the thought of her brother.

"I'm an actress," she stated with as much decisiveness as she could muster.

"Of course you are," the woman replied, not unkindly, but sounding a little disappointed. "The motion-picture industry attracts a great many young people to California." Her tone was melancholy, as if this were less than a thrilling prospect.

After a short period of silence, Miss Mears peered at Helen with concern. "So, Miss Helen of Illinois, do you know anyone in Los Angeles? Have you found a safe place to stay?"

"No to the first question, and not yet to the second. But I'm going to look up the YWCA first thing."

Miss Mears's countenance brightened. "Oh, the YWCA runs an excellent facility. The Hotel Figueroa, on Figueroa Avenue at Tenth. It's perfectly respectable. In fact, I've recommended it to several businesswomen traveling alone. I know a few women on the board. You'll be absolutely safe and sound there. One can't be too careful, you know. Los Angeles has plenty of mashers and evildoers waiting to prey on vulnerable young women."

Sounds like Frances, Helen thought, refusing to succumb to such fears. Every big city had its criminal element. Small towns did, too. She scrambled in her handbag for a paper and pen. "Tenth and Figueroa." She actually had a place to go. A plan. "Thank you so much."

"You're welcome. And when it comes time to look for a church, I recommend First Presbyterian of Hollywood." Miss Mears smiled. "That's where I attend, and where I work as well."

"Oh! I certainly will." Helen scribbled another note onto the paper. Maybe if she found a good church right away, Marjorie wouldn't be quite so furious with her.

"And if I may be so bold, I have one more suggestion for you."

"I'm all ears."

"When you've found work, or even before you do, try to find a prayer group of people who work in the industry. Or form one of your own. People of faith are a rare breed and you need to encourage one another and stick together."

"That sounds like a good idea," Helen told her. "Thanks."

A comfortable silence ensued as the miles rolled past. What would Hollywood be like? Would most other Californians be as friendly as the two she'd already met?

"Los Angeles, California," the conductor called as he strolled through the car. "Next stop, Los Angeles, California. End of the line."

All around her, passengers stirred, grabbing their suitcases. With a deep shiver of excitement, Helen rummaged in her purse and dug out her gloves. Soon she'd step off the train and into the glorious California sunshine.

Her big adventure was about to begin.

CHAPTER FOURTEEN

When Helen stepped off the train at the Los Angeles station, following closely on the sturdy heels of Henrietta Mears, her first impression was that the entire building was under construction, with sections roped off from the public, ladders and drop-cloths strewn about, the woodsy smell of sawdust and sharp tang of fresh paint, the ringing thud of hammers and whine of saws, and the voices of burly men in paint-stained overalls as they shouted back and forth.

"Goodness. Are they remodeling the whole place?" She lifted her gloved hand to her nose to block the dust as she and Miss Mears waited for their checked bags to be unloaded.

The kindly teacher shook her head. "They're fixing damage from the earthquake last March." When Helen didn't reply, she added with a note of surprise, "Hadn't you heard of it?"

Feeling sheepish, Helen admitted she hadn't. She wasn't much for reading newspapers, other than the movie section.

"California is prone to earthquakes, you know." Miss Mears's penetrating glance was owlish behind her thick glasses.

"I didn't know that." Come to think of it, Helen knew little about her new home state, other than that it counted the motion-picture capital of the world among its glories. "I do remember learning something in school about a giant earthquake that practically leveled San Francisco some thirty years ago, but I guess I assumed that a disaster like that doesn't happen very often."

"Well, it doesn't," Miss Mears reassured her. "Not at that magnitude. This quake last March wasn't nearly as bad as the one in

San Francisco, but it did do quite a lot of damage around the city, as you'll soon see."

After they collected their bags, they stepped out of the station into the warm morning sunshine. Helen detected a sweet aroma unlike anything she'd ever smelled before—so sweet it carried above the diesel and exhaust fumes and other city odors.

"What's that smell?" She took a deep sniff.

"Which smell?"

"Sweet. Sort of flowery."

"Oh, you must be smelling the orange groves." Miss Mears smiled. "I'm so used to them, I don't notice anymore. There are miles and miles of them surrounding the city. We passed a large grove about twenty minutes ago. I should have pointed it out to you, but you were busy."

Helen had indeed been busy, repairing the damage the journey had wreaked on her make-up and hair. She couldn't arrive in her new town looking like a bedraggled mess. Even so, glancing around the exterior of the station, she noted nearly every pedestrian looked sharper and better-dressed than she was used to. Many people had a tanned and athletic look about them. She assumed those were the Californians, while the pasty ones like herself were out-of-towners. And everyone was rushing to get somewhere. As it was not quite eight o'clock in the morning, she imagined most everyone was on their way to work in the tall office buildings or low-slung factories that surrounded the station.

Despite her travel-weary state, she felt a thrill to be among them. *Someday I will have somewhere important to go*, she promised herself, *and, Lord, sooner rather than later, please.* But right now, her most important task was to find a safe place to stay.

Miss Mears occupied herself with giving a tip to the porter. Then she waved and smiled at a woman of similar age who approached her and gave her a quick hug.

She turned to Helen. "Here's where we part ways, my dear," she said with a look of concern. "I'm sorry that I must rush off. I wish we could drive you to your hotel, but I'm afraid I've got to run straight off to a speaking engagement in the opposite direction." She touched Helen's arm. "Do you think you can manage all right on your own?"

"Of course," Helen answered with more confidence than she felt. She appreciated the woman's motherly concern. "Thank you for recommending a place to stay. You've been very kind to help me get my bearings."

"You're very welcome. May the Lord be with you. And do look up Hollywood Presbyterian. It's not far from the Hotel Figueroa." Miss Mears shook Helen's hand. "I look forward to seeing you there."

Helen promised she would, and Miss Mears hurried off with her companion.

Helen hoisted her suitcase, pulled out the piece of paper with the hotel's address on it, and looked around the vast station in search of where to go next.

Standing in the middle of the concourse, she felt the peculiar sensation of someone's eyes watching her. A tall man appeared to be eyeing her from the shadow of a pillar. There was nothing remarkable about his appearance. In his trench coat and fedora, he looked like an ordinary commuter, except that he seemed to be staring at her. When he noticed her staring back, he vanished behind the pillar. Irritated, she turned her back toward the spot where he'd stood.

She didn't enjoy being stared at—at least when she wasn't on stage. Perhaps the man merely thought she was pretty, or mistook her for someone else. After all, if the red-haired man on the train had made that mistake, maybe others could too. Even so, it wasn't polite to stare.

Moments later when she glanced back over her shoulder, she no longer saw the man, but the chill of uneasiness hadn't left her. Miss Mears's warning about mashers and evildoers, still fresh in her mind, made her jumpy. She shot up a quick prayer for protection in this new, strange city, and wondered where to go next.

Many travelers seemed to be heading toward a particular exit marked *Taxicabs*, so Helen headed that way too. As she passed a cigar stand, she caught a glimpse of the strange man again, presumably buying a cigar but still glancing in her direction, and her spine chilled. Goodness, why was he taking such an interest? He wasn't *following* her, was he?

To her great relief, just at that moment a familiar head of coppery hair appeared just a few feet ahead. She quickened her pace. While the screenwriter was virtually a stranger as well, she considered him a friendly presence. Operating on the principle that it was better to act first and ask forgiveness later, she trotted up to him, dropped her suitcase on the ground, and flung her arms around his neck.

"Darling! It's so good to see you!"

Standing in line at a newsstand, waiting to buy a pack of gum, Rusty caught a glimpse of Helen Corrigan crossing the terminal at a distance. He lifted his palm in greeting, but she didn't appear to see him. But in the mere seconds it took for him to complete his transaction and look up again, she was headed straight toward him at a brisk pace, a frown creasing her brow. In that instant, she reminded Rusty of an angry buffalo. He could practically hear her snort. Golly, she couldn't still be mad at him for yelling at her, could she? He'd said he was sorry.

No, he told himself, that wasn't it. She'd probably just thought of more questions to ask him about life in Hollywood, which was understandable. More troubling would be if she'd ask him to introduce her to influential people at the studio, assuming he'd know some. Troubling because he didn't know that many influential people. And troubling because he'd met her type before, bright-eyed young starlets eager to get on his good side, hoping to ride his coattails, so to speak, to gain access to the studio. This type of woman was never actually interested in Rusty, just in his so-called connections. Well, he should have made it clear to Helen Corrigan that he was low man on the totem pole at Cooperman Studios and wouldn't be able to—

"Darling!" she cried, barreling into him. She dropped her suitcase on the floor and flung her arms around his neck. "It's so good to see you!"

He couldn't have been more shocked if she'd hoisted her skirt and danced the can-can. Taken aback, he stood stiff as a tin soldier, arms at his sides.

"I think someone's following me," she hissed in his ear. "Please, act like we know each other. Pretend you're my boyfriend."

"Um... okay." Too stunned to argue, Rusty obeyed. He wrapped his arms around her waist and blurted, "Sweetheart! I thought I'd never see you again."

They stood locked in the awkward embrace for several moments as passengers scurried around them, beaming or scowling at the effusive spectacle. Then Helen turned her head to take a surreptitious peek over her shoulder. The scent of something sweet and appealing wafted from her blond hair. Rusty inhaled. Lilacs, maybe. Something soft and spring-like. Heat crept up his neck.

"I think he's gone. At least, I don't see him anymore," she murmured, turning back to face Rusty. She tried to take a step back. When he held his grip, she placed her hands on his shoulders and gave him a gentle push. "You can let go of me now," she stage-whispered. "*Darling.*"

"Oh. Okay." Rusty dropped his arms, unaccountably let down that the charade was over. He'd rather enjoyed the feeling of holding her in his arms. He scanned the waiting room as his blood pressure returned to normal. "Hey, are you—is everything all right now?"

"I think so." She gave her blond bob a self-conscious pat. "I don't see him anymore. I'm pretty sure he's gone. It was probably nothing. Just some random creep. Or my overactive imagination." A faint blush crept into her cheeks. "Sorry about ambushing you like that."

"Glad I could be of service to a lady," he said. "And I must say, for an aspiring actress, you did an excellent job of make-believe just now. If you can pull that off in a screen test, you'll do fine."

"Thanks. For what it's worth, so did you. I really appreciate it." She stood and looked at him for a long moment as if waiting for him to say something. "Well, I suppose I must be going."

"Can I help you with your bags?"

"This is it." She lifted the dropped suitcase in one hand. "This is all I brought with me. I travel light."

"Can I give you a ride somewhere?"

"No, thanks. I'm looking forward to taking a taxi to the Hotel Filip—er." She consulted the paper. "Figueroa." She smiled. "Well, thanks again."

"Are you sure you'll be all right?"

"I'll be fine. I just—I had a little scare, that's all. Silly me." She started to walk toward the sign marked *Taxicabs.*

"Hey. wait."

She turned. Against his better judgment, he broke his own rule about helping young starlets.

"There's a cattle call every Friday at Cooperman Studios."

"A what?"

"An open audition. That's when they cast extras for new films. It's a good way to start. You should go."

"Really?" She walked back to him. "What time on Fridays?"

"Nine a.m. sharp. Here's the address." He pulled a slightly tattered business card from the pocket of his jacket.

She looked at it. "Zachary P. Noble. Screenwriter, Cooperman Studios," she read aloud. Her brows rose. "Zachary? This is you?"

He nodded.

"You don't look like a Zachary."

"What do I look like?"

She tilted her head and peered up at him. "I don't know. Not a Zachary, though."

"Most people call me Rusty. Because of the hair."

"Might I see you there? At a cattle call?"

"Oh, no," he scoffed. "I stay as far away from those things as I can. They're pure chaos."

"Oh, I see." She smiled and tucked the card into her handbag. "Well, Rusty Noble, thank you very much for the information. And for being here when I needed you."

Something tightened in his chest. "If you get a part, look me up. Or even if you don't." He couldn't have kept the note of eagerness out of his voice, even if he'd wanted to.

"Maybe." She smiled again, then turned away.

He watched her walk toward the taxi stand. Nice kid. Good-looking, and clever too. Maybe she'd turn out to be the one in a million who'd beat the odds. From a practical standpoint, he knew she'd probably wash out. Be gone within six months, if not sooner.

But to his surprise, he found himself praying she wouldn't.

CHAPTER FIFTEEN

For several minutes Helen watched people getting in and out of taxis, then navigated the task herself and found the process wasn't as daunting as it first appeared.

"The Hotel Figueroa, please," she told the driver.

"Hotel Figueroa, eh?" the cab driver confirmed, glancing at Helen in the rear-view mirror.

"Yes, please. At the corner of Tenth and Figueroa."

"I know where it is," the cabbie said, his voice genial. "Take lots of you business ladies there all the time."

Again she felt a rush of pleasure at being called a business lady. Soon she'd have to learn to navigate the public trolley system—expensive cab rides would eat through her savings in no time—but today wasn't the day. For now she was content to stare out the cab window at the billboards, tall buildings, and glamorous-looking pedestrians, wondering if any of them were famous and planning what she would say to a movie star if she did indeed encounter one in the flesh. Marjorie had met the silent-screen star John Gilbert once at the Avalon Ballroom in Chicago, and she'd made Helen laugh with her story of the humiliation of being tongue-tied in his presence. Helen had been appalled at the wasted opportunity and vowed that such a tragedy would not happen to her, should she be lucky enough to meet the likes of someone like John Gilbert. Although these days it would more likely be Gary Cooper or Clark Gable. John Gilbert, sadly, hadn't made a very successful transition from silent films to the talkies.

She marveled at the palm trees lining boulevards and swaying in the gentle early-morning breeze. Buildings encased in scaffolding looked to be undergoing construction, maybe repairs from the recent earthquake or simply new buildings going up to accommodate the swelling population. A magazine article she'd read on the train stated that Los Angeles was one of the fastest-growing cities in the country.

By the time the cab pulled up to the Hotel Figueroa, the early mist had burned off and the summer sun had taken on a harsh quality, though not nearly as searing as in Arizona. Nowhere, Helen decided, could be as hot as Arizona. Still, the sun shone brighter in California than it did back in the Midwest. Her new sunglasses would get a lot of use.

She paid the cab driver, stepped out onto the sidewalk, and took a good look at the hotel's exterior. Based on Marjorie's description of the Chicago YWCA, Helen had expected a rather plain, utilitarian structure, or perhaps an older building—not that anything in Los Angeles seemed very old. But the building standing before her was an imposing example of Spanish Colonial splendor, apparently undamaged by the earthquake. Creamy stone walls rose ten stories tall, adorned with carved pillars, arched windows, and black wrought-iron embellishments. How could such an elegant structure suit a traveler on a strict budget, like her?

Turned out, it couldn't.

"I'm sorry," the clerk at the reception desk said with an apologetic smile. "This hotel was indeed founded by the YWCA, but it hasn't been run by that organization for several years now."

Apparently, Miss Mears hadn't been aware of this new development. And why should she be? Helen chided herself, refusing to be annoyed with the kind woman who had only been trying to help her. The clerk paged through a leather-bound ledger. "But we have a few rooms available, should you wish to stay." She glanced at Helen over the top of her spectacles. "We host a great many lady travelers like yourself. You'd feel quite comfortable here."

It pleased Helen to be perceived as a "lady traveler" instead of the country bumpkin she felt herself to be. Even so, the price the clerk quoted was well over her budget. But maybe for just a night or two…just until she got her bearings in this strange new city.

Her decision was swayed by the hotel's lobby, decorated with Spanish-style charm with wrought iron decorations, a cool tile floor, and the promise of a swimming pool down an arched passageway. Besides, she was so very tired of traveling, and in desperate need of a hot bath and a long nap.

And so she paid the daily rate, and a uniformed bellhop carried her suitcase as he showed her to her room, a spare but very clean space, brightly lit by an east-facing, multi-paned window. To her delight, the room contained its own small, private bathroom in which she promptly luxuriated in the much-anticipated bath.

When her skin was suitably wrinkly, she stepped out of the tub, toweled herself off, and slipped into her nightgown, even though it was now the middle of the day. She needed to sleep before doing anything else, including finding food. But first she did the one thing even more important than napping.

She opened a drawer in a small wooden desk, extracted a sheet of hotel stationery, and composed a letter to Marjorie. Trying not to over-explain, she told her sister where she was, and why, and assured her all was well. She very nearly closed with a cringing apology for the havoc her unplanned absence was sure to cause, but decided against it.

She was not sorry. And she wouldn't insult Marjorie by lying to her. So she simply wrote, "I hope you can understand and, in time, forgive me. I promise to write soon and let you know how things are going. In the meantime, please keep me in your prayers, as I will keep you in mine. All my love, Helen."

She folded the letter, slipped it into an envelope, and addressed it. She set it on top of her purse to mail at the first opportunity. Then she shut the drapes, slid between the cool white sheets, and closed her eyes. Thoughts about the "cattle call" audition scrolled across her imagination like a movie. What would it be like? What would be expected of her?

Her last vision, as she slipped into blissful sleep, was of a herd of dairy cattle, dancing across a barn floor in top hats and tap shoes.

CHAPTER SIXTEEN

Rusty got to the writers' bungalow early and typed out his resignation letter. While he didn't yet have the financial means to open his own studio, he knew the writing was on the wall. As soon as Cynthia made her accusations to Stanley Cooperman, Rusty would be thrown out on his ear. He preferred to leave on his own terms rather than have a firing on his record.

Behind Midge's desk, Cooperman's door was shut tight, meaning he was in conference with somebody.

"It's his brother," Midge told him in an exaggerated stage whisper, eyes huge behind her cat's-eye glasses. "Leroy Cooperman."

"I haven't met him," Rusty replied, "but I've seen him lurking around the set a time or two. What's his angle?"

Midge pushed her glasses up the bridge of her nose and leaned toward Rusty as if she were telling him a secret, even though they were the only two in the room. "He did time, you know."

"Time?"

"You know. Prison." She leaned closer. "They say he got in trouble with the mob. Committed an armed robbery or grand theft auto or something."

"Who's 'they'?" Rusty found it hard to imagine a brother of Stanley Cooperman getting into such deep trouble with the law.

Midge shrugged. "Everybody."

"So it's just a rumor then." Rusty kept his eyes on Cooperman's closed door. The last thing they needed was to be caught gossiping about the Cooperman brothers right there in the chief's office.

"It's a pretty accurate rumor, if you ask me. A man that quiet and shady-looking has got to be hiding something."

She looked ready to launch into further juicy speculations, so Rusty hastily formulated a question about her recent vacation. Slouching into a chair, he listened to her rave about a dude ranch near Rocky Mountain National Park while he waited for Cooperman to finish his meeting.

At last the door edged open and Leroy Cooperman came out, followed by Stanley. Midge quickly resumed typing. Rusty stood and nodded to Leroy as he passed. The brothers' appearances were completely opposite. Where Stanley was pale, pudgy, and balding with a loud voice, Leroy was thin to the point of skeletal, dark-haired, and carried an air of brooding. Rusty had to admit Midge was right. The man did look kind of shady.

As Leroy left the office, the chief looked surprised to see Rusty.

"Noble? You must have read my mind. I was about to have Midge summon you. Come in."

Here it comes, thought Rusty as he followed Cooperman into the inner sanctum. He fully expected to be given the hatchet. Cynthia must have telephoned Cooperman from Arizona and given him the score. Only from her perspective, of course. No matter. In a few minutes he'd hand over his resignation letter, and his career at Cooperman Studios would be over.

Cooperman motioned for Rusty to sit and took his place behind the massive oak desk. "I've heard all about what went on in Tucson," the chief began. "Now I want to hear your version."

"My version, sir?" Rusty's voice came out a squeak.

"What did you think of Cynthia's performance?"

"Her performance?" Rusty swallowed. "Well, sir, I—"

With an impatient wave of his hand, Cooperman snapped, "Confound it, Noble, don't beat around the bush. Tell it to me straight. Can the woman act or not?"

"Can she—can she what, sir?"

"Jean-Luc Renard told me her acting was appallingly bad," Cooperman said. "Is that your opinion as well?"

Rusty's mind raced. *What to say, what to say?* "Well, sir, Jean-Luc's the director. I'm just the scriptwriter." He tried to be diplomatic. "I do think that if Miss Starling could be persuaded to be a bit more, well, *restrained* in her delivery, it would suit the character of Annabel Brewster much better."

"I see." Cooperman looked at him. "Well, I'm in your debt on two counts. For one, her infatuation with Mark St. Ives appears to have faded."

"That's good news, sir. But I had nothing to do with that." He hoped his words were true.

"You kept them from being alone together. Don't think I'm not grateful for that."

Rusty didn't feel deserving of the man's praise, but he let it slide. "And the second thing, sir?" Perhaps now he'd give Rusty the long-awaited promotion.

"Jean-Luc spoke highly of you. He told me you were a big help to him on location."

"Thank you, sir. It was my pleasure."

"I predict that someday you'll make a very effective assistant director."

Rusty's heart sank. "Someday, sir?" Hadn't he proven himself worthy of the title in Tucson? "B-but you said, sir, that if I did well in Tucson, you'd give me the promotion."

Cooperman looked at Rusty as if he'd just announced a Martian spaceship landing on the front lawn.

"You must have misheard. Or misunderstood."

Rusty stood firm. "I'm quite sure I didn't, sir. You said very distinctly that—"

"Oh, come now, Noble." Only Cooperman could speak in a voice that was one part soothing, one part threatening. "Why would I move you to a different position now? Why, you're the very best scriptwriter we have. I need you out there in the writers' bungalow, keeping those other dimwits in line." As he spoke, he stood and walked toward Rusty, who soon found himself being herded toward the door.

"But—"

"Thank you, Noble. Now back to work."

The door swung shut in Rusty's face. He stood for a moment, staring at Midge's empty desk, grateful she wasn't there to witness his humiliation.

Later that evening, when he removed his jacket and hung it in the closet, the resignation letter was still in the pocket. He pulled it out and stared at it, then tore it in half and dropped it into the wastebasket. He hadn't been fired, as he'd feared he would. On the other hand, he hadn't been given the promised promotion, either. And it *had* been promised. Rusty was sure of it.

If anything, Cooperman's caginess had strengthened Rusty's resolve to open his own studio. Someday. But today was not the day.

Helen sat on a sofa in the lobby of the Hotel Figueroa, sipping a steaming cup of black coffee. That was about all she could afford, with the pricey hotel eating a chunk of her budget. She'd have to find cheaper accommodations as soon as possible. But for the time being, at least, she could enjoy the moment and pretend she was a fine woman accustomed to taking her coffee amid such luxury.

She didn't think her stomach could handle more than coffee, anyway. Not this morning. Not with the butterflies flapping around her intestines. For today was Friday, the day of "cattle call" auditions at Cooperman Studios, and Helen's first day of working at a real, honest-to-goodness Hollywood studio, even if the work didn't yet come with a paycheck attached. She was a real actress, going to a real audition.

She'd taken her time bathing and dressing in a pretty dress her stepmother had purchased for her in a Tucson department store.

"It's for your birthday," Frances had insisted over Helen's protests, even though her birthday was months away. Helen had thanked her. Now she silently thanked her again, as the simple, flattering dress seemed the perfect thing to wear to a professional audition.

After seeking directions from the desk clerk, she stood on the busy sidewalk, bathed in the brilliance of a California morning, waiting for the trolley that the clerk had promised would take her to Cooperman Studios. She didn't mind the wait, as the spot was the perfect vantage point from which to people-watch.

Without warning, she spotted a familiar figure across the street, and her stomach lurched. It was the fellow in an oversized trench coat and fedora, the mysterious man she'd seen at the train station. What was he doing, hanging around outside the Hotel

Figueroa? The coincidence seemed uncanny. He couldn't really be following her—could he?

Just then a bus rumbled by, and when it had passed, the man had vanished again.

CHAPTER SEVENTEEN

H elen ruminated about the mystery man during the entire trolley ride. Why would someone be following her? She was a nobody. Was he even following her, or was her overactive imagination creating a situation that didn't exist?

By the time she stepped off the trolley in front of the famed Cooperman Studios, she'd convinced herself that she was imagining things concerning the mystery man. The sight of the studio pushed him completely from her mind. She stood in awe on the sidewalk outside the stately main building.

She'd finally made it. She was here!

For a few minutes, she walked up and down the street, admiring the palm trees and the cacti growing helter-skelter out of the ground, while she gathered her wits about her. Then she strode with an air of confidence up the front steps of the building and to the reception desk.

A sleek, well-groomed woman seated behind the desk looked up as she entered the lobby. Goodness, was every last person in California sleek and well-groomed?

The woman smiled at her approach. "May I help you?"

"How do you do," Helen said. "My name is Helen Corrigan. I'm an actress, and I'm here to try out for a motion picture."

"Which one?"

"I beg your pardon?" She hadn't expected to be given a choice.

The receptionist picked up a clipboard from a rack on her desk and consulted it. "Are you here for Goforth, Cranfield, or DeJong?"

Helen gave her a blank stare. "Those are motion pictures?"

The woman returned her stare, one plucked eyebrow raised in disdain or amusement or both. Helen couldn't tell which.

"Those are the directors' names, dear. Those are the ones running auditions today." Her red-painted lips clearly enunciated the words, as if Helen were hard of hearing, or a non-native speaker of English.

"Oh. Um, I'm not sure. Any of them, I suppose."

The receptionist heaved a long-suffering sigh and set down the clipboard. "Have you an appointment?"

"No, I don't." Helen swallowed. "I was hoping that—"

The shrill ring of the telephone on the desk made her jump.

"I'm sorry," the woman said to Helen as she reached for the receiver. "Cooperman Studios allows auditions by appointment only."

Helen placed a gloved hand on the desk and leaned toward the woman. "Can I make an appointment then?"

The receptionist placed her hand over the mouthpiece. "We only make appointments through talent agents. Have your agent phone us." She rolled her chair so her shoulder was to Helen and spoke into the telephone. "Cooperman Studios. How may I help you?"

Clearly, the conversation was over.

Dejected, Helen trudged back out to the sidewalk. Now what? True, there were plenty of other studios to try. But would they all tell her the same thing—that she needed an appointment to audition, and needed an agent to get her that appointment before they'd even let her try out? She supposed that to find out, she'd just have to try the next studio on her list.

But first she needed lunch. Her stomach was growling after her inadequate breakfast of coffee plus nothing. She needed food, as well as a pause to catch her breath, gather her courage and steel herself to be more forceful at the next studio.

She crossed the street to a small, busy luncheonette. All the tables were occupied, so she took a seat at the counter. She studied the menu, seeking out the lowest-priced items.

"I'll have a bowl of chicken noodle soup," she told the waitress. "With a few crackers, please. And a glass of water."

While waiting for her food, she went to the ladies' room. She was washing her hands when a young woman about her age with fluffy dark hair burst in, wetted a handkerchief, and dabbed furiously at her chest.

"Hell's bells," she muttered, grabbing Helen's attention.

"What's the matter?"

"Oh, I've spilled tomato juice on my blouse and just *look*," the woman wailed. "The stain's not coming out. Right in front, too, where it shows the most." She stared at her reflection in the mirror, her face a mask of despair. "I can't go back to the office looking like this."

"Here." Helen reached into her handbag and produced a small bottle of cleaning solution. "Try this."

The woman took the bottle. "Gosh, thanks. You're certainly well-prepared."

Helen had to chuckle at that remark. Of all the adjectives her family might use to describe her, *well-prepared* was not one of them. "Not always, believe me. You can thank my sister in this case. She reminds me all the time to keep my handbag well stocked for such emergencies. She knows how clumsy I am." Then she grew hot with embarrassment. "Not that I'm saying you're clumsy. I just mean—"

The dark-haired woman smiled. "I know what you mean. And it's true—I *am* clumsy sometimes." She looked down at her blouse. "It's working. That must be some magical potion you've got there." She capped the bottle and handed it back to Helen, then continued to dab at her blouse with the hankie. "Well, thanks again. You're a real lifesaver."

Helen dropped the bottle into her handbag. "You're very welcome. If I were in your shoes, I'd hope someone would do the same for me." As a final gesture of camaraderie, she twirled and asked. "Is my petticoat showing?" The woman assured her it was not.

Helen left the restroom and returned to the lunch counter, where she ate her humble meal, feeling quite alone. The brief encounter with the friendly woman highlighted the fact that, apart from desk clerks and waitresses, she hadn't had a real conversation with anyone since leaving Miss Mears and Rusty Noble behind at the train station.

Rusty Noble. She patted the pocket where she'd placed his business card for safekeeping. She must remember to write and thank him, if and when she managed to obtain an audition. Or even if she didn't. He'd tried to be helpful, and that was what mattered.

The dark-haired woman had rejoined her friends, a group of five or six women chattering excitedly around a table behind Helen. She wished she were among them. She'd never enjoyed eating alone, unlike Marjorie, who seemed perfectly content to spend lots of time alone. Helen preferred company—the more, the merrier.

The thought of her sister brought a sharp ache to her throat. How would Marjorie react when she received Helen's letter? She'd be furious, more than likely. Would Helen be welcome to return home, if this Hollywood adventure didn't work out?

Fiercely she bit into a cracker. It *had* to work out. There was no other option.

All at once the group of girls behind her broke into song.

"Happy birthday, dear Myrtle! Happy birthday to you!"

Helen swiveled around on her stool, smiling at the spectacle in spite of her bleak mood. A cake with candles sat at the center of the table, with several wrapped gifts off to one side, piled in front of the presumed birthday girl, a diminutive blonde with large blue eyes.

"Come on, Myrtle, make a wish," her friend coaxed. Blushing, the guest of honor took a deep breath and blew out the candles amid much cheering and applause.

"What'd you wish for?"

"I'll bet it had something to do with a certain key grip," another girl said, and Myrtle's blush deepened from pink to crimson.

"Don't you dare tell your wish! If you tell, it won't come true," warned a red-haired girl, her eyes wide with alarm. Apparently, she took this wishing business seriously.

Helen slowly turned back to her soup. Maybe someday she'd have a group of friends like that, friends she could eat with and laugh with. At least one good friend, like Nanette back home. Surely, she'd make at least one friend, if she stayed in Los Angeles long enough. If she didn't give up and go home before she'd even had time to meet anyone.

"Would you care for a piece of cake?" A hand appeared next to Helen's soup bowl, holding out a slice of chocolate cake on a plate. She glanced past the hand and up a bracelet-laden arm to a familiar face framed by dark wavy hair. It was the young woman she'd met in the restroom.

"Oh, no, thank you," was Helen's automatic response, even though the cake looked delicious.

"Please take it." The woman set the plate on the counter. "We have way too much for just ourselves. It's our friend's birthday," she added unnecessarily. "Anyway, it's the least I could do, since you helped me out back there."

"All right. Thank you very much." Helen accepted the plate with a smile. As the woman returned to her table, Helen kept facing the group in case someone might invite her to sit with them, but of course no one did. In any case, there was no extra room at their table. But it was kind of them to think of her, just the same. Glancing around, she noticed that several other patrons were being offered cake as well. She turned back to the counter and savored the sweet treat, taking small bites and chewing slowly to make it last.

Someone at the table said, "We'd better be heading back." It was the voice of the dark-haired woman who'd given her the cake. "Mr. Goforth's holding auditions this afternoon, and Blackie'll have my head on a platter if I'm late."

Helen's ears perked up. Goforth was one of the names the snooty receptionist had mentioned earlier. Perhaps these women worked at Cooperman Studios. Maybe they were office workers. They didn't look like actresses, but in her everyday dress and hat, Helen supposed she didn't look much like an actress, either.

"What's the project?" asked one of the tablemates.

"A pirate romance with Ramon Novarro," the dark-haired woman replied.

Something fluttered in Helen's chest. Ramon Novarro! *The* Ramon Novarro?

"We'd better get going then."

The group stood, gathering up handbags and scraping chairs. Helen hastily paid her bill and left the restaurant, then followed the women at a discreet distance as they crossed the street and headed toward the studio. To her relief they didn't go inside the main building, where the snooty receptionist would surely have recognized Helen and tossed her out, but to a gated entrance at the side of the building.

A uniformed guard stood in a small wooden shelter beside a grand metal gate, letting cars and pedestrians in and out. Helen's heart pounded. How was she going to get past the guard? Would he expect her to show a pass or something? Was he going to block her entrance as the receptionist had? She quickened her pace and nearly caught up with the rear of the group, but still lagged far enough behind that they wouldn't notice her tagging along. Or so she hoped.

The bold redhead was leading the way. "Hi, Mike," she said breezily as she passed through the gate.

The grizzled guardian at the gate tipped his hat. "Had a fine lunch out, did ye, ladies?" He spoke in a genial Irish brogue.

"That we did. It's Myrtle's birthday," the redhead said.

"Is it now? Well, sure and a happy birthday to ye, Myrtle."

Trotting along at the tail end of the group, Helen hoped to pass unnoticed, but the guard glanced at her. Then glanced again, frowning slightly. Before he could say anything, she pasted on her biggest smile and said, "Hi, Mike. Nice day, isn't it?"

She could have kicked herself for the inane comment. This was Southern California, after all. *Every* day was nice.

But it did the trick. He nodded then, seeming a little uncertain, but he let her pass through with the group. And all at once, she was in!

But now what?

The studio lot looked like a strange sort of city, with a wide, busy thoroughfare connecting several boxy buildings, some tall, some short. Green lawns edged with red flowers flanked the buildings, and palm trees stood like sentries. Here and there, modest-sized bungalows painted in pastel tones contrasted with the square white warehouse-looking buildings.

Helen continued to follow the girls until they broke off into smaller groups, heading for different buildings. She continued to follow the one who'd talked about working for Goforth, the one who'd offered her the cake, sensing she was kind enough not to throw her out on her ear.

Soon she found herself in what looked like an empty waiting room. Miss Chocolate Cake nodded to an older woman monitoring the waiting room from behind a desk.

"Sorry I'm late, Mrs. Black."

The woman gave a cool nod. "Miss Gibson."

Miss Chocolate Cake—who now had a name, Miss Gibson—continued to the back of the room. She went to a desk in the corner, slid her handbag into a drawer, sat down, rolled a sheet of paper into a black typewriter, and began typing at impressive speed.

Helen approached the reception desk with as much confidence as she could muster. A framed photograph of a sweet-faced tabby cat caught her eye.

"Good afternoon, Mrs. Black. Cute kitty," she added, hoping to butter the woman up.

It didn't work. Mrs. Black's unsmiling countenance remained passive. "Yes? May I help you?"

"I'm here for the—the Goforth audition."

Mrs. Black consulted a clipboard. "You've found it. Name?"

"I'm Helen Corrigan."

"Not *your* name. The name of your agent."

Here we go again.

Helen steeled herself to perform her first major role, Young Actress Going on a Movie Audition.

She blurted the first name that popped into her mind.

"Mr. Whisker." Her horror was immediate. Why on earth had she thought of Marjorie's cat at that moment? Because of that stupid photograph, that's why.

The receptionist lifted one eyebrow. "Mr. Whisker?"

Helen cringed inside. My goodness, she could have come up with a better name than that! But what was done, was done. She straightened her shoulders in an attempt to appear confident and self-assured.

"Yes. Mr. C. Whittaker Whisker. Of the—of the Whittaker-Whisker Agency."

The woman made a note on her pad. "I've never heard of him."

"He's new in town."

"From where?"

"Kansas City." A town she'd passed through on the first leg of her train trip. Where in tarnation this ruse was coming from, Helen had no idea, but apparently Mrs. Black was buying it.

"I see." Mrs. Black consulted her clipboard. "Did Mr.—er—Whiskey—"

"Whisker."

"—did he make an appointment? I see neither your name or his name on my list."

Warming to her role, Helen drew herself up into what she hoped was a regal stance worthy of Sarah Bernhardt. "I'm quite certain he did. He told me quite specifically that he'd arranged for me to try out for the Goforth project."

"Which role?"

Oh, brother. "The—the ingenue role." There was always an ingenue role.

At that moment a door opened. Women of all ages, but mostly young, began spilling out into the room and heading toward the exit.

"Looks like you're too late," Mrs. Black said, sounding relieved. "The audition's over."

"It's over? Already?" Helen sagged in disappointment. Just her luck.

"Mr. Goforth must have made his choice quickly. Sometimes it takes longer. As you would know, with your vast experience of auditions." Mrs. Black's stern, skeptical expression softened into one of pity. "Look, Miss Corrigan. There's another casting call next Tuesday for a similar role. I'll add your name to the list, tentatively, but do ask Mr. Whisker to give me a call. We only accept agented actresses."

"I understand that. Yes, I will. I mean, he will." Helen paused to catch her breath. "Thank you."

"Tuesday at ten a.m. sharp, reading for the part of Matilda." Mrs. Black handed her a sheet of paper with some dialogue typed on it. "Prepare this reading beforehand. And don't forget—Mr. Whiskey absolutely *must* call and introduce himself to us before Tuesday. Otherwise, I'll have to scratch you off the list."

"He will." Elated by the prospect of an audition, Helen didn't bother to correct the woman. In fact, she barely gave a thought to how she'd conjure up the fictional Mr. Whisker, or Whiskey, or whomever, to make such a call. That detail could be dealt with later. Perhaps the white lie would even be overlooked, although she knew for certain God had heard it loud and clear. She'd have to confess. But for now, she was scheduled for an audition.

She floated out of the building on the sea of young actresses and was about to head for the trolley to take her back to the Hotel Figueroa when she felt a hand on her arm.

"Hold on a minute."

She wheeled around, fully expecting to be called out as a fraud and ordered to leave the premises. But it was only Miss Gibson, who'd followed her out of the building.

"That was quite a performance back there."

Helen's face burned. She'd been found out.

"What do you mean?" she stammered.

"I mean, you've never even seen a movie audition, have you?"

"No," Helen admitted.

"And you don't have an agent, either."

Helen shifted from one foot to the other. "I might have one."

Miss Gibson raised a skeptical eyebrow. "Mr. Whisker?"

There was a brief pause, then both women burst into giggles.

"Mr. Whisker is my sister's cat," Helen admitted.

"I figured as much." Miss Gibson grinned at her. "Look, I like you. I can tell you're a good egg. After all, you helped me out at the luncheonette. Now I'm going to return the favor." She scribbled something on a piece of paper. "I'm Florence Gibson, but my friends call me Flo. Come over tonight and rehearse with my roommate and me. We'll tell you all about what to expect."

"You're actresses too?"

Flo gave her a sideways smile. "Aren't we all, in one way or another?"

CHAPTER EIGHTEEN

That evening Helen took the trolley to visit Flo at her apartment in the Hollywood Studio Club. Located on Lodi Place in the heart of Tinseltown, the Studio Club was a large building in a similar Mediterranean style to the Hotel Figueroa, with beige stucco walls accented in green and coral. The center section, flanked by wings on either side, featured decorative archways and a painted mural above the main entrance.

Inside, the place had a friendly, homey atmosphere, with a communal parlor that, Flo explained, could be shared by all the residents, especially when entertaining male callers, who weren't allowed in the apartments.

Flo's apartment, while tidy and comfortable, was not much bigger than Helen's bedroom back in Kerryville. She shared it with an aspiring actress, a dark-haired, dark-eyed beauty named Donna Delmonico.

"It's not luxurious, but it's safe and affordable, and it's loads of fun to live here," Flo said. She'd changed from her office clothes to overalls and a cotton shirt. "It's like a sorority, I guess." She giggled. "Or as I imagine a sorority would be, having never been to college. We get two meals a day, and there are dances and teas and talent shows."

"And chaperones. Don't forget the chaperones," Donna added in a droll tone. She was a statuesque beauty whom Helen remembered seeing coming out of the audition, and hadn't yet seen crack a smile. She hadn't been cast in the Goforth picture, and Helen wasn't able to tell if her annoyed demeanor was due to that particular disappointment, or to a negative frame of mind in general.

"How many girls live here?" Helen asked.

"Close to a hundred, I guess," Flo said.

"And they're all actresses?"

"Actresses and aspiring actresses. Could be at any stage of their career, from tadpoles to full-grown bullfrogs. So to speak." Flo sat back on the worn sofa and crossed her long legs, Indian-style. "And not only actresses, but singers, script girls, cutters, writers, designers, dancers, stenos like me... as long as you're pursuing a career in the motion picture business, you're in."

"As long as there's a vacancy," Donna added, "which I don't think there is right now."

"Oh. I see." Helen swallowed her disappointment. In her mind she'd already been collecting her things from the Hotel Figueroa and moving into the Studio Club. But that would have to wait.

"But something's bound to open up soon," the ever-optimistic Flo chimed in. "Residents are only allowed to live here for three years, tops, so there's a constant turnover. In the meantime, you could stay here with us. Couldn't she, Donna?"

Donna opened her mouth as if to say something. Then she closed her mouth and shrugged.

"Temporarily, I mean," Flo explained. "Just until an apartment opens up. We'd appreciate some help with the rent, and I guarantee it's way cheaper than wherever it is you're staying."

She was right about that.

"Of course, we don't have a real bed for you. But you're welcome to sleep on the sofa."

The three spent the rest of the evening discussing the audition process, with Flo and Donna offering tips to Helen.

"If there's one key piece of advice I can give you, it's this," Flo said at the end of the evening as she walked Helen to the trolley stop. "You just have to keep trying, and when that doesn't work, get back in the saddle jend try again."

Helen vowed then and there to cling to the saddle for dear life, no matter how bumpy the ride, no matter how long it took.

***

Rusty was still sound asleep when the telephone jangled at his bedside.

"Noble, get in here! Now." Cooperman's voice boomed over the wire.

"What's wrong?" Rusty groped for the alarm clock in an effort to check the time, but knocked it to the floor. Probably just as well he didn't know.

"We have an emergency. I need you here at the studio, now."

Rusty fumbled into his clothes and raced to the studio, wound tighter than a two-dollar clock. Was Cooperman going to fire him after all? But why call him in the middle of the night? And on a weekend, too. Why not wait until Monday morning?

He was still groggy when he passed Midge's empty desk and stumbled into Cooperman's office. The great man looked as if he'd had a rough night. His jowly face was pale except for a shadow of stubble and the dark pouches under his eyes. One whiff told Rusty he'd been drinking, probably heavily.

"What's the matter, sir? I got here as soon as I could."

"Cynthia's gone," Cooperman said with a sorrowful shake of his head.

Rusty's blood ran cold. "What do you mean gone, sir?" Much as he didn't like Cynthia, he'd never wish anything bad to happen to her. "Has there been an accident?"

Cooperman raised his head. "An accident? No, you fool. She's gone. Gone!"

Rusty swallowed. "I don't understand, sir."

"She's run off to Mexico."

Rusty's breath hitched. "Mexico. With Mark St. Ives?"

"No, dang it." Cooperman pounded his fist on the desk as if Rusty were being purposefully obtuse. "With some two-bit cattle rustler she met down in Tucson. When you were supposed to be keeping an eye on her," he added in an accusatory tone.

Indignation rose in Rusty's chest. "I *did* keep an eye on her, sir, exactly as you'd asked. You told me to let you know if anything transpired between her and Mark St. Ives, so I kept a close eye on the situation, and I assure you—"

Cooperman waved a dismissive hand. "That's not important now, Noble. Water under the bridge. What is important is that she's quit the picture. Gone and left us completely in the lurch."

Rusty's jaw dropped. "She quit *Annabel Brewster*? But we're so close to being finished."

"I've spent a fortune on that picture. A *fortune*, I tell you. We have to finish it, or the backers will howl. I'll have a devil of a time getting them to invest in any future pictures, and we need the money badly."

"But how can we finish it without Cynthia? There are still several scenes left to film, and most of them involve her. Besides, the publicity's already gone out with Cynthia's name all over it."

Cooperman began to pace the room, rubbing his five-o-clock shadow. "We'll just have to hire another actress, someone who looks like Cynthia, and have her take over."

"But what about all the scenes we shot in Tucson? Will those have to be redone?" Rusty hated the thought of being sent back so soon to that godforsaken, rattlesnake-filled desert, but if that's what it took to save the picture, by golly, he'd do it.

"No. We're behind schedule and over budget as it is." Cooperman thought for a minute. Then he said, "We'll keep everything we can from Tucson, and all the close-ups of Cynthia's face. Anything shot from a distance, or with her back to the camera can be shot with a different actress. One we can convince the audience is Cynthia." He sat behind his desk. "If there are close-ups we don't have yet, you'll have to rewrite the script to eliminate them. And tell Central Casting to find me a Cynthia lookalike."

Rusty doubted they could pull it off, but he wasn't about to tell Cooperman that. "Who do you have in mind, sir?"

"I don't know. Someone blond. Get me Jean Harlow."

"Jean's under contract to MGM, and they're not too keen on lending her out."

"Well, then, Carole Lombard."

"Lombard's on location in Morocco."

Cooperman pounded the desk again. "Confound it, Noble. Figure it out. Take care of it, and keep me informed."

"Yes, sir." A random image entered his mind. An image of the actress he'd met on the train. The woman who looked enough like Cynthia that Rusty had gotten them confused. Though she'd called herself an actress, of course he had no way of knowing if she could truly act. But this was no time for quibbling. He snapped his fingers. "I think I have a solution. I met a girl who looks almost exactly like Cynthia. Could be her body double. If I can find her."

"Well, what are you waiting for, Noble?"

"Yes, sir, I'm on it."

He backed out of Cooperman's office, then sprinted through the early dawn to the writers' bungalow. What was her name? Helen something. Cortland. Corman. He had no idea how to find her, but he had to try. If Cooperman Studios was to salvage *The Courage of Annabel Brewster*, there wasn't a moment to lose.

His frantic mind produced a snippet of their final conversation. She'd said something about going to the Hotel Figueroa. Rusty had no idea if that's where she'd ended up, or if she'd still be there after so many days had passed. But it was the first place he'd try.

CHAPTER NINETEEN

Helen moved into Flo and Donna's apartment at the Studio Club on Saturday morning. That afternoon, Flo worked on Helen's face with her pots and pencils, then prevailed on a neighbor, a fledgling photographer, to take a roll of headshots for cheap, in exchange for helping the photographer build her portfolio. As a favor to Flo, the neighbor worked late into the night to develop the photos in her closet/darkroom, and Helen was pleased with the results.

"You made my eyelashes look so long," she said to Flo.

"The right combination of makeup and lighting can work magic," Flo responded. "You're blessed with good bone structure. The camera loves you. Many girls, even very beautiful girls, aren't so lucky."

On Monday night, Helen had a fitful night's sleep on Flo's sofa covered with a thin blanket, and the next morning she accompanied her new roommates to Cooperman Studios, feeling much more confident. Flo was unfailingly cheerful and friendly, but Donna's smile barely concealed a biting sense of humor and strong competitive streak. She seemed to resent Helen's presence from the start, but she didn't say so outright.

This time her name was printed on Mike's magic list, thanks to Mrs. Black, and he waved her past the gate. Her only trepidation was that she hadn't been able to produce a "Mr. Whisker," much less get him to call the studio. She hoped she wouldn't be thrown out on that account. Maybe Mrs. Black would have forgotten all about the phantom agent.

Once inside the gate, Donna peeled off to her own audition. Since they had a little time to kill before Helen's audition started, Flo took her on a quick tour of the backlot. Helen marveled at entire city blocks built to look like New York and Midwestern small towns that were the very image of Kerryville, picket fences and all. The streets were empty of vehicles but filled with people practicing dance steps or rehearsing dialogue. She marveled at the sight of a Revolutionary War figure in a powdered wig immersed in deep conversation with a cowgirl dressed in fringe and boots.

With Flo's help, Helen found the correct soundstage in a white, windowless building three stories tall. The huge sliding door stood open and a crowd milled around outside, apparently waiting to be told what to do.

"Will you be all right if I leave you here?" Flo asked. "I need to get to my desk."

"Sure, I'll be fine," Helen assured her. It made her heart beat faster to be around other actors and actresses, even at the giant casting calls like this one, where the hordes of actresses reminded her of dairy cows back in Illinois, being herded here and there. A man with a clipboard began calling directions. All the actresses trying out for the part of Matilda were instructed to pass through the soundstage to some rooms at the back, and wait on folding chairs against the wall.

The soundstage was enormous, with decorated walls that ended abruptly despite the lack of a ceiling, and several tons of lighting strung on wires overhead. The walls were padded and covered with chicken wire to keep the noise locked inside. The room was warm, despite the presence of large electric fans, and Helen's throat felt dry.

The folding chair grew hard beneath her as auditioning women were called into the room one by one, in groups of three. The others sat still, as if waiting for a doctor's appointment or a bus.

When her turn came, Helen entered the room. Three casting directors sat at a long table. As instructed, she slipped her headshot and registration form across the table to one of the casting directors, who looked her up and down, barely making eye contact. When he gave her the instruction, she backed up a few feet and began to read her lines. Once she opened her mouth and began to speak, her nervousness melted away. She was in her element.

When Helen's reading was over, the casting director merely said, "Thank you," and she was ushered out of the room. The man with the clipboard intercepted her.

"Tryouts for the chorus are over there." He pointed toward a distant corner of the soundstage, where a row of young women were dancing to bright music from a piano.

"But I'm not here to try out for the chorus. I tried out for Matilda."

The man narrowed his eyes. "Look, sister, you wanna try out or not?"

"But—"

The man looked weary. "Look, try out or don't try out. Your call." He turned and walked away. Bewildered, Helen made her way over to the chorus.

Rusty checked the time on the wall clock, pushed himself away from his typewriter, and stood.

"I'm headed over to Soundstage B."

"They're holding cattle calls today, you know," Smitty called from his desk across the room. "It'll be a madhouse over there."

"Yes, I know. That's why I'm going. Gotta talk to the casting director. Cooperman wants me to find somebody who looks like Cynthia."

"Good luck with that," Smitty said with a look of doubt, and turned back to his typewriter.

Rusty hurried to the soundstage, hoping against hope that Helen would show up. He doubted it—she'd only just arrived in town, after all, and surely was getting her bearings in a strange place. But he could hope. He'd had no luck tracking her down at the Hotel Figueroa. The desk clerk had acknowledged that a woman fitting her description had stayed at the hotel, but that she'd checked out the day before.

He entered the soundstage and scanned the swarms of young starlets waiting their turn.

"And one, two, three, go! Step, hop, turn, pause. Smile, ladies!" The casting director's shouted direction drew Rusty's attention to the group currently undergoing evaluation.

He spotted her, second from the left in the back row. She'd actually shown up! Amazed at his good fortune, he walked over to the casting director, Bert Small.

"Hey, Bert. Say, what's the name of the blonde?"

Bert rolled his eyes. "You kidding me? Which blonde? I got six blondes up there."

"Back row, second from the left."

Bert squinted at the dancers, then consulted his clipboard. "Name's Helen Corrigan."

Corrigan. That was it. Helen Corrigan.

Bert smirked. "You thinking of trying to get a date?"

"*Pfft.* No," Rusty scoffed. He'd had enough of eager blonde starlets to last a lifetime. When he thought about settling down at all, which wasn't often, he had in mind a down-to-earth girl, a girl who shared his love of the Lord. The kind of girl, he'd convinced himself, who didn't exist in Hollywood. He didn't know how he'd meet her, tethered as he was to Tinseltown. But if it was meant to be, somehow, God would work it out. He had to believe that. Meanwhile, he was too busy building his career and trying to keep Cooperman happy to worry about the lack of a girlfriend. Lonely as Hollywood could be at times, family ties represented a burden he didn't need.

But at the moment he kept his eyes riveted on Helen, lest he lose her again. Boy, that girl sure could dance. She had great legs, and an excellent sense of rhythm. Rusty nudged Bert and pointed to Helen. "That one's worth keeping an eye on. She's got something."

"*Hm.*" The director's reply was noncommittal, but he made some notes on the clipboard.

Rusty watched the remainder of the number and caught Helen's eye. He gave her the thumbs-up signal. The smile she gave him in return made him go a little wobbly in the knees.

Bert stashed his clipboard under his arm and clapped his hands. The piano music stopped. "All right, ladies, thank you. We'll be in touch. Next group up, please. Form two lines."

Rusty strode over to where Helen dabbed her forehead with a hankie. Her face bore an attractive flush from the exertion, and her eyes sparkled.

"Rusty! So good to see you," she exclaimed. "So what did you think of the audition?"

"You did great. How do you think it went?"

She shrugged. "I felt pretty good about it. Guess it all depends on what they're looking for."

He grasped her elbow. "If you're all done here, you need to come with me."

She recoiled. "What? Where?"

"Hold on to your hat. You're about to meet Mr. Cooperman."

"What?" She pulled her arm away from his grasp. "Not now! I can't meet him looking like this."

"It's too important to wait." He grabbed her arm again and tried to steer her toward the door.

"But I'm all sweaty," she protested. "I need to redo my makeup and change my clothes."

"You look great." She did, too. Besides, it would be good for Cooperman to see her in her audition clothes. It'd make it easier for him to picture her as a working actress if she *looked* like a working actress. "Sorry, no time. Plus I'm not letting you out of my sight. You're a hard one to track down."

She planted her feet. "At least let me change my shoes."

He yanked her along. "You'll thank me later. You'll see."

He hurried Helen out the door of the soundstage and down the sidewalk, the taps on her shoes clicking on the pavement, to Cooperman's office in the main headquarters building.

"Midge, is he here? This is urgent."

The secretary huffed. "I hope that whatever you've got to tell him will cheer him up. He's been Chief Thundercloud ever since Cynthia gave him the slip." She pressed the intercom button on her desk. "Mr. Cooperman, Rusty Noble's here to see you." She seemed to take no notice of Helen.

Cooperman's voice crackled over the intercom. "Send him in."

Midge cocked her head toward the inner office, and Rusty went through, tugging a reluctant Helen behind him.

"Here she is," he announced to Mr. Cooperman. "This is the girl I told you about. The one who can stand in for Cynthia."

Cooperman stood and walked around his desk, examining Helen from head to toe with a critical eye.

"*Hm.* Turn around." He made a twirling motion with his hand. Then, "Walk over there. Now turn and walk back."

Helen followed all his instructions.

At last he said, "Close enough. She'll have to do. We need to get that picture finished, come hell or high water. What's your name, dear?"

"Helen Corrigan."

The boss was silent for a moment, as if thinking, and Rusty wondered whether he'd tell her to change it. But at last he extended his hand and said, "Well, Helen Corrigan, looks like you've got yourself a job."

CHAPTER TWENTY

T he contract was a truncated one, only covering specific scenes of *The Courage of Annabel Brewster* with no promise of future work. Even so, Helen was ecstatic. Her name was listed on a studio contract signed by Stanley Cooperman himself, with her neat schoolgirl handwriting directly beneath his illegible scrawl. And the payment listed was more money than she would have seen in a whole month of working at Corrigan's Dry Goods. She could barely contain her excitement. Just wait until she told Marjorie!

Without a chance to catch her breath or tidy her hair, Helen was shunted off to the costume department. Work started the very next day. The process of filming turned out to be much more grueling than she'd imagined. While she didn't have to speak any lines, her role as a stand-in was literal, meaning she had to stand on her feet for hours as the cameras shot and reshot scenes of her walking, running, crouching behind rocks, and climbing over fences, all the while heeding the chalk marks on the soundstage floor. The exertion wore her out.

But frankly, if they'd asked her to turn cartwheels and handsprings, she would have done it, so thrilled was she to be working on a movie. She owed it all to Rusty Noble. And to God Who, after all, had blessed her with the fortuitous resemblance to Cynthia Starling.

The only scene Helen truly disliked required her to take a swim in a pool of water meant to be a creek, wearing a flesh-colored bathing suit. From the audience's perspective, she'd look as if she were wearing nothing at all. She'd been mighty uncomfortable with that scene but tried to talk herself into it by telling herself it was historically accurate. After all, on the Oregon Trail, the creek would have offered the only option for Annabel Brewster to take a bath.

The director, Mr. Renard, assured her she'd only be seen at a distance and thus would be unrecognizable, and furthermore, audiences would assume she was Cynthia Starling. When those facts didn't persuade her, he reminded her of her contractual obligation. That did the trick. Even so, she hated giving the impression that she'd filmed a scene without any clothes on and vowed to never get caught in that kind of situation again. She'd rather resign from a picture than compromise her moral values.

On a rare occasion when Mr. Renard told her she wouldn't be needed for the afternoon, she popped over to the writers' bungalow.

"I never properly thanked you for getting me this job," she told Rusty. He stared as if she'd just started speaking Chinese. "I mean, if you hadn't introduced me to Mr. Cooperman."

"You could thank me by letting me take you on a tour of the backlots," he blurted. He shot to his feet, knocking over a can filled with pencils. As they clattered to the floor and he bent to pick them up, two other writers sitting near him looked at Helen, then looked at each other, then shared a grin.

So they thought this was funny, did they?

"Why, Rusty, I'd like nothing better," she purred, giving him her sweetest smile. "Shall we go right now?"

"Um... sure." He fumbled the last pencil into place, then gave her a dumbfounded look, as if, in the moment, he didn't quite remember where the backlots were located.

Helen made a show of slipping her arm through his as though it were the most natural thing in the world. As they strolled out of the building together, the shocked expressions on his coworkers' faces were a joy to behold.

As for the look on Rusty's face... she knew she'd made the right move.

Rusty hadn't expected her to say an immediate yes to his offer of a tour, but he regrouped quickly. The project he was working on could wait for an hour or so. Heck, he wouldn't have been able to concentrate, anyway.

Not after she'd smiled at him that way.

"Come on," he said. "There are some things I want to show you."

As they walked to a neighboring soundstage, she let go of his arm. He understood. She'd only taken his arm to put on a show for Jim and Smitty, to put them in their places. Nonetheless, he felt the same disappointment he'd felt at the train station when she broke their pretend embrace. She was an actress. She pretended. That's what actresses did.

He led her to a soundstage where a stagehand was strewing a miniature mountain landscape with material from a bucket, creating the effect of a snowy winter wilderness.

"It looks incredibly realistic. What's that he's using?" Helen pointed to the bucket.

Her amazement amused Rusty. "It's a magical combination. Flour and kitty litter."

"Really?" Helen laughed. "I never would have guessed."

"Most people don't. That's why the model makers' work is shrouded in secrecy. People watching the movie need to believe they really are in a city under attack, for example, or in a battle at sea. Speaking of which, come look at this."

He took her to a workshop where sets were being built for a war picture. He showed her a large tub of water backed by a painted sky. In the water floated toy boats similar to those her nephew Bobby enjoyed playing with in the bath, only much more intricate and lifelike.

"When the battle scene is shot," Rusty explained, "the water will be churned with egg beaters. And I'll give you three guesses where the smoke comes from for the burning ships."

"I don't know," she admitted. "Smoke machines?"

"From the producer's cigars." He grinned at the stunned look on her face. "They lean down close to the surface of the water and puff away."

"Whenever I've watched a battle scene in a movie, I've assumed the ships were real ones and the scene was shot on the ocean," she said.

Rusty shook his head. "That would be way too expensive, and too time-consuming."

"I wasn't considering the practical aspects. I'll never look the same way at a battle scene again."

He loved how her laugh came from deep inside. She didn't giggle and twitter in a silly, superficial way like most starlets he knew.

In another part of the workshop, he showed her a miniature Midwestern town constructed out of nothing more than paint and plywood, with autumn-tinged trees constructed out of shredded cardboard. It was like a doll town, only better. As they watched, a model train clanged through, making Helen again think of Bobby and Barbara. How they would love to see, or better yet play with, these miniature sets!

"Producers save money by not building huge sets that they aren't going to use very much," Rusty told her. "Sets like this one can be used over and over. And unlike the full-size replicas outside, it's not subject to the weather."

"Oh, it's charming, and perfect in every detail," she breathed. "But I don't understand something. How do the actors work on these sets without towering over them? They'd look like monsters."

"They film the actors against a black backdrop. Then they film the miniature set and combine the two pieces of footage. And speaking of monsters, it was a miniature set that King Kong destroyed, and King Kong himself was an amazing triumph of puppetry. I assume you saw it."

"Oh, I did. I was terrified." Helen frowned. "So, tell me... all those scenes where the giant ape was towering over Fay Wray and she was screaming her head off... ?"

"They weren't even in the same room at the same time. They were filmed separately, then combined later."

"Golly." Helen looked as if a whole new world was opening before her.

"And if you think that's interesting, wait until you see *The Invisible Man*." Rusty nearly bounced on his toes, like a kid responding to an adult's interest in his pet project.

"I've seen the previews. I'm wondering how they'll pull that one off," Helen said.

"Do you really want to know?" Rusty asked. "Or will it spoil the movie for you?"

"I really want to know."

He stopped and turned to her, practically bursting with excitement, as if he was about to reveal the secret of Tutankhamin's tomb. "They filmed Ray Milland wrapped in black velvet, against a black screen. This created a sort of negative effect. Then they filmed the rest of the scene, and made a composite of the two."

"Fascinating!" Helen's face bore a look of astonishment. "It's amazing they can do things like that."

"But don't tell anybody. You're sworn to secrecy."

"Sworn to secrecy." She lifted three fingers as if reciting a scout oath. Somehow Rusty knew deep down that he could trust her.

"It opens next week," he blurted. "*The Invisible Man*. Maybe you'd like to go? With me, I mean."

"I'd love to." Helen beamed at him.

As he walked her to the studio gates, Rusty worried he'd been overly enthusiastic, that he'd overwhelmed her with arcane details of the movie business. He could get that way sometimes, like an eager puppy aiming to please.

"Seriously," he said, "I hope I haven't ruined any movies for you by telling you how some of these effects are produced. Sometimes people don't really care to know how the sausage is made, if you know what I mean."

She assured him of her fascination. "I'm here to learn. I want to know everything about how films are made. All the gory details. Although, in all honesty," she added, "I much prefer the less gory ones."

Rusty's insides warmed. She shared his deep interest in moviemaking, in making pictures seem as much like real life as possible. She seemed interested in the whole process of filmmaking, not just the acting. In his experience, most starlets didn't take much notice of the parts of moviemaking in which they weren't directly involved.

And it also seemed quite possible, all of a sudden, that Helen Corrigan was his kind of girl.

Maybe he wasn't meant to spend the rest of his life alone, after all.

CHAPTER TWENTY-ONE

When she got back to the apartment after a full day of filming, Helen typically was so exhausted, she felt like doing nothing more than eating a quiet supper in her pajamas and reading a good novel until an early bedtime.

The studio had other plans for her.

"You need to get yourself out there in public," Mr. Cooperman had told her when he'd hired her. "We need our actors and actresses to be the faces of Cooperman Studios, both here in Los Angeles and in the nationwide press. Plus, we've got to keep the investors happy."

Part of keeping the investors happy included wining and dining them at lavish, star-studded parties. After one particularly grueling Friday when Helen dragged herself home, Donna and Flo met her at the door of the apartment, dressed to the teeth.

"Come on, doll. Put on your glad rags, and make it snappy," Donna ordered. "We've been invited to a studio party at Cooperman's house, and anyone who's anyone will be there. We might just see some real stars!"

"How does he expect us to shine after he works us like mules all day?" Helen grumbled.

"Welcome to the magic of Hollywood," Flo said with a sympathetic smile. "Now hurry up. We'll wait for you."

Helen's energy returned after taking a cool shower. She refreshed her makeup, brushed her blond bob, and put on the only fancy dress that she'd brought with her—a geranium-pink number that had formerly belonged to Dot and was only a few years old—and a pair of summery tan sandals.

When she entered the living room, Donna took one look at her and wrinkled her nose as if detecting a bad smell. "You're not wearing *that*, are you?"

Helen looked down at her dress, perplexed. "What's wrong with it?"

"Everything." Donna was not one to mince words. "For one thing, it's entirely the wrong season to be wearing bright pink. You look like a tulip."

"What difference does it make? Los Angeles doesn't have seasons," Helen replied, feeling defensive. "It's warm and sunny here all the time."

"That doesn't matter. Fall is fall. And for another thing, that style has not been in fashion for at least—"

"Don't worry, sweetie," Flo broke in. "I've got something you can borrow." She spoke in a soothing tone, cutting off Donna's torrent of criticism. "You and I wear about the same size, don't you think?"

She led Helen to the bedroom closet and pulled out a dark blue silk gown, simple and elegant. "This one, I think, to bring out your eyes. And silver sandals to go with it. You'll be the belle of the ball. Now get changed, and *hurry*!"

Helen thanked her and rushed to change, leaving her pink dress in a heap on the floor. The three roommates shared a taxi to the Cooperman mansion in Bel-Air. Helen couldn't help but gape at the sprawling structure built in the style of a French chateau. Golden light blazed from every window. The taxi joined a line of sleek, shiny limousines and sedans gliding up the curved driveway past sculpted gardens, toward the impressive front entrance.

"Let's get out here and walk the rest of the way," Helen suggested. "I want to get a closer look at that garden before the light's completely gone." In reality, she wasn't so much interested in the gardens as in casting off the heavy cloak of anxiety that had settled around her shoulders at the thought of meeting all those larger-than-life celebrities and important studio people. Walking in the fresh air would help, even in her borrowed sandals, which pinched a little. Better a bit too snug than too big, she reasoned, at the risk of flying off her foot like Cinderella's slipper.

After paying the driver, the three women exited the taxi and strolled through the twilight glow of the garden, admiring the sculpted hedges and geometrical arrangements of flowers, most of which were unfamiliar to Helen. "Not your garden-variety garden, is it?" she quipped. As she suspected, the gentle walk calmed her nerves and helped her get her bearings.

They entered through the French doors and followed the crowd to a ballroom packed with people in formal attire. Women wore floor-length gowns of all colors of the spectrum—including pink, Helen noted with a surge of resentment toward Donna—and sparkling jewelry. The men, by contrast, looked virtually alike in black tuxedos, distinguishable from one another only by their age, girth, and hair, or lack thereof.

As soon as they entered the ballroom, Donna shot off across the room without a backward glance. Helen touched Flo on the arm. "I'm going to find something to drink. Be right back."

Flo nodded, her eyes already sweeping the room. "I'll meet you over there." She pointed and set off in the opposite direction.

After smoothing out her wrinkled skirt and tucking a few errant strands of hair behind her ears, Helen approached the bar and smiled at the bartender. "Ginger ale with ice." She accepted the drink gratefully and took several sips to soothe her parched throat and calm her jitters.

The intimidation factor was high. The guest list included a lot of famous people, as well as studio executives, make-up artists, cameramen, and costumers. Those who weren't stars looked almost as glamorous as those who were. Myrna Loy did the foxtrot with a genial newcomer named Jimmy Stewart. Claudette Colbert and Frederic March spun in the center of the dance floor while several other couples glided around them like planets circling the sun. Other guests, like Helen, clung to the edges of the room like barnacles to a ship's hull.

A waiter materialized at Helen's side, offering champagne. She waved him away, happy with her soft drink. She felt like the Invisible Woman, drifting unnoticed among the glittering crowd, circling the edges of conversations, catching snatches of industry gossip about various actors' tryouts and dry-outs. Some spoke in loud, animated voices to studio executives who might be able to finance a new project or otherwise crack open a door of opportunity. In spite of the star power present, the truly honored guests were the deep-pocketed investors and studio backers for whom the party was held.

She observed the scene like a naturalist in the wild, making mental notes of the species she recognized. No one took any notice of her, and she preferred it that way.

The room was warm in spite of the electric fans lining the walls. Her feet ached. She longed to slip off her sandals and stand barefoot on the cool parquet floor.

Someone approached her from the right and brushed her shoulder.

"Well, you're a welcome sight."

Rusty Noble smiled at her with a look of surprise on his face, as if she were the last person he expected to find standing in Mr. Cooperman's ballroom. He seemed pleased about it, though.

"Thank you," she said. "I was just thinking about how I don't know a soul here except Flo and Donna."

"You know me."

"Thank goodness for that." She smiled up at him. "I'm glad you're here. I want to thank you for giving me that fascinating backstage tour. I've been thinking about it ever since." In truth, she'd been thinking about *him* ever since. But he didn't need to know that.

"It's I who should be thanking you," he replied. "For putting up with my lectures on cinematography. I do get carried away sometimes." His expression turned serious. "And for saving *The Courage of Annabel Brewster.*"

Heat crept up her neck. "Oh, I'd hardly say I saved it."

"I would. Without your strong resemblance to Cynthia Starling, we'd really be up a creek."

Helen took a sip of her drink. "Why didn't she finish the picture? Did she get sick?"

"No, nothing like that." His expression registered distaste. "Let's just say she saw a better opportunity and seized it."

That seemed irresponsible of Cynthia, but Helen didn't say so, not wanting to gossip.

"Well, I'm sorry to hear it. But not *too* sorry," she confessed, "as it made an opening for me to step into."

Rusty raised his glass. "To Tinseltown, and to seizing opportunities when they appear."

They clinked glasses, then Helen asked him, "What else are you working on?"

"Another Western," he said. "I'm calling this one *Stormy River Serenade.* But Cooperman will probably change the title."

"How's it going?"

"I've sent him my synopsis of the story. We'll see what he says. Meanwhile we're breaking down the story line into dialogue."

"Sounds like an interesting job," she said.

"It has its moments."

She tilted her head. "You must like Westerns, since you write so many. Are you making a name for yourself in cowboy films?"

"Audiences like Westerns. Which, in turn, makes Cooperman like Westerns. That's the bottom line in this business—what do audiences want?"

"And there's a part for me in this new script of yours?" she asked, only half joking.

"Of course," he said. "There's a part you'd be perfect for, as a rancher's daughter. It's the main supporting role."

"Not the leading role?" she teased.

"The leading role needs to be a teenager," he said. "You look young, but not *that* young."

"Okay, then." She waited a moment for his comment to settle, to consider whether or not to be offended. She decided his blunt response was acceptable, under the circumstances. "Who do you hope will play the lead?"

He answered without hesitation. "Debbie Fagan."

"Oh, I like her. She was so fun to work with in *Annabel*. And who else?"

"St. Ives for the male lead, probably. He's a bit of a dunce, but audiences like him. Although it would be great if Cooperman would negotiate for John Wayne."

"That new guy over at Fox? He's good. My sister and I saw him in *The Big Trail*."

"Whoever it ends up being, I hope Cooperman decides soon. Until I know which actor's playing which part, it's hard for me to get a real handle on the script."

"If you could write anything, what would you write?"

He blinked. "Gee. Give me a minute. Nobody's ever asked me that before. Not in a long time, anyway." He sipped his drink. "I want to make good movies. Thought-provoking movies. Movies that uphold truth, beauty, and goodness, that honor God." His face reddened. "That probably sounds pretty corny."

"Not at all," she assured him. "Those are the kinds of movies I want to make, too. Tell me more."

As he spoke, his intense hazel eyes focused on her without looking away. His reddish-brown hair swooped backward, slicked with pomade. He looked much more handsome here at the party than he had on the train, or even at the studio. When he smiled, he displayed slightly crooked teeth, which she hadn't noticed before and which endeared him to her. After seeing hordes of blinding white, dentist-perfect teeth, an imperfect smile like Rusty's made him seem genuinely likable. Like most of the men present, he was dressed in a black dinner jacket, but he'd added an olive-green pocket square that complemented his coloring.

Too soon, Rusty was called away, and she was left standing alone again. Condensation formed along the sides of her glass and threatened drip onto her dark silk dress. On *Flo's* dark silk dress. Maybe even ruin it. She looked for a place to deposit her drink, but before she could, Flo approached her, accompanied by a tall, tanned man with short salt-and-pepper hair. His horn-rimmed glasses gave him a serious demeanor.

"Helen, I'd like to introduce you to Phil Fairmont. Phil, this is my new roommate, Helen Corrigan."

"How do you do, Mr. Fairmont." Helen extended her hand, conscious of its dampness.

The man didn't seem to notice as he shook her hand. "Please, call me Phil."

"Phil's an *agent*," Flo informed Helen with a meaningful inflection in her voice. "He works very closely with Cooperman Studios, among others. He's very well connected. I thought you two would enjoy meeting one another. Now, if you'll excuse me, I see a friend I need to catch up with." She winked at Helen, then walked away.

Helen turned to Phil Fairmont, tongue-tied. What was one supposed to say to an agent?

Fortunately, Phil picked up the thread of conversation.

"Flo tells me you've only recently arrived in Hollywood, yet you've already managed to land a role, all on your own. You must know how very rare that is."

"Well, it can hardly be called a role," Helen admitted. "I am a stand-in for Cynthia Starling."

His gaze swept over her in an appraising way. "I can see why. There's a powerful resemblance."

She started to thank him, then thought the better of it. Her physical resemblance to Cynthia wasn't something she could take credit for. It was just the face and figure God had given her. "I hope to get a speaking part soon, however minor. It's small, but a step up, I think."

"I'd say so," Phil Fairmont said in a dismissive tone. "Here's my card. Call me when you've gotten a little more experience under your belt."

That he didn't want to sign her on as a client right then and there caused a twinge of disappointment, but then she chided herself for being unrealistic. Beginning actresses like her were a dime a dozen in Hollywood. She'd have to prove her worth before a big agent like Phil Fairmont—*well connected*, Flo had called him—would start paying attention. But he would someday. She was sure of it. At least they had been introduced. She made a mental note to thank Flo for that.

She was scanning the room for a tray on which to deposit her empty glass when an older man appeared before her.

"Say, aren't you a pretty one?" He leaned a little too close, the stench of whiskey strong on his breath. "Why, for a minute there, from a distance, I thought you were Cynthia Starling. Has anyone ever told you that?"

Helen took a step back. "Once or twice." She could scarcely believe it, but being constantly compared to Cynthia Starling was getting a bit tiresome.

"I'm Herbert Jones." The man slurred his words. He bore a look of self-importance, as though the name was supposed to mean something to her.

It didn't.

"How do you do," she said in a cool tone, not offering her hand, lest she encourage him to continue talking to her. She wasn't in the mood to talk to any drunken men tonight. She surveyed the space over his shoulder. If only she could find Rusty again, or Flo, or even Donna. Just about anyone would do.

"Say, toots... " the man said. "Come here. I want to tell you a secret."

She recoiled as he leaned forward and whispered something in her ear, his hot moist breath unpleasant against her skin. At first, she didn't understand what he'd said. Then, as the words unspooled themselves in her brain, she took another step back, looked him square in the eye, and slapped him hard across the face.

From across the room, Rusty kept stealing glances back at Helen. Even in a town crowded with stunning women, she stood out, at least to Rusty's eyes. She had a fresh, unspoiled quality that so many starlets lacked. He hoped the harsh realities of Hollywood wouldn't scratch away that glow of innocence. Rusty had seen that happen far too often.

He was glad to see her talking to Phil Fairmont. Now there was a guy who could really help her out, if he took a shine to her. And why wouldn't he? Anybody could see that she had that star quality—unmistakable, yet hard to define.

As Rusty watched, Phil handed Helen his card—a great sign! A good agent wouldn't hand his card out freely to struggling actors and actresses. Rusty wanted to tell her so, to give her a word of encouragement. When it appeared the two had ended their conversation, he pushed his way through the crowd toward her, but some bigwig investor from New York got to her first. Rusty paused, not wanting to interrupt, but something seemed off. Why would a fat cat like that guy want to speak to Helen?

Seconds later, he knew why. With a salacious grin, the man bent his head toward Helen's and murmured something in her ear. Without hesitation, she drew her hand back, then decked him straight across the face with a resounding *smack*.

"How dare you!"

The interloper reeled back, hand to his cheek, expression of pure shock.

A momentary tension fell over the ballroom as people turned to see what caused the commotion. Even the band paused when the leader turned around to see what his musicians were gawking at.

The bigwig's face contorted. "You—!" He shouted a name not usually heard in polite society. Helen looked as shocked as he had.

Chaos broke out as some onlookers began shouting at the investor and others shouted at Helen.

From his vantage point, Rusty spotted Stanley Cooperman hurrying toward the scene. Rusty pushed his way through the crowd and grabbed Helen's hand.

"Quick. Follow me."

"But—"

"No arguments."

He led her through the crowd and out a set of French doors to the conservatory. Finding a quiet bench in the shadow of a giant potted palm, he beckoned for her to sit, then hovered solicitously.

"Are you all right? Can I get you a glass of water? Or something else?"

She had a dazed look. "I'm all right."

"He had it coming. Who cares if he's one of Cooperman Studio's biggest investors?"

"Ha, ha. Very funny."

"No, really," Rusty insisted. "He's the head of some financial firm that's heavily invested in the studio. He and Stanley Cooperman go way back."

She groaned and dropped her head into her hands. "Oh, no! I can't believe I did that."

"Did what? Slapped a guy who got fresh with you?" Rusty took a seat beside her.

"Slapped an *investor*. A major backer of the place that employs me." She looked at Rusty, horrified. "What if he withdraws all his support? What if I get fired?"

"You won't get fired," Rusty said with confidence, even though he had no idea whether it was true. "Clearly the guy deserved it. I don't know what he said to you, but it must have been a terrible insult."

"It was."

Rusty took the liberty of patting her knee. "Believe me, the guy will get over it. Why, a fellow like that probably gets himself slapped once a day and twice on Sundays. He's probably already moving on to his next target as we speak."

"I hope you're wrong," Helen said. "No woman deserves to be spoken to like that."

"No, she doesn't. And neither do you. I'm afraid that sort of behavior is all too common in Hollywood, though."

"Is it?" Helen shook her head. "I had no idea. Everyone I've met thus far has been very nice to me."

"Most people are nice, but there's definitely a smarmy element you want to stay away from."

"That's what people back home have told me." Helen groaned. "I thought they were exaggerating. Maybe I should have listened better."

"That's why some people start their own studios. So they don't have to play that game." Rusty looked at her, weighing how much of his dream was safe to confide in her. Part of him longed to tell her all about his plans. On the other hand, he didn't know her well enough yet to spill the beans completely.

She straightened and faced him, her chagrin over slapping an important investor apparently forgotten. "I've been mulling over what we talked about the other day, about wanting to make better-quality movies. My father told me Hollywood needs Christians making movies. He says it's just as much a mission field as anyplace else where people need to hear the good news."

Rusty's heart pounded. She wanted exactly what he wanted. At last, a woman whose vision for the movies aligned with his. "Your father sounds like a wise man. I'd like to meet him one day."

"He says Hollywood is having a huge impact on the world, and that Christians should come here and try to make a difference." Helen slumped back against the bench. "Well, I'd been feeling discouraged, not seeing what kind of a difference I could make. I'm only one person." She turned her head and smiled at Rusty. "But now I know there are at least two of us."

"There are plenty of people who feel that way. If enough of us—enough people, I mean—banded together and formed our own studio, I believe we could truly make a positive difference on the kinds of movies that are made," Rusty said, careful to stop short of saying that he was already planning to do exactly this. "My dream is a studio where people of faith have full creative control over everything: the stories we choose to tell, the scripts, the casting, even the crew. We need more studios producing good films that are also a good place to work. Offering fair contracts, like the kind the Screen Writers' Guild has fought so hard for. Reasonable working hours. A place where actors and actresses, along with everybody else, are treated with respect as hardworking, talented professionals, not as pawns to be admired and traded and tossed out at will."

Her eyes shone in the moonlight. "I'd love to work for a studio like that," she breathed. "Do you know of any here in Hollywood?"

Mine, he wanted to shout. Instead he said, "If I did, I'd already be working there." He paused. "For now, it's just a beautiful dream. It's no easy thing to start up a studio. It takes money and plenty of it, for one thing. A crew of like-minded talent, technicians, cameramen... and then you gotta go up against the major studios, like David facing Goliath."

"David won though, in the end," Helen reminded him. "God gave him the power. And maybe God would help a struggling studio, too, if it were doing His work. Making movies that honored Him."

Rusty pondered her words. He hadn't thought of it that way before. "That's it, of course. I just don't like the direction the major studios are taking, including Cooperman. Too much sex and violence. They say that's what audiences want, but I'm not so sure. I think audiences want movies they can watch together as a family. Good stories, well told, with solid moral values." He paused for breath, realizing he was talking too much. "Sorry for preaching your ear off. I'll get off my soapbox now."

"You're not preaching," Helen assured him. "It's obviously something you feel passionate about."

He was ready to burst with gratitude that she understood. "I just feel like, as an industry, we can do a better job. I want to do my part."

"Well, if you ever do hear of a studio like that, I hope you'll let me know," Helen said. "I'd love to work on movies like those you've described."

Rusty gave an internal cheer, and vowed that if ever he was able to get his studio up and running, Helen would be the first actress hired. But he couldn't tell her of his plans. Not yet.

Not until he had something more solid to offer her.

As they continued to talk about the peculiarities of being Christians in Hollywood, Flo appeared through the French doors, silhouetted against the light. When she spotted Helen and Rusty sitting in the shadows, she hurried over as quickly as her high-heeled dancing slippers would allow.

"Helen! Thank goodness. I've been looking everywhere for you. Are you all right? What on earth happened back there?"

Helen gave Flo a brief explanation of events. Then she stood. "I can't go back in there," she pleaded. "Can't we just go home?"

Flo enfolded her into a hug. "Of course we can."

"I'll take you both," Rusty offered.

"Oh, no." Helen placed a hand on his forearm. "You're very kind. I've enjoyed our conversation. It's important for you to stay here and talk about your ideas. To find more people who think the way we do." She gave him a little wink that set his blood racing.

"You wait here," Flo told Helen. "I'll go get Donna and we'll be off."

When she'd gone inside, Rusty turned to Helen and gently grasped her arm.

"Are you sure you don't want me to drive you all home?" At that moment, he couldn't think of anything he'd rather do than keep talking to her.

But she shook her head. "If we're going to convince people of the need for cleaner movies, we need to strengthen our contacts in the industry, which starts by hobnobbing with all the right people at events like this one."

His heart warmed at her use of the term "we." "Very well then. Let the hobnobbing begin." He wanted to wrap her in his arms, but that seemed entirely too forward. So he settled for a handshake, relishing the warmth of her hand in his.

Flo returned without Donna. "She wants to stay. She says she'll get a ride home with someone else."

Helen shrugged. "All right."

The three of them left the conservatory through a side door that led to the sculpted gardens, and from there to the entrance. Rusty approached a white Packard touring car parked along the circular drive and rapped his knuckles on the window. He said something to the driver, passed him some bills from his wallet, then opened the rear passenger door and beckoned Helen and Flo to get in.

"We can't take someone else's car," Helen protested. "That's like stealing."

"The driver says he'll return straight away after dropping you off," Rusty said. "Now get in and be good."

Helen smiled her thanks. "Good night, then."

"Good night."

Helen slid across the leather seat, marveling at the car's luxurious interior. Flo followed.

"Wow," she breathed, looking around. "Donna will be sorry she missed *this*."

The driver turned toward them, touched the brim of his hat, and said, "Where to, ladies?"

Flo gave him the address, and the car pulled away from the curb.

From the safety of the Packard, Helen looked up at the chandelier-lighted front entrance to the mansion. Too bad such a fun evening had to end on such a sour note. But Rusty had been so kind, had rescued her from that boorish man.

Her reverie was interrupted by a glimpse of a familiar figure emerging through the doorway, dressed this time in evening clothes instead of a trench coat and fedora.

The Stalker.

"Look, Flo." She pointed through the limousine's window. "Do you know who that man is?"

Flo leaned across Helen to look out the window. "Who?"

"That man standing in the doorway, facing this way."

But a pair of bright headlights momentarily blinded Helen, and when she turned back, he was nowhere to be seen.

CHAPTER TWENTY-TWO

Late the next morning, the three bathrobe-clad roommates draped themselves around the apartment's living room, discussing the events of the previous night over mugs of strong coffee. Flo praised Helen for standing up for herself against the amorous party guest the night before.

"You did the right thing," she said with conviction. "If more women stood up to those lecherous creeps, maybe all of us would get treated with more respect."

"Mr. Cooperman isn't going to like it," Donna said in an ominous voice. "He expects the actresses to treat the investors well. And the secretaries. Especially the pretty ones." She slid a glance toward Flo. "And especially the really rich investors, like Herbert Jones. His family's in oil."

"He ought to be boiled in oil," Helen murmured.

"Well, even if that's true about Mr. Cooperman, he's wrong to condone such behavior." Flo sounded as if she didn't quite believe it. "We're professionals and deserve to be treated as such."

"In any case," Helen added, "I've never been one to put up with that sort of malarkey. Years ago I slugged a fellow who got fresh with me at a Fourth of July picnic at Lake Michigan." She couldn't help a whisper of pride at the memory. "He saw fireworks, all right. And I was just a kid then."

"Such ladylike behavior," Donna drawled.

"Hey, it beats letting rude fellows like that take advantage of us," Helen said. "Nothing says we have to abandon our moral standards when we cross the Hollywood city limits."

"Maybe so, but sadly, it's how the game is played." Flo gave a rueful shake of her dark head. "The pressure to conform, and the temptations to stray from what we know is right, can be awfully hard to resist. Even though I'm not an actress, I feel like one sometimes. Like when Mr. Cooperman wants all the secretaries to attend black-tie parties like the one last night. For goodness' sake, I was hired for my typing speed, not my ability to slink around in an evening gown."

"You sure looked like you were having a good time," Donna remarked.

Flo blushed. "Well, yes. I do enjoy going to parties. But it shouldn't be an obligatory part of the job."

Helen shifted on the sofa and folded her legs underneath her. "We should band together to keep our morale up and our standards high. That's why I'm thinking of starting a prayer group at the studio."

"A what?" Donna stared at her as if she'd started speaking a foreign language.

"A prayer group. You know, a group to meet together before work, maybe once a week or so, to share concerns and pray for each other. To encourage one another and help us stay strong in the faith."

Donna tilted her head as if dumbfounded at the very idea. "Like a church service? But at work?"

"Not a church service," Helen clarified. "Just prayer. Maybe fifteen or twenty minutes. A half hour at most."

"I think that's a great idea." Flo's enthusiasm made up for Donna's disbelieving smirk. "I'd love to participate in something like that."

"It wasn't my idea," Helen admitted. "I met a lady on the train coming here, a Bible teacher, and she suggested it."

"Sounds corny to me. Count me out." Donna made a scoffing noise, then carried her coffee cup to the sink and turned on the faucet full blast.

Helen ignored her and turned to Flo, raising her voice to be heard over the running water. "Speaking of church services, the lady I'm talking about works for a church here in Hollywood. I looked up the address and it's not far from here. I'm thinking of going there in the morning to check it out. Want to come with me?"

Flo nodded. "Sure. It would do me good to get back into the churchgoing habit."

"Me too." Helen hugged herself, happy to have committed to attending church again.

Even happier to have someone to go with her.

The next morning Helen and Flo left the apartment early and located the church. They enjoyed the service, and afterward sought out Miss Mears during the coffee hour.

"I don't know if you remember me," Helen said. "Helen Corrigan. We met on the train from Tucson."

Miss Mears's blue eyes shone behind her spectacles. "Of course I remember you, Miss Corrigan. How nice to see you here."

Helen introduced Flo, then briefly brought Miss Mears up to speed on their work with Cooperman Studios.

"We're going to start a prayer group, like you suggested."

"That's a wonderful idea." The older woman gave them a few pointers on how to organize and publicize the group. "Keep me posted on how it goes."

The following Monday at the studio, word had gotten around about how Helen Corrigan slugged one of the VIPs. A few people followed Donna's lead in mocking Helen for being prissy and stuck-up.

"You're going to have to be friendlier with important people if you want to get anywhere in this industry," one older actress told her with a jaded expression.

"Oh, yeah?" Helen gave herself an internal kick for not having a snappier comeback.

"Don't worry about her," Gilda Miller murmured as the mature actress strode away. "I thought you were great."

"You were there?"

"Yeah. But next time, there are subtler ways to make your point. We'll work on it." Gilda winked.

Helen sincerely hoped there wouldn't be a next time.

At break, a cameraman named Howard beckoned her aside. She braced herself for more criticism.

"Hey, Helen," he mumbled, as if he were keeping a secret, "I just wanted to tell you, I was there at the party the other night. And I was proud of you for giving that guy what he had coming."

"Thanks." She spied a small gold cross hanging around Howard's neck, peeking out of the open collar of his shirt.

"Some of us are starting up a prayer group," she told him. "We're going to get together in the commissary every Monday morning before the workday starts."

"Great idea," Howard said.

"Please spread the word to anyone else you think might be interested."

"I will."

Helen grinned in satisfaction. So that made three prayer-group participants so far. Howard, Flo, and herself.

The break was nearly over. She had to get back to work. But as soon as she was free, she'd head to the writers' bungalow in search of Number Four.

The one person she most hoped would join.

For purposes of prayer, of course.

And also because she couldn't get him out of her mind.

The first meeting of the Cooperman Studios prayer group consisted of six people sitting around a table. Helen, Flo, Gilda, Howard the cameraman, the young actress Debbie Fagan, and an older actor named Simon Jarrow.

Helen welcomed everyone. "Just a brief reminder why we're here," she said. "We're going to meet every Monday before work and pray for each other, for Cooperman Studios, and for our industry. We'll each say our requests, then all pray together. Now, who'd like to go first?

Her invitation was met with silence.

"Come on, now. Don't be shy. Who has something they'd like to pray about?"

"I do," Flo ventured. "I pray that my supervisor, Mrs. Black, will find some relief for her rheumatism. It's really been giving her trouble lately."

Helen jotted a note on her pad. "Okay. Others?"

"I'd like prayer for my wife," Howard said. "She lost her mother recently and she's devastated."

"Let's pray for Mr. Cooperman." Simon cleared his throat. "For all the tough decisions he has to make. And for his brother, Leroy, and his adjustment to life on the outside."

It took Helen a minute to figure out what Simon meant. Outside? Then she remembered the gossip about a brother who'd spent time in prison for embezzlement, or something like that. She made a note.

"Anything else?"

When all the requests had been stated, Helen said, "Simon, will you pray for us?" She handed him the list of requests. All bowed their heads and closed their eyes while Simon prayed out loud.

Shortly before they'd finished, Helen heard a shuffling noise as a seventh person joined them at the table. When she opened her eyes after Simon's *amen*, she was delighted to see Rusty.

"Well, hi, there," she said warmly.

"Hi. Sorry I'm late. Sounds like I missed it." He ran a hand through his hair, making his cowlick stand straight up.

"That's okay. We're glad you're here. We've finished praying, but is there anything we can pray for you about?"

He shrugged. "Just, you know, for our movies to, you know, promote good morals and stuff." He stumbled over his words as if embarrassed. Clearly, he wasn't used to expressing himself about matters of faith. Not at work, anyway.

"Got it covered." Howard smiled at Rusty.

Having agreed to meet again the following week, the group dispersed. Helen caught up to Rusty.

"It's great to see you here," she said.

"Just wanted to see what it was all about."

"Now that you know, will you come back next time?"

His hazel eyes looked warmly into hers. "I sure will."

"That's great!" Helen kept her response friendly and professional as they parted for their separate workspaces. But for the rest of the day, her spirit soared, even when Jean-Luc Renard had her crawling through "zee mud" as they wrapped up filming *Annabel*.

Just like that, Monday morning became the brightest spot in her week.

CHAPTER TWENTY-THREE

With the filming of *The Courage of Annabel Brewster* completed, Helen went on a few auditions, but none of them panned out. While the stand-in job had paid well, especially by Kerryville standards, she needed to stretch her earnings to last as long as possible. Not only that, she had the added expense of a round-trip train ticket to Kerryville for Nanette's wedding.

When she didn't start landing roles immediately, she knew she had to replenish her fast-dwindling savings somehow, so she turned to the one thing she was qualified to do. Working in a retail store. Thanks to a fellow Studio Club resident who'd been willing to put in a good word, she managed to land a part-time job clerking at Bullock's Wilshire Department Store for the Christmas shopping season.

Given that steady acting work wasn't yet in the cards for her, Helen couldn't have been more pleased with this Plan B. After years of working at Corrigan's Dry Goods, she was good at helping people spend their money. But the similarities ended there.

In contrast to Corrigan's modest Main Street storefront, Bullock's flagship store had more in common with Chicago's elegant Marshall Field & Company, where both Marjorie and Dot had worked back in their single days, but more modern and up-to-date. Bullock's was housed in a beautiful Art Deco-style building, seven stories tall, on Los Angeles's fashionable Wilshire Boulevard. Shoppers could exit their vehicles under an elaborate *porte-cochère* at the rear of the building, where valets in livery greeted them and parked their cars.

Helen had never seen anything like it.

The store's interior was equally luxurious, the kind of place where the soft crackle of expensive leather, the whisper of silk and lace, and the rustle of hundred-dollar bills were often the loudest sounds to be heard. Clothes were displayed on rosewood stands, their costly accessories in low glass cases. The Louis XVI Room sold dresses by designers Helen had never even heard of. There was even a Doggery department that carried every canine accessory imaginable, and a Saddle Shop for the horsey set.

To Helen's delight and awe, she'd been assigned to the fragrance department on the main floor, the loftily titled Perfume Hall, that featured vaulted ceilings, glossy granite floors and veined marble walls polished to a shine, like in a museum.

On a December evening shortly before closing time, Perfume Hall had grown quiet and void of customers. The front display, which Helen was charged with keeping free of dust, was lined with sparkling crystal bottles of every shape and size, filled with amber, cobalt, and emerald-colored liquids and labeled with graceful fonts.

She almost didn't want to touch some of the bottles, they were so expensive. Her hands trembled as she carefully removed them from the shelf to dust under and around them. She liked to pronounce the names out loud, akin to taking a crash course in French. *L'Heure Bleue. Nuit de Noël.* She also loved to sniff the testers, ranging from fresh and springlike scents to those that were more sultry and mysterious. Her favorite was the store's signature blend of lemon, rose, and lilac.

Helen's supervisor, Mrs. Carroll, was a tall, thin woman with a prominent nose that seemed particularly well suited for a person in charge of the fragrance department.

"Make sure you don't leave fingerprints on the glass," she remarked. "It does no good to remove the dust and leave finger-prints behind."

"Yes, ma'am," Helen responded, feeling like a five-year-old.

"I'll be in the stockroom for a few minutes," Mrs. Carroll said. "I don't think we'll have many more customers tonight."

Helen finished dusting the shelves, then kneeled behind the counter to ferret through some boxes, looking for extra stock to replace a few bottles that had been sold.

A pair of silk-stockinged legs appeared in her line of vision, and an imperious voice said, "Miss, I'd like some help."

Helen straightened up. But before she could ask, "How may I help you?" the customer said, "Oh, it's you." It was Donna, dressed in a silk dress and a fur stole Helen hadn't seen before. Donna glanced around Perfume Hall as if she'd never laid eyes on it before. Perhaps she hadn't.

"I forgot you work here," she said in a bored tone. "I forgot you're a shop girl."

"Yes, I am." Helen ignored the implied insult. "How can I help you, Donna?" She hoped the transaction wouldn't take too long.

"I'm interested in this scent." Donna picked up a tester of an expensive fragrance. "You can go ahead and wrap it up. My *boyfriend* will be along any minute to buy it for me. Just like he bought me this stole.." She petted the piece of fur gracing her shoulder.

Donna had a boyfriend? Not that Helen cared, but she did a double take when Herbert Jones, the lecherous investor from Mr. Cooperman's party, came striding up. "I'm ready to go."

Donna turned to him and waved her wrist under his nose. "What do you think of this one, Herbie? Isn't it delicious?"

He jerked his head back and made a face. "Smells like insect repellent."

Donna looked at the tester. "But it's one of the most expensive ones here."

"Buy it or don't buy it," Herbert said with a tone of indifference. "Then let's get the heck out of this dump." He turned and walked away.

A fleeting look of dismay crossed Donna's face. Then she composed her features. She set the tester on the counter.

"On second thought, I don't like it at all." She gave her chin a snooty lift. "It smells cheap." She turned on her kitten heel and followed Herbert out the door.

Helen watched them walk away, then returned the tester to its proper place on the counter, feeling troubled and sorry for Donna. Nothing was worth letting a man talk to her that way. Certainly not a fur stole or silk stockings. Especially not a bottle of overpriced perfume.

Rusty sat at his desk and gnawed on his pencil, finding it impossible to concentrate on the scenario he was writing. Jim and Smitty, already given over to the holiday spirit, were playing a noisy game of wastebasket-ball with a little toy reindeer that one of the secretaries had placed in the bungalow in an effort to jolly it up.

"Look alive, Rusty," Smitty hollered as the reindeer sailed past his head.

It was no use. He threw down his pencil, picked up the reindeer, and pitched it back to Smitty. "Hey, the three of us should get together over the break and go over plans for the new studio," he said. "What do you say? We won't have Cooperman breathing down our necks."

"Can't do it," Smitty said. "Going to visit the folks in Bakersfield."

"Me too," Jim said. "Home sweet home. You're staying in town, right, Rusty?"

Rusty nodded. He'd probably spend the time off working. The way he spent most holidays.

"What does your new girlfriend think of your dream to open a studio?" Smitty tossed the reindeer up and down.

"What girlfriend?"

"The blonde number with the eyes."

Irritation crept up Rusty's neck. "She's not a number, she's a lady. Show some respect. And she's not my girlfriend." *Yet.*

"Sorry." Smitty returned the reindeer to its perch on a windowsill covered in flocked snow. "All I meant was, if we had someone like her on our team, as our lead actress, it would set us ahead."

"How do you know?" Rusty challenged. "You haven't seen her act. How do you know she has any skills?"

"We've seen her around the set, jumping through hoops for Renard," Jim said. "We've seen her work hard and take direction well. She's the polar opposite of Cynthia Starling."

"You can say that again." Rusty agreed.

"And she likes you," Jim said. "So maybe she'd be willing to live in poverty for a while, until things get moving at the studio."

The room grew warmer. Rusty hoped Helen liked him. She seemed to. And he sure liked her.

"Plus, we heard she decked some obnoxious bigwig at Cooperman's party," Jim added. "She could double as our security guard."

"Golly, I wish I'd been there to see that," Smitty said.

"She's something, all right." Rusty did his best to sound noncommittal. But the inside of his chest was as wobbly as Santa's bowlful of jelly.

If everything she'd said to him at the party had been true, Helen Corrigan was as beautiful on the inside as she was on the outside. Would she consider joining the new studio? To work side by side with Rusty, making the kinds of movies they wanted to watch?

To just plain be at his side?

There was only one way to find out.

CHAPTER TWENTY-FOUR

Cooperman Studios closed for two weeks at Christmas, and many of the Studio Club residents left town over the break. Helen planned to as well. Under ordinary circumstances, she would not have afforded herself the money to travel all the way to Illinois merely to spend the holidays. But as a member of the bridal party, she needed—no, she *wanted*—to be there for Nanette's wedding to Ted Barber, as well as to relax and reconnect with her family. She especially wanted to mend fences with darling Marjorie, whom she'd hurt so deeply by running off to Hollywood with no warning.

The Friday before leaving, she scavenged Bullock's on her lunch break to load up on California-themed Christmas presents to tuck into her luggage. With the help of her employee discount, she bought a set of kitchen towels decorated with palm trees for Marjorie. Boxes of date candy for Charlie and Peter. A genuine Max Factor eye liner pencil for Dot. A Shirley Temple doll for Barbara, and a toy movie camera for Bobby.

Her spirits buoyed by her purchases, Helen returned to the sales floor with renewed energy.

"This is our best seller," she assured a mink-draped customer as she held the spray bottle over the counter.

All at once, Helen's breath hitched. A familiar figure appeared beyond the customer's head—the mysterious man who appeared to be stalking her. He was examining a pair of men's shoes in the department that bordered the perfume department. Helen's indignation overruled her fear. Who was he to keep showing up wherever she was? The man might have had a legitimate reason for being there, looking for a new pair of oxford brogues. Still, she found it a mighty strange coincidence. Was she imagining things?

In any case, she was no longer afraid of him. Surely if he meant to do her harm, he'd have done so by now. If he merely wanted to meet her, he should introduce himself and get it over with. His persistence in trailing her around—if that was indeed what he was doing—was getting annoying.

Well, enough was enough. As soon as she finished helping the customer, she'd march straight up and ask him to explain himself.

But Mink Stole took longer than expected to make her selection. By the time Helen wrapped up the transaction and crossed the aisle to find her stalker, he was nowhere to be found.

Next time he wouldn't be so lucky.

If there was a next time.

"I've been pleased with your work here, Miss Corrigan," Mrs. Carroll told Helen before she clocked out at the end of her shift. "If you'd like to continue to work here when you return from your journey, there will be a place for you."

Helen expressed her gratitude. Privately, she hoped to get so much more acting work in the new year that there'd be no time—and no need—for a retail job. But she was grateful to have a fallback in case the hoped-for torrent of acting opportunities took longer than expected.

Walking to the streetcar stop that evening with all her parcels, it seemed strange to be thinking about Christmas in such warm, sunny weather, with Salvation Army Santas sweating in their red suits, ringing bells under the palm trees.

Her next stop was the studio, where Mr. Cooperman gathered the staff in the pink stucco commissary building and distributed Christmas gifts to all the employees and contracted players of Cooperman Studios. Even though Helen was no longer under contract, she'd been included in the gathering because of her work on *Annabel.* Like most of the women on staff, she received a bottle of spray cologne that she knew was expensive from her work at Bullock's. Rusty was given a silver tie clip marked with the Cooperman Studios logo.

"It's like a brand," he quipped later when he and Helen were alone, seated on the sofa in the Hollywood Studio Club parlor. He showed her the tie clip nestled inside a blue box. "It signifies that he owns me."

"It signifies no such thing," Helen replied. "It signifies nothing more than 'Merry Christmas.' I think it's quite handsome." *Like you.* "And I think it's wonderful that Mr. Cooperman gave us gifts. He didn't have to." She scooted a little closer to Rusty on the sofa, thankful that of the few residents who remained in the building, none of them seemed inclined to enter the parlor. They had the room to themselves.

He stretched, then slid his arm across the back of the sofa in a casual manner. She shifted even closer, so close their legs almost touched.

He laid a light, seemingly tentative arm across her shoulders. When she didn't move away, he let it rest there, to her great delight.

They gazed at the lighted Christmas tree some of the residents had decorated and listened to Christmas music on the tinny electric radio. Even though Helen was eager to travel home and see her family, this moment, being here next to Rusty, couldn't have felt more right, more perfect.

Well, actually, it could be a little more perfect. If he'd kiss her, then it would be *perfectly* perfect. She glanced at the doorway in search of mistletoe. Not a sprig to be seen.

Darn it.

After several minutes, Rusty set the little blue box on an end table. He seemed to have something on his mind.

He cleared his throat. "Um. Helen?"

"Hm?"

"You know how we've been talking about the need for better movies? Movies that uphold good values, and stuff like that?"

"Sure. You want to produce movies that honor God," Helen said simply.

He nodded.

She lifted her head and looked at him, her expression sincere. "That's exactly what I want, too."

"I hope you truly mean that," Rusty said. "Because with your looks and talent, we could really go places."

She cocked her head. "We?"

"You asked me to tell you if I heard about a studio that specialized in those kinds of movies."

She turned to him with a flutter of anticipation. "You've heard of one?"

"Yeah." He returned her smile. "Mine."

She drew back a little, confused. "Yours? Your what?"

His words came out in a rush. "A new studio. Some friends plan to go in with me. We've been talking about it for a while now. And our conversations over the last few weeks have solidified it in my mind. I'm thinking that in six months, maybe a year, we'll be ready to make our first film. If we can manage to get some financial backing, that is." He removed his arm from her shoulders, turned to face her, and took both her hands in his. "The thing is, Helen, I'd like you to consider coming on board with us. With me."

A new sense of understanding clicked into place. She stared at him, open-mouthed. "You mean it? You want me?"

He gave a vigorous nod.

She had to be sure. "In what way?"

"Well, to act, of course. To star in our movies. When we *have* some movies."

Her spirit drooped a little. Once again, she'd let her heart leap ahead to envisioning romantic intentions on his part, when all he really wanted was her acting skill. And probably her looks. Would she ever learn to put the brakes on? To guard her heart?

Through the fog of disappointment she realized he was still talking and forced herself to concentrate on his words. "Until then, we'll all probably need to do a little of everything. Answer phones, scout for good stories. You can help me write scripts. You're great at coming up with clever dialogue. Can you type?"

"A little," she whispered. Not very well. But she could learn. She'd do whatever she could to help him.

"Don't you see?" he said with urgency. "We want all the same things. We'd be perfect together."

"All the same things." She pondered his words for a moment, speechless. Then she found her voice. "Rusty Noble, I'd be honored to work for your movie studio," she said, as solemnly as if she were accepting a proposal of marriage.

For a moment, they stared at each other. The next thing she knew, he was slipping his arms around her, drawing her close. He kissed her, gently at first, then with increasing firmness.

Trembling, she kissed him right back.
No mistletoe required.
She hadn't misread his feelings, after all.

A little while later, they sat back on the sofa, admiring the Christmas tree, and each other, in breathless wonder. Finally he spoke.

"You have no idea how much I've been hoping that would happen." He sounded a little breathless, as if he were as surprised as anyone that he'd kissed her.

"I'm glad you did," she assured him.

"And I'm glad you agreed." He gazed at her for a moment as if he were going to kiss her again. Then he cleared his throat and, with seeming reluctance, released his embrace. "But maybe we'd better talk about other things for a while."

She understood. No sense throwing gasoline on a smoldering fire. "Then let's talk about the pictures we'll make together." She sighed with happiness. "Excellent pictures."

"We'll show the naysayers what movies are capable of, that they can disseminate wholesome ideas just as well, or even better, than tawdry ones." A shadow dimmed his smile. "There's one important thing I have to tell you, though. Very important."

Concern stabbed Helen's heart. *Oh, no.* She didn't like the sound of that. He wasn't going to tell her something unpleasant, was he? Like he already had a girlfriend?

Or a wife?

Nonsense. She knew him well enough to know he wasn't married.

But then again, she thought she'd known Chet well, too.

She braced herself to hear the worst.

He gave her a solemn look. "You have to promise me you won't breathe a word of this to anyone. About the new studio, I mean."

Relief poured through her. Was that all? "I won't," she promised.

"Because if word gets back to Mr. Cooperman, I could lose my job."

"I understand. My lips are sealed."

He ran his thumb along the side of her face. "I knew I could trust you."

They turned back to face the tree, snuggling together like lovebirds on a chilly night.

"It'll be a while until I have enough money to go out on my own. Until I can get out from under Cooperman's thumb."

"I know. I can wait." The tie-clip box on the table caught Helen's eye. "If Mr. Cooperman had chosen the perfect gift for you, what would you have wanted?"

"Good question." He was silent for a moment, then said, "Lincoln Logs."

She tilted her head slightly to see his expression. "Lincoln Logs? You mean those little wooden logs that fit together to make cabins and things?" She returned her gaze to the Christmas tree. "I think my nephew has a set of those."

"When I was a kid, that was all I ever wanted. Never got 'em."

"Your family couldn't afford them?"

"Didn't have a family."

"No family?" She sat up straight and gaped at him in surprise. Over the weeks they'd been getting acquainted, she'd told him stories about her family back in Kerryville, lots of stories, but hadn't realized until now that they'd never spoken about Rusty's upbringing. Somehow whenever the topic came up, he managed to change the subject. To Helen, it seemed as if he'd somehow simply emerged on that train in Tucson, fully grown.

"You must have had parents at some point," she said. "What happened?" When he didn't answer right away, she softened her tone. "That's a nosy question. I'm sorry. You don't have to tell me if you don't want to." She settled back down next to him.

"No, it's all right. It's just been a while since I've talked to anyone about it. In fact, I can't remember ever talking about it."

She remained silent, giving him time to collect his thoughts.

"My earliest memories are of an orphanage in Philadelphia," he began. "I never knew my parents. I lived at the orphanage until I was nine or so. Then they put me and several of my buddies on a train bound for the West. At every stop they'd put us off the train and gather us together, and the townspeople could come and look us over. Some of us got kept."

"I've heard of that. The orphan train, they called it. The people who ran it hoped to find families to adopt the orphans."

He stared at the lights on the Christmas tree, his expression granite. "Yeah, well, that's what they intended. Sometimes it worked out and sometimes it didn't. Some of the people were good, but a lot of them didn't want kids to raise. They wanted farmhands and housekeeping help."

Her heart melted in sympathy. "How sad."

He shrugged. "In most cases, we weren't any worse off than we'd been at the orphanage we left behind. It just didn't always pan out into the cozy family life the founders had envisioned."

"So where did you end up?"

"I was a scrawny kid, so I guess I didn't look like I could handle much work. The bigger boys got picked before me. I ended up all the way out here in California, where an orange grower took me on. From then on, I picked oranges in season and did other jobs around the groves and barns when they weren't."

"Did they treat you well?"

He shrugged again. "As well as could be expected, I suppose. I mean, the owner didn't beat me or anything. But that first Christmas I was with them, the man's son got a set of Lincoln Logs. They were the most fascinating thing I'd ever seen. But the boy wouldn't let me play with them. The one time I tried, he punched me."

"What a bully." Helen reached over and took his hand. "Did they have a present for you?"

He snorted. "Oranges."

Helen didn't know what to say. The gifts in her Christmas stocking had always included an orange, and it had been a welcome treat, a real splurge in the Midwest during wintertime. But she didn't imagine they'd be so to a boy who spent most of his time picking them off the trees.

"How did you end up working for Cooperman?"

"It was pretty simple," he explained. "When Cooperman came out to build his studio, he bought the orange groves I was working on and razed them to the ground. When the family I was living with moved on, I had no desire to move with them. So I applied to Cooperman for a job. First he gave me odd jobs around the place. Then I proved to be pretty good at synopsizing books for him that I thought would make good pictures—I've always been an avid reader."

"So Mr. Cooperman rescued you, in a way."

"It was more than that. To this day, he treats me like practically one of the family, almost."

"Like family?" The astonished word slipped out of Helen's mouth before she could grab it back. She couldn't imagine being on such familiar terms with the intimidating Mr. Cooperman.

"Don't get me wrong," Rusty hastened to explain. "He didn't adopt me or anything like that. Most of the time I'm just another one of his employees. But he became sort of an uncle figure to me. He and the late Mrs. Cooperman always treated me well, inviting me over for Thanksgiving dinner and whatnot if I didn't have anywhere else to go." He shrugged. "I'm sure they would have done the same for anyone else in need."

Helen was pretty certain they wouldn't have, that Rusty had earned their kindness by being hardworking and loyal.

The conversation appeared to be making him melancholy. She tried to lighten the mood.

"At the very least, surely you can buy yourself a set of Lincoln Logs, if you still want them."

He snorted. "What use would they be to me now? They're a kids' toy."

She shrugged. "Who knows? Maybe someday you'll have a son, and you can buy a set for him."

He shook his head. "Not me. I don't see myself ever settling down and having a family."

Like a bucket of cold water, a sensation of unpleasant surprise settled over Helen's chest. "No family?" She couldn't imagine such a thing.

"No need. I do better on my own with no encumbrances."

His revelation left her speechless. He kissed the top of her head, but her cheerful, loving mood had faded. Was that all she meant to him? Nothing more than an encumbrance?

Maybe she'd misunderstood his intentions.

Maybe they didn't want all the same things, after all.

CHAPTER TWENTY-FIVE

"**M**erry Christmas, sleepyhead." Clad in her faded apron of rooster-printed cotton, Marjorie greeted Helen as she stumbled into the kitchen. The dear, familiar, bacon-scented Kerryville kitchen with its drugstore calendar and grinning Kit-Kat clock ticking on the wall. "Sleep well?"

"Yes, I did. Merry Christmas to you, too." Helen reached for the coffeepot. She'd forgotten how aggressively cheerful her sister could be in the morning—almost as bad as Flo. "Are you the only one up?"

"Yes, except for Peter. He worked the night shift and should be home soon. I'm hoping it was a quiet night for him, being Christmas Eve." Marjorie's arm muscles flexed as she pressed a piece of fruit through the juicer. "Thanks for these oranges—they're a real treat."

Helen was glad she'd had the last-minute idea to bring home a box of California oranges. Rusty's story of working the groves reminded her that citrus was hard to come by in Illinois, expensive and not nearly as tasty. She made a mental note to ship another box home as soon as she returned to Los Angeles, maybe grapefruit or lemons. During these times of hardship, sending fruit was the least she could do to help her family stretch the household budget.

Thinking of Rusty made her happy and sad at the same time. Happy about his kisses. Happy that he wanted her to come and work with him at his studio.

Sad that he didn't seem to want any more than that.

Pushing thoughts of Rusty aside, she took a seat at the table. "I'm glad we're alone for a few minutes, Marjie. We haven't had a good heart-to-heart chat in a while."

"Our hearts haven't been in the same time zone for months." Marjorie placed the pitcher of orange juice in the icebox and pulled out a carton of eggs. "And you've only been home a day and a half. I'm so glad you are," she added, tossing a smile in Helen's direction.

"Me, too." Helen hesitated to bring up a potentially tender subject, but wanted to lay her cards on the table before Peter returned and the others woke up. "I just wanted to make sure there are no hard feelings between us."

Marjorie cracked an egg. "Why would there be hard feelings?"

Is she serious? "Because I moved to Hollywood against your wishes. Because I didn't go to teacher's college like you wanted."

Marjorie took a long moment to reply. Then she sighed. "I'll admit, I was angry at first. And hurt that you confided in Pop and had him break the news to me over the telephone, instead of telling me yourself. That part stung a bit."

"I am sorry. I suppose that must have seemed cowardly," Helen admitted. "I did try to tell you. But you kept trying to talk me out of it."

"I know." Marjorie whisked the eggs with great vigor. "But I'm over it now."

"Are you? Really and truly?"

Marjorie stopped whisking and heaved a sigh. "What do you want me to say, Helen? Do I wish you hadn't moved so far away? Yes. Do I wish you'd gone to college and trained for a stable career? Yes." She turned to face Helen, whisk in hand. "But, sweetie, you're an adult now. I can't tell you what to do anymore. You're free to make your own choices."

That's it? Helen waited for her sister to elaborate, but nothing more was said. "Okay. Thank you."

Marjorie turned back to the counter and continued whisking the eggs, a little more calmly this time. "Besides, I get it. Pop's always been the family peacemaker."

"Yes, he is. He was remarkably patient with me about the whole thing."

"I remember when he ran interference between Frances and me when there was tension between us over my moving to Chicago to work at Marshall Field."

"And thank goodness for that. Otherwise you might have married Richard instead of Peter, which would have been a disaster."

"Not a *disaster*, necessarily." Marjorie poured the eggs into a pan. "Richard was a nice enough man. Just not the right man for me."

"Well, I'm sure glad things turned out the way they did."

"Me, too."

Helen rose and rested her chin on Marjorie's shoulder. "So are we all right? I don't want there to be any tension between us."

Marjorie reached up and patted her head. "There's not, sweetie. Really. I'm over it."

"Forgive me?"

Marjorie gave a heart-melting smile. "There's nothing to forgive."

"I'm so glad to hear it." Helen embraced her sister. Marjorie held her for a moment, then released her. She returned to the stove, lifting the pan off the burner and sliding the eggs into a ceramic bowl.

"We'd better wake the rest of the family," she said briskly. "Breakfast will be ready soon."

"I can't believe the twins aren't already awake and tearing into their stockings," Helen said. "Remember how crazy we'd get on Christmas morning when we were kids?"

"They're a little young yet to anticipate the hoopla."

"Well, I'll make sure everyone's up," Helen volunteered.

As she climbed the stairs, she sent up a prayer of thanksgiving for her sister's softened attitude, and for the privilege of spending Christmas at home in Kerryville. It warmed her heart to be surrounded by her family for an entire luxurious week.

Although she had to admit, if only to herself, that a piece of her heart had remained back in Hollywood, waiting for her return. Did Rusty mean what he'd said about encumbrances? Did he really not want this kind of life? Warm, happy mornings surrounded by family?

Maybe he simply didn't know what he was missing.

Maybe he needed someone like Helen to show him.

Being "practically family" to Stanley Cooperman meant Rusty was granted the privilege of joining the Cooperman household for Christmas dinner. The tradition had started back when he'd been a homeless teenager cleaning floors at the studio, and had continued through the years, even though Mrs. Cooperman, who'd behaved like a kindly aunt toward him, had passed away several years ago.

The already luxurious living and dining rooms were festooned with glittering crystal and gold streamers. The enormous tree standing in the living room caught his attention.

The Christmas dinner guests included the two grown Cooperman children, Max and Serena, and their respective spouses and children, as well as Stanley's brother, Leroy, and director Jean-Luc Renard, whose family lived in France. Twelve people in all.

Rusty was seated next to Leroy at the dinner table. He worried about this at first. He found Leroy intimidating, with his criminal past and perpetual scowl. What would they find to talk about? What did one chitchat about to an ex-con? He would have preferred to have been seated next to Jean-Luc, with whom he had something in common, but didn't want to commit a breach of etiquette by altering the seating arrangement.

He needn't have worried. The younger Cooperman brother turned out to be a lot more talkative and outgoing than he first appeared.

"My brother tells me you're the best writer at the studio," Leroy said after a polite exchange of pleasantries.

The last bit of Rusty's trepidation melted into gratitude toward his boss for speaking kindly of his work. "Oh, I don't know about that," he said with modesty. "There are several talented writers on staff. But it's nice to hear, just the same."

"You won't get anywhere in Hollywood by being modest." Leroy picked up his knife and fork. "Tell me. Do you ever take on freelance work apart from your work for Cooperman Studios?"

Rusty's trepidation crept back. Was this a genuine question, or was Leroy some kind of spy for his brother, trying to sniff out Rusty's loyalty to the studio? He decided to proceed with caution.

"What kind of work are you referring to?" he asked, keeping his answer deliberately noncommittal.

"A certain project I have in mind. A film project. Something Stanley's not interested in taking on." Leroy glanced toward the end of the table at his brother, who was engaged in lively conversation with Jean-Luc. "Can I take you to lunch sometime to talk about it?"

"I don't know," Rusty said. "They keep me awfully busy at Cooperman. I don't normally take on outside projects."

"I think you'll like this one," Leroy said. "One of your fellow writers recommended you as the best man for the job."

Rusty pondered this. Who could have recommended him? Smitty? Jim? Both men knew of Rusty's desire to start his own studio. Maybe this was a pathway to getting his first assignment as an independent producer. After all, even if Cooperman found out, he wouldn't fire Rusty for helping out his own brother. Would he?

He supposed it wouldn't hurt to hear the man out, although the prospect of being caught freelancing in violation of his contract made him uncomfortable.

But not so uncomfortable that he wasn't making plans to open his own studio as soon as he had the resources. Maybe this potential new project was God's way of giving him the green light to go out on his own.

"I guess we could have a meeting sometime," Rusty said slowly. "Give me a call when you're ready."

After all, what harm could it do just to talk to the man?

CHAPTER TWENTY-SIX

On the day after Christmas, Helen and Marjorie went to the Orpheum to see Helen's grand debut on the silver screen. Dot and Charlie joined them, leaving the twins with Mrs. Brown next door.

When they got to the theater, Peter was in the lobby, still in his police uniform, buying popcorn for everyone.

Thrilled, Helen ran toward him. "I'm so glad you're here. I thought you had to work."

"I did, but I swapped shifts with Murphy." He gave her a hug. "Couldn't stand to miss out on my sister-in-law's big screen debut."

The rest of the family gathered around, greeting Peter and grabbing bags of popcorn.

Abruptly, Helen stopped short. Her stomach dropped to her knees as she gripped Peter's arm.

"Hey, what's the matter?" He frowned. "You look as if you've seen a rat or something."

Speechless, Helen pointed to a man standing near the concession stand. It was *him*—the man from Los Angeles. The man who'd been stalking her all over town. What was he doing here in Kerryville?

A shiver ran down her spine. Had he been following her all this time, even to her hometown? Was she in danger? Was her *family* in danger?

In that moment, anger and fiery indignation incinerated the fear in Helen's heart. She dropped Peter's arm and stalked toward the man, ready to demand an explanation.

"Hey! You!" she shouted.

But before she reached him, Peter intercepted her.

"Hold on there, hot foot."

She thrust a finger at the man. "Peter, arrest this person. He's been stalking me for months."

But to her consternation, the man did not look the least bit concerned. He merely grinned and waved at Peter.

"Hey, Bucky," Peter said. "Long time, no see."

Helen parked her fists on her hips. "You know this man?" she demanded.

Peter's eyebrows rose.

"Sure. This is John Buck. We worked together with the Feds back in Chicago." He turned back to John. "How are you doing, buddy?"

The man started to say something, but Helen interrupted. "I've seen you in L.A., *John Buck,*" she snapped. "If that's even your real name."

Peter looked at her in surprise. "Hey, Helen, what gives?"

"What's going on here?" Charlie put a protective arm around Helen's shoulder.

She shrugged it off and took a step toward John Buck. "You've been following me all over Los Angeles. And now you're here in Kerryville. Who are you and what do you want?"

Peter stared at his friend in apparent confusion. "Bucky? What's she talking about?"

John Buck winced and shrank a little. "You weren't supposed to notice me," he said to Helen.

"Well, I did."

"So it's true? You've been trailing her?" Peter frowned at his friend. "What the heck, John?"

Marjorie stepped forward and placed a hand on Peter's arm, her face red as a holly berry. "I think I can explain."

Helen crossed her arms and looked at her sister. "Oh?"

"Yes." Marjorie swallowed. "You see, I hired him to keep an eye on you. I never thought you'd find out." She turned toward John with an accusatory glare. "You were supposed to be invisible."

His shoulders slumped. "Sorry. I'd never worked in L.A. before. I was off my game."

Helen wheeled on Marjorie. "You *hired* him?" she screeched. "To *spy* on me? What about all that song-and-dance about how I'm all grown up now?"

"You are grown up," Marjorie wailed. "I meant what I said yesterday. This was—this happened *before*, when I wasn't sure. I was so worried about you."

"Pipe down, you two." Peter warned. "We're in public. Marjorie, perhaps you'd better explain."

Marjorie wrung her hands. "When Pop called to say Helen wouldn't be coming home, I panicked. I had to reassure myself that she was safe. John was the only detective I knew, other than you, Peter. He happened to be available to fly out to California right away. And he agreed to discount his fee."

All eyes turned to John Buck.

"I was lucky enough to get a spot on a mail plane," he said, as if this explained everything. "A little cramped, but I got there before Helen's train did. The wonders of air travel, eh?"

Peter's jaw flexed as he glared at John. "You didn't think I might want to know about this?"

"Don't blame John," Marjorie interjected. "I asked him not to say anything."

"What can I say?" John shrugged. "I've always liked Marjorie. Ever since she helped us crack that liquor ring back in Chicago. Remember, Pete? And I'm a sucker for a good sister story." He smiled, sheepish. "And, hey, it was L.A. I made a vacation out of it."

"Are you people coming?" Dot called from across the lobby. Having ducked into the ladies' room, she'd missed the whole exchange.

"Go on in and save some seats," Marjorie called back. "We'll be right there."

Helen remained unappeased. "Marjorie, how could you? You said you trusted me."

"I'm sorry, sweetie," Marjorie said, her voice laced with apology. "I admit it was a mistake. It's just that... well, you're so young, and Los Angeles is crawling with criminals. "

Helen waved her hands. "So is Chicago. So is New York. So is—well, *everywhere*, except for Kerryville."

"You'd be surprised," Peter muttered.

"I'm sorry, Helen. I was so frantic, I didn't know what to do. I acted in haste." Marjorie's voice quivered as though she might cry.

Helen lifted her chin, determined to remain unmoved. "Well, now you know I can take care of myself."

"I see that now." Marjorie's eyes glistened. "You're no longer that flighty girl with stars in her eyes. You're a serious actress making her mark on Hollywood. Hiring a detective was a really dumb thing to do. Can you forgive me? Please don't be angry. I meant well."

Helen looked at her sister and sighed. Her heart softened, just a little. "I'm not angry, Marjie. I'm just—" For a moment she struggled to find words. Then she gave up. "I mean, *honestly*, Marjorie." She waved an impatient hand in John Buck's direction. "You couldn't find a detective who's a little more... undetectable?"

A round of laughter broke the tension. Helen's fury dissipated in light of her sister's heartfelt apology. She could foresee some future day when the story would become just another piece of family legend trotted out for everyone's amusement.

The Time Charlie Threw a Baseball Through Mrs. Brown's Window.

The Time Helen Tried to Baptize the Neighbor's Cat.

The Time Marjorie Hired a Detective to Spy on Helen.

Someday it would be hilarious.

Today was not yet that day.

"Will you join us, John?" Marjorie asked as they turned toward the theater.

"Thanks, but my date's inside. She'll be wondering where I've gone. I'd rather she not hear how badly I dropped the ball."

"Don't feel bad, Bucky." Peter put a hand on his friend's shoulder, with a wink at Marjorie. "You couldn't possibly have known who you were dealing with." Together they crossed the lobby. "So what brings you to Kerryville tonight?"

"To meet up with Marjorie and give her my final report."

"When did you do that?" Helen demanded.

Marjorie blushed. "This afternoon, when I told you I had to run an errand."

Helen shook her head. "From now on, I'm never believing any of you when you say you're just going out for a walk."

As the opening credits rolled, the family settled into their seats with a buzz of anticipation.

"Now don't expect too much," Helen had warned them ahead of time. "As a body double, I don't speak any lines. There are no close-ups of my face. You're supposed to think you're watching Cynthia Starling the whole time."

"Sure, kid," Charlie said with a snicker. "You've been stealing the limelight since the day you were born."

They thought she was exaggerating about the insignificance of her role.

They were wrong.

Even Helen was appalled at the amount of strenuous running, crawling, and leaping that had gotten left behind on the cutting-room floor. Now and then she nudged Marjorie and whispered, "Those are my feet," or, "There's the back of my head," and Marjorie dutifully passed the word down the row, like a game of telephone.

But at the embarrassing bathing-in-the-creek scene, Helen kept her mouth shut and her eyes firmly planted on the screen, refusing to even look at her sister, much less take credit for that bit of cheesecake.

For the most part, any evidence of Helen's contribution to the film was negligible. For all intents and purposes, audiences would believe they were watching Cynthia Starling the whole time. *Which is the point of a body double*, Helen reminded herself, setting aside her disappointment. She couldn't help making the comparison, however, that the last time she'd been at the Orpheum, she'd been the star of the show. Her critically acclaimed performance had brought the house down. And her heart had been left shattered in pieces on a backstage floor.

Unwilling to think about Chet, she tried to relax and enjoy the film, looking at it through the public's eyes. She hadn't viewed the finished product before leaving California, and the scenes had been shot out of order, so it was interesting to watch the story play out the way it was meant to be viewed. The movie's audience appeal was due as much to Rusty's skilled scriptwriting as anything else. Certainly more than to Cynthia Starling's clumsy acting.

After the closing credits, which didn't include Helen's name, the family hurried home through the cold, their breath crystallizing on the frosty air.

"Thanks for coming, everyone. Sorry there wasn't more of me to see." Helen trudged along slightly behind the rest of her family, sensing their disappointment that there hadn't been more recognizable shots of their sister. She'd tried to warn them.

"It was a very good movie," Marjorie said in an overly hearty voice. "I like pioneer stories."

"Yeah. That shootout with the bandits was something else," Charlie added. "Say, anyone up for hot chocolate?"

Helen sensed they were trying to make her feel better. Dot dropped back to walk beside her. Never one to beat around the bush, she asked Helen outright, "Did you work hard on that film?"

"Yes."

"Did you get paid for it?"

"Yes."

"Will you get credit for it when you apply for your next picture?"

"I suppose so."

Dot slipped her arm through Helen's. "Then you are a working actress. And don't let anybody try to make you feel otherwise."

Helen's throat constricted. At least one Corrigan believed in her, understood what she was trying to achieve and what it took to get there.

Well, two Corrigans. Dot and Pop.

And that would have to be enough.

For now.

The following Saturday, the whole Corrigan clan attended Nanette Johnson's wedding. Helen thought Nanette looked like a fairy-tale princess in a bias-cut gown of champagne rayon with long, sweeping lines and full-length sleeves. Her misty tulle veil swept back from a Juliet cap framing her sweet face.

She took special pride, though, in the dark green velveteen dresses, which had been home-sewn using fabric purchased at

Corrigan's. Marjorie, an accomplished seamstress, had been a dear and sewn Helen's for her in her absence.

"Although, let's face it," Helen had confided to Nanette. "She would have had to make mine even if I'd been right here in Kerryville the whole time. I'm all thumbs with a sewing machine."

The simple ceremony was followed by a festive cake-and-punch reception in the church parlor. Helen enjoyed catching up with friends from high school and other people she'd known growing up. Most of them were eager to hear all about her new life in Hollywood.

"I can't believe it," her friend Sheila said. "You had an actual part in a motion picture!"

"Not a speaking part," Helen was quick to clarify. "Just a walk-on." But she felt proud of herself just the same.

"I always knew you'd be a star," Sheila gushed. "You were so good in all the high-school and community productions."

Helen thanked her.

"Speaking of community productions," Sheila said, "I read in the paper that the play you were in last summer made a huge splash in Chicago this fall." When Helen didn't comment, she pressed on. "You know, Helen, that one you starred in. *Under the Burning Bush.*"

"*Under the Flaming Oak,*" Helen muttered under her breath.

"That's it. Well, I guess the director's a real bigshot now. Did you know he wrote it, too?"

"I did know that." Helen looked around for an opportunity to make her escape.

"And to think it premiered right here in little Kerryville," Sheila gushed.

Helen did not want to talk about the play, and even less about Chet. "If you'll excuse me," she said to Sheila, "I'm going to go over there and say hello to Mrs. Varney." She moved to another table where Mrs. Varney, her former Sunday school teacher, was seated. That turned out to not be the best move, either.

"There are so many terrible influences in Hollywood, dear," the older woman said. "And few find success in such a tough field. I fear that your spirit will harden and you'll become jaded. Are you quite sure you know what you're doing?"

Helen assured her she did. She told Mrs. Varney about meeting Henrietta Mears on the train, and how she'd formed a prayer group that was meeting together before work at the studio.

"It sounds like you're doing all the right things. Just be aware of the company you keep," Mrs. Varney warned. "Remember that sin is like the force of gravity. It's much easier for poor companions to pull you down to their level than for you to pull them up to yours."

"Yes, ma'am. I'll remember," Helen promised.

"I'll continue to pray for you," Mrs. Varney added, "as I pray for all missionaries serving in hostile territories."

Helen thanked her, but was taken aback. She hadn't thought of herself as a missionary serving in hostile territory, but first Pop and now Mrs. Varney had made that same comparison. She supposed it had some merit. It was certainly no cakewalk to stand up for Christian beliefs in Hollywood. Thank goodness she had the support of a good church and the Monday-morning prayer group.

The day after the wedding, Helen rang in 1934 with her family. And the day after that, she was on a train headed back to California, her whirlwind vacation over. Though she was sorry to say goodbye to her family, her departure felt completely different than it had the previous summer. This time, rather than feeling like she was sneaking off to do something naughty, she left for Hollywood with a song in her heart, eager to return to her job, her friends, and Rusty. Her close relationship with Marjorie had been restored, and all was right with the world.

Well, almost right.

There was still a certain red-haired gentleman who thought he wanted to remain unencumbered. The fool.

She made it her goal to convince him otherwise.

CHAPTER TWENTY-SEVEN

When work resumed after the holidays, Rusty got called into Mr. Cooperman's office.

"I like the preliminary work you've done on *Stormy River Serenade*," the boss said. "DeJong's locked in to direct. Full steam ahead."

Rusty released his breath in a rush. He hadn't realized he'd been holding it. "That's great news. Thank you, sir." He hesitated, then asked, "Have you thought through the casting yet?"

Cooperman looked thoughtful. "I'm thinking of St. Ives for the male lead."

"St. Ives?" Rusty tried and failed to keep the disappointment out of his voice.

Cooperman eyed him. "Something wrong?"

"No, sir. It's just that the studio has used Mark so much lately. Might be time for a fresh face. I'm thinking somebody like John Wayne would make a good lead."

"I tried." Cooperman grimaced. "Fox has him sewn up tight."

"Too bad. Well, St. Ives will do an adequate job. And for the female lead?"

"Debbie Fagan for the girl. Haven't quite made up my mind on the secondary lead, though. The girl's older cousin, Virginia. Got any ideas?"

Did he ever! "Helen Corrigan would be ideal, I think." He struggled to sound calm and cool-headed, as if this were purely a business decision.

"Who?"

"Helen Corrigan. You remember, she took over for Cynthia on *The Courage of Annabel Brewster*."

"Oh. Her." Cooperman waved a dismissive hand. "No. I want a brunette this time."

"A brunette?" That didn't seem right. "But Debbie Fagan's a blonde. Shouldn't there be a family resemblance between her and her cousin?"

"Blond is boring. I'm thinking Virginia should be dark. A Myrna Loy type. Maybe you can write some Cherokee into the character's heritage."

"I see." Cherokee? That odd detail would add nothing to the story, and possibly even detract from it, but Rusty knew arguing would be pointless. Helen looked nothing like Myrna Loy. Well, he'd tried. Maybe he should speak to the director, Julian DeJong. The director usually had the final say on casting, and Rusty and Julian were on pretty good terms. Maybe Julian could talk some sense into Cooperman.

From under his bushy eyebrows, Cooperman peered at Rusty. "It's coming back to me now. You've championed that Corrigan girl before, Noble, but I must say, I don't really care for her."

Rusty gaped at him in surprise. How could anyone not like Helen? "Why not, sir?"

"Looks too much like Cynthia Starling."

It was the first and only time Rusty'd heard Helen's resemblance to Cynthia cast in negative terms. Her appearance had opened one door. Now it was closing another.

Such was Hollywood.

Cooperman still kept a silver-framed photograph of Cynthia on his credenza. He was looking at it now with a melancholy expression on his face. Clearly his rejection of Helen in the role of Virginia had nothing to do with Helen, and everything to do with Cynthia's betrayal on both the personal and professional levels. Even so, it hurt Rusty's heart to hear it.

"Well, if that's all, sir, I'll be going." He turned to leave.

"Loyalty, Noble."

He turned back. "Sir?"

"Loyalty is what truly matters," Cooperman said in a sad voice, his eyes still fixed on Cynthia's photograph. "It's becoming an old-fashioned virtue. Nobody's loyal anymore."

Rusty didn't know what to say. He left the office under a cloud of guilt.

He wasn't planning to remain loyal to Cooperman, either, if loyalty meant working for him forever.

He was excited about his plans for the new studio.

But in that moment, he felt like a heel.

When Helen stepped off the train at Central Station, Rusty was waiting for her. He greeted her with a warm embrace—a real one this time, not a pretend one. Then he took her to lunch at their favorite diner near the studio.

"I'm so happy you're back," he said after she'd told him all about her trip and Nanette's wedding. She had an animated, dramatic way of telling stories that held him in fascination. No wonder she was a good actress. "It feels as if you've been away for months."

"It felt that way for me, too," she assured him, pressing his hand across the table. "It's strange, but in a way, being with you feels like coming home." She paused and released his hand as the waitress served their meals, a cheeseburger for him and a bacon-lettuce-and-tomato sandwich for her. Then she said, "How are things at the studio?"

"Okay. Pretty quiet since the holidays." He chose not to say anything about *Stormy River Serenade* for the time being. He'd had a conversation with Julian DeJong and suggested Helen for the role. Now the result would be up to Julian. He didn't want to raise Helen's hopes unnecessarily.

"Have there been any developments toward opening your own studio? *Our* own studio?"

Rusty dipped a French fry in a dollop of ketchup. "I had an interesting conversation with Leroy Cooperman."

"Leroy?" Her brow creased. "What did he want?"

"He asked me if I ever took on extra screenwriting projects. He didn't give me details, but it's something Stanley apparently doesn't want to produce."

"What did you tell him?"

"I said I'd meet with him and talk about it. Depending on what it is, it could turn out to be our first film, the one that launches our studio. Or..." He stirred the French fry in the ketchup, forgetting to eat it.

"Or... ?" Helen prompted.

"Or he could report back to his brother about our plans to start a studio. In which case—" He drew a finger across his throat.

"Golly. That is a dilemma." Helen bit into her sandwich and took her time chewing, as if taking time to think. Then she swallowed and said, "It might be worth a conversation, just to find out what he has in mind."

Rusty's heart leaped in gratitude they were on the same page. "That's what I thought. I can at least talk to the fellow. Find out what he's thinking." He popped the French fry into his mouth and chewed it. "I'd hate to pass up what could be our first film project, out of fear. On the other hand, I can't afford to lose my job prematurely. I need the cash."

"It's a narrow line," Helen acknowledged, "but I have a good feeling about it. When do you think you'll meet with Leroy?"

"He's supposed to contact me when he's ready. The ball's in his court."

That was the thing about this business, Rusty mused. Whether it was Julian or Leroy or somebody else, the ball was always in somebody else's court.

But the day was coming when it would be in his court.

He could hardly wait.

After lunch, he drove her home to Flo and Donna's apartment at the Studio Club and gave her a sweet kiss goodbye with a promise to take her to a movie later in the week.

"Want me to carry in your suitcase for you?" he offered.

"Thanks, but you're not allowed upstairs," she reminded him.

"Ah, yes." He lifted her chin and gave her another quick kiss. "Just as well, I suppose."

She waved goodbye as he drove off, then climbed the stairs to the apartment, suitcase banging along the railing. Until she could afford a place of her own, she'd continue sleeping on a fold-out sofa that gave her a backache. Not that she wasn't grateful. Affordable housing was hard to come by in Tinseltown, and for now the fold-out sofa was adequate to her needs.

The most irritating thing about the living arrangement was sharing the single bathroom, which wouldn't have been as much of a problem if Donna had any sense of time.

"Hurry up in there! I'm going to be late for work," Helen had been forced to holler more than once, while pounding on the door.

For the time being, the "work" she risked being late for meant her part-time job at Bullock's. She wished it meant work at a movie studio—*any* movie studio—but without an agent, auditions were hard to come by. And agent representation was even harder to come by.

Until that shining day came, she got used to standing on the unforgiving granite floor of Perfume Hall with a spritzer in her hand. "A sample of Bourjois today, madam? A light spray of Chanel?"

Helen wondered if Marjorie had felt this way when she worked at Marshall Field. Surely her customers there couldn't have been any more spoiled and demanding than those who patronized Bullock's Wilshire.

"You're doing good work, Miss Corrigan," Mrs. Carroll often said in a tone of grudging respect. "Keep it up."

All those years toiling in the family dry-goods store were paying off. If Helen had wanted to work the rest of her life in retail, she'd be all set.

Alas, she had other ambitions. But as long as she had to sell perfume to support herself, she tried her best to put a positive spin on it.

"There's a lot of acting involved in retail," she explained to Flo one night after work. "Selling requires you to have a sort of script in your head. Not one you memorize, but one you can tailor to your own voice."

"What do you mean?"

"It's like I'm playing a character, in a way—a different character for every customer. By adjusting my voice or the way I'm standing, I can convince a customer of the merits of one scent over another, based on what they're looking for."

"How do you know what they're looking for?"

"I don't know." Helen lifted her shoulders. "I just do."

"Golly." Flo regarded at her as if she'd just revealed some deep secret of the ages. "I'll never look at salespeople the same way again."

But more than serving customers, Helen loved being around other actors, even at the giant casting calls where she was little more than an anonymous pair of legs ending in tap shoes. She tried out to be a dancer in a saloon, a college coed, a girl sleuth.

She didn't seem to be what the studios were looking for, though.

The California sunshine mocked her as, dejected, she returned home to the Studio Club from yet another failed screen test. Eight times now she'd attended open casting calls for young women that were listed in *Variety*, and eight times she'd been disappointed.

"How did it go?" Donna asked on the eighth time. Too bad it was only Donna and not Flo at home to greet her. Flo had a way of helping Helen see the bright side of nearly every situation, while Donna seemed to take pleasure in poking pins into any small balloon of hope.

"Terrible," Helen admitted. "The movies are so completely different from the stage. I don't know what I'm doing. I haven't gotten so much as a nibble." She kicked off her shoes and threw her purse and then herself onto the sofa. "I don't know exactly what the studios are looking for, but it's obviously not someone like me."

"Give it time," Donna encouraged her in a suspiciously un-Donnalike way. "Don't give up."

Helen cast a wary eye on her roommate. Donna was never this friendly to her. Something was up.

"I have no intention of giving up," she said. She laid her head back against the sofa cushion and closed her eyes. No, she wouldn't give up. But naively, she'd thought that the toughest challenge was going to be trying to make it in Hollywood without compromising her Christian values. It hadn't occurred to her that Hollywood might not have a spot for her in the first place. But she wasn't about to give Donna the satisfaction of knowing it. Her roommate wouldn't understand, anyway. She had no qualms about lowering her standards if it moved her ahead a square or two on the Hollywood game board. She found Helen's convictions to be stuffy and old-fashioned and wasn't shy about saying so.

Donna's skirt rustled as she sat on the ottoman opposite Helen. Sensing herself being stared at, Helen cracked open one eye. "What is it?"

Donna bit her lower lip. "I have news."

Helen opened her other eye. "Oh? Tell me."

"You know that part we both tried out for? That new picture that Goforth's directing?"

"Uh-huh."

"I got it." Donna managed to sound both giddy and apologetic at the same time. "Don't be mad."

Helen's mood plummeted, but she sat up and forced a smile. "I'm not mad, Donna. Why would I be mad? A little jealous, maybe. But never mad. I'm proud of you!"

Donna looked relieved. "It's just that, well... you've been going on audition after audition with no luck at all, and then here I just waltzed in and—"

"Remind me what sort of picture it is," Helen broke in, unwilling to hear too many details of Donna's glowing success. Likely her rich benefactor, Herbert Jones, had put in a good word for her with Mr. Cooperman. *That's how the game is played.* Helen bit her cheek to stop herself from giving Donna a piece of her mind.

Donna's dark eyes shone. "It's a pirate adventure story. I'm going to be filming it out of town on location in Oregon for at least three weeks."

"Three weeks? That's great news," Helen assured her. And it *was* great news—three weeks without Donna making snide comments and hogging the bathroom? Bliss!

Her pleased expression stayed on her face by sheer force of will. But deep inside, envy gnawed at her midsection. When would she ever experience that kind of success?

After Donna left, a discouraged Helen fished in her purse for the card Henrietta Mears had given her and called the number. She made an appointment with a secretary to meet with Miss Mears at First Presbyterian. Miss Mears seemed like a God-fearing, honest, level-headed woman. Although she wasn't involved in the movie industry, she counseled lots of young people who were. Maybe she could advise Helen on what to do.

On the appointed afternoon, Miss Mears welcomed Helen into her sun-filled office. After exchanging the customary pleasantries, Helen got down to the purpose of her visit.

"My faith in God is the anchor of my life," Helen said. "It's an integral part of who I am."

"I'm glad to hear that," Miss Mears said. "It will stand you in good stead when times get tough."

"I'm afraid they already have gotten tough." Helen told Miss Mears about her struggles to find acting jobs, and her dismay at some of the questionable things actresses were expected to do.

"Hollywood tests your faith." Miss Mears refilled Helen's teacup from a steaming pot. "It gives you an opportunity to make right or wrong decisions. A while back you told me you were starting a prayer group of Christian actors and crew. How is that going?"

Helen shrugged. "It was going great before I went home for Christmas, but since then..." Her voice trailed off. "I no longer work at Cooperman Studios, so I haven't been back. Flo and Rusty tell me it's still meeting, though."

"Try to keep participating, even though you're out of work. Especially when you're out of work," Miss Mears advised. "I'm sure that would make you feel better, and it would help you keep your eyes focused on Jesus and not the ups and downs of auditions and such."

Helen promised she would. She hoped her expired pass would still gain her admittance to the studio. If not, maybe Flo or Rusty could sign her in as a guest. One way or another, she'd be there.

At the end of their meeting, she and Miss Mears prayed together. Helen fervently prayed to be shown the next step in her career. She came home buoyed by fresh resolve not to give up on her dream, and equally fresh resolve to rejoin the prayer group at Cooperman Studios, certain that God would take care of her and guide her course.

One evening not long after, she arrived home after her shift at Bullock's to a ringing telephone. She hurried and picked it up.

"Hello," a brisk male voice said. "May I please speak to Donna Delmonico?"

"I'm sorry, Donna's not here. May I take a message?"

"This is Phil Fairmont calling." Helen tightened her grip on the phone. "Will you please have Miss Delmonico call me back right away?"

"I'm sorry, Mr. Fairmont. Donna—I mean, Miss Delmonico—is out of town for at least three weeks."

"That's no good," Mr. Fairmont huffed. "She's needed right away. Some gal here twisted her ankle, and I wanted to recommend Miss Delmonico as a replacement."

"I'd be happy to come down and audition, Mr. Fairmont. I'm her roommate, Helen Corrigan, and I'm good at standing in for people."

Helen couldn't believe her own boldness.

"Helen Corrigan, you say?" Mr. Fairmont hesitated as if rifling through his memory to place the name.

"Yes," Helen prompted, trying her best to sound like a cool professional and failing miserably. "We met at a party at Mr. Cooperman's house last fall. I'm the girl—the *actress*—who was hired to fill in for Cynthia Starling in *The Courage of Annabel Brewster*."

"Oh, yes. I remember." After a pause, Mr. Fairmont said, "Well, in this case, I suppose one girl's as good as another. All right. Come down to the studio first thing tomorrow morning. I'll leave word with the guard that you're to be allowed in. Soundstage B. There'll be an audition involved, but you should do fine."

The next morning, Helen dressed with extreme care. Her fingers were cold, her palms clammy. She prayed that she was doing the right thing. She told herself she wasn't cheating Donna out of a part. After all, Donna was all the way up in Oregon, where she couldn't possibly do the screen test. Even so, Helen would have found the situation much more to her liking if Mr. Fairmont had called asking for Helen instead.

All the way to the studio, she fought with herself. On the plus side, she was excited to have another audition. On the downside, after her recent string of failed attempts to capture a casting director's attention, she was afraid to get her hopes up about this one. She'd heard Julian DeJong was extremely demanding.

She needn't have worried. When she got to the studio, to her surprise, she was whisked inside, puffed, powdered, and positioned before the cameras for a screen test. No one even suggested she audition for the chorus. And by the end of the day, she had landed a fairly substantial role—a speaking role, no less, as Debbie Fagan's older cousin—in a new Western called *Stormy River Serenade*, with a screenplay written by the incomparable Zachary P. Noble.

"Well, well, Miss Corrigan," Julian DeJong said as he told her the good news. "Let's see how you live up to your reputation for hard work."

CHAPTER TWENTY-EIGHT

"**P**laces, everyone," the assistant director called through his megaphone. "*Stormy River Serenade*, scene twelve, take one."

Helen took her place on the set, a modified horse stable.

Simon Jarrow, playing Helen's character's father, strode onto the set wearing the most ridiculous costume Helen had ever seen, consisting of a tomato-red jacket and brilliant yellow riding breeches. Helen's eyes nearly popped out of their sockets. What were the costumers thinking?

Rusty, standing nearby to make notes on the dialogue, caught her expression and chuckled. "Sometimes on lower-budget films like this one, the costume department has to improvise," he explained. "Happily, the picture will be in black and white."

"He's giving Beau Brummell a run for his money."

They both laughed.

"Quiet on the set," the assistant director barked. At Julian DeJong's signal, the cameras began to roll.

Simon turned Helen with a flourish. "What say you, daughter?"

"Oh, Father." Helen as Virginia clasped her hands over her beribboned bodice. "I don't think I've ever been so happy."

The words she spoke were true in real life, for the most part. Helen loved making movies. But if she had thought that filling in for Cynthia Starling had been hard, it was nothing compared to her first speaking role. The director, Julian DeJong, was even a tougher taskmaster than Jean-Luc Renard had been.

"Tone it *down*, Helen," he barked through the megaphone. "How many times do I have to tell you? There's no need to project your voice to the last row. In fact, there *is* no back row."

Phil Fairmont had told her that Cooperman had wanted a brunette for the part, but that DeJong had championed Helen. In gratitude, she did her best to please the demanding director. But for Helen, learning to practically whisper into the microphone was difficult indeed. And that wasn't the only thing she needed to learn, and unlearn.

"There are so many differences between acting in live theater and in motion pictures," she told Rusty on one of their dates.

"Like what?"

"Well, at the Orpheum, every performance was a little different from the last. We always made adjustments according to how we were feeling on stage, or what the other actors were doing, or how the audience was reacting. No two performances were exactly alike. And once we got started, the play rolled on, no matter what went wrong."

"And movies?"

"On a movie set, we repeat the same words and actions over and over again, a dozen times over, from various angles, with close-ups and long shots and overhead views. It can be so tedious. And the scenes are shot out of order, so you have no sense of continuity. And the actors have to speak much more quietly." As Mr. DeJong kept reminding her.

At the midmorning break, Mr. Cooperman's secretary, Midge, approached Helen.

"Mark St. Ives wants to take you out to dinner this week."

"I'm not interested," Helen replied.

Midge's eyes sparkled behind her cat's-eye glasses. "Let me rephrase that. *Mr. Cooperman* wants you to go on a date with Mark St. Ives. For publicity purposes. He thinks it will make both you and he look more enticing."

"Oh, I see. So it's a command performance." Helen emphasized the word *performance*. "Just so it's clear, I have no romantic interest in Mark St. Ives, nor does he have any in me."

"You don't have to," Midge assured her. "By the same token, the fans who devour *Movie Classic* and *Screenland* magazines don't need to know that."

Helen nodded. "Gotcha." If she were interested in having dinner with any man, it would be with the one who was now standing a few feet away, coaching Debbie Fagan on one of her lines.

A particular bright spot of *Stormy River Serenade* was working in close proximity to Rusty. As the movie's screenwriter, he was on hand to work with the director and producer to make dialogue changes as necessary. And while he wasn't required to be on set every single day, Helen found, to her delight, that he very nearly was.

They soon found they worked great together as a team. Helen freely made suggestions for how Rusty could improve dialogue, often adding a touch of humor or sparkle to an otherwise prosaic line. The two of them collaborated together on improving her role. Gradually, and with Julian DeJong's full directorial approval, they increased her part from a minor role to a more substantial one. Not so substantial that she outshone the lead, of course. But substantial enough to show audiences—and directors, and anybody else whose opinion mattered—the kind of work she was capable of.

And when the working day was done, more often than not, they spent their evenings together. Sometimes they saw a movie and dissected it afterward over milkshakes. Sometimes they talked about their castle-in-the-air plans for a studio, sometimes about other hopes and dreams they harbored. Sometimes they didn't talk much at all, just enjoyed one another's company.

Rusty hadn't made any more remarks about encumbrances and his lack of desire for a family. Even so, Helen made sure to emphasize the joys of family life whenever she talked about hers back in Kerryville.

Just in case he was still on the fence about it.

CHAPTER TWENTY-NINE

On the evening of Helen's "date" with Mark St. Ives, he picked her up at the Studio Club in a chauffeured limousine. As she joined him in the spacious passenger area, they exchanged greetings with all the polite repartee of two coworkers on their way to a business dinner, which is exactly what they were. In the soft lighting Helen admired the immaculate seats upholstered in cozy brown suede and the door panels trimmed in shiny polished wood. She could get used to this kind of luxury, although it would be more fun to experience it with Rusty than with Mark. Even so, she could live without it, if it meant being with Rusty. Unlike so many in the business, she wasn't in it for the luxury, but for the challenge. And for the chance to make the kinds of movies that were good for the soul which, she realized, weren't always the most lucrative. Scandalous content sold tickets. But wholesome content could sell tickets, too, to the right audience. She was sure of it.

"I thought filming went well today, didn't it?" she said to Mark, referring to their recently completed workday.

"Yes," Mark agreed. "It did."

Their conversational duty thus completed, Helen leaned back against the seat, enjoying the view through tinted windows as they sped past the gaudy panorama of Hollywood at night.

When they reached the restaurant, men with cameras lined the sidewalk, ready to snap photos of famous people as they arrived or departed from the various nightspots, photos they could later sell to the tabloids. Some stood alert, poised and eager, ready for action, while others—the older, more jaded ones, Helen guessed—lounged against fences, joking and smoking and only occasionally lifting their cameras.

However, at the first glimpse of Mark St. Ives stepping out onto the pavement, all the photographers sprang into action. The camera flashes and popping noises momentarily disoriented Helen as she accepted the hand Mark held out to her and unfolded herself from the back seat of the limousine as gracefully as she could. She was grateful for the loan of another of Flo's dresses, this one a slinky silver number which sparkled every time she moved. She'd asked to borrow the same dark blue gown she'd worn to the party at Mr. Cooperman's, but Flo had nixed that idea.

"You can't show up to two events spaced so closely together, wearing the same dress," Flo had scoffed with infinite practicality. "People will think you haven't got anything else."

"But I *haven't* got anything else," Helen had replied.

"We'll go shopping on Saturday," Flo said. "We might still be able to pick up an end-of-season bargain." But Saturday was too far away to help her with tonight's sartorial dilemma, so Helen had accepted the loan of the silver gown, grateful she and Flo wore the same size.

Mark stood tall for a moment and posed for the paparazzi, making sure to turn what he thought was his best angle toward the cameras. He wore a tailored suit on his six-foot frame, his broad shoulders straining at the buttons. His hair was slicked back and his eyes were electric blue from the contact lenses he wore. When at last the photographers shifted their cameras toward the next limousine to pull up to the curb, he turned to Helen and offered her his arm. His expensive shoes clicked on the pavement as they approached the restaurant.

As a valet held open the door, one of the bystanders, an older woman wearing a headscarf, pushed forward and asked Helen, "Hey, are you somebody?"

Taken aback, Helen stared at the woman for a moment, then purred in a serene manner, "What do you suppose?" and swept past her into the vestibule. Her conscience nipped at her. In spite of the woman's rudeness, she ought to have made a kinder response. She'd have to work on that, to be better prepared for life in the public eye.

Dinner was a tedious affair of stilted conversation amid the stares and whispers of other diners and the occasional flash of a camera bulb. People stopped by the table at regular intervals to speak to Mark in hope of getting a greeting, an autograph, a few precious moments basking in the warm glow of his reflected glory.

"The salmon is good, isn't it?" he remarked to Helen.

She reached for her water glass and took a sip. "Yes. I've never had salmon prepared this way before."

The salmon turned out to be a more scintillating conversational partner than Mark. Now and then he tossed a smile her way, his teeth white and perfect, but she had the feeling he did it more for the cameras than for her. For her part, she forced a feminine giggle now and then, as if he'd made some witty comment. She thought the meal would never end.

At last dinner drew to a close. As Helen relished the last few spoonfuls of her cherries jubilee and looked forward to spending the rest of the evening with her new Willa Cather novel, Mark asked, "Would you care to dance?"

Helen shook her head and feigned a yawn. "No, thank you, Mark. Dinner was lovely, but it's been a long day for both of us. I think it's time to go home."

His handsome face bore the same confused expression as it did whenever he forgot his lines during rehearsal, which was often.

He leaned forward and said in a quiet voice, "I think they expect us to dance."

"They?" It was Helen's turn to be confused. Then she remembered what this really was—a publicity opportunity, not an actual date. *They* were the people in the publicity department at Cooperman Studios, who would be scouring the morning newspaper for photos of Mark and Helen kicking up their heels.

"All right," she said, silently adding *Let's get this over with*. He led her to the dance floor, where they performed for the cameras a dutiful fox trot, followed by a lindy hop, smiling at each other all the while. Helen's cheeks ached with the effort. Thankfully Mark was a halfway decent dancer. She wondered if Rusty liked to dance.

By the time the limousine dropped her off at the Studio Club, she was too tuckered out even for Willa Cather. She set aside Flo's dress to take to the French cleaners, then she put on her nightgown, washed her face, brushed her teeth, and dabbed on a new skin tonic called Moondrop Miracle that Bullock's had start-ed carrying. Gilda Miller had recommended it. Skeptical about most highly touted cosmetics, Helen found this one really did help diminish the ravages of heavy stage make-up.

The evening had been a colossal bore. But at least the dancing had given her some exercise to burn off the cherries jubilee. She wouldn't be able to borrow Flo's gowns much longer if she continued to eat her way through Hollywood.

CHAPTER THIRTY

The next day, while devouring a ham on rye and a chocolate soda at a diner not far from the studio, Rusty perused coverage of Helen's arranged date in the daily newspaper. A gossip columnist's brief observation of "Mark St. Ives dining and dancing with an unknown blonde" accompanied a large photo of Helen and Mark St. Ives gazing blissfully into one another's eyes on the dance floor.

Rusty found the description of an "unknown blonde" both irksome and amusing. Amusing because it would be only a matter of time before the name "Helen Corrigan" was on everyone's lips. He was sure of it. And irksome because... well, just because. The image of her and Mark together annoyed him to no end, but he couldn't put his finger on why. What did he care if Helen went out on the town with Mark on the studio's dime? It was no concern of Rusty's. Studios set people up all the time. Still, she did look as if she was having an awfully good time.

Pushing aside the newspaper and his empty soda glass, he pulled out his copy of the *Stormy River Serenade* script and began reviewing his notes, making a notation here and there to change a bit of dialogue.

"Looks like you and I had the same idea." He looked up from his work just as the Unknown Blonde herself slid into the seat across from him. "I couldn't take one more soggy sandwich from the commissary, could you?" She lifted her hand to signal the waitress.

Rusty set aside his script. "I highly recommend the ham on rye."

Despite his recommendation, she ordered a salad and a glass of iced tea. When the waitress walked away, she confessed with a roll of her eyes, "I'm dying for a cheeseburger, but that costume has no mercy."

"Well, you don't need to fit into it this afternoon. Julian's given everyone the rest of the day off so he can work with the extras."

"I know. Even so, discipline is good for the soul." She eyed the dregs of his chocolate soda.

"I see you're becoming famous." Rusty slid the newspaper toward Helen with the photograph showing. She glanced at it, winced, and slid it back to him.

"Isn't it awful? Flo showed me this morning."

"What, awful? It's a nice picture of you."

"You're sweet to say so." She paused while the waitress returned with her tea, then she took a long sip. "But I guess getting my picture in the paper is worth something. Even if they didn't bother to find out my name. The publicity department's going to have a fit about that. Getting my name in the paper was the whole point of sending me out with Mark."

"Well?" Rusty prodded. "Was it fun?"

"Was what fun?"

"Your date with Mark."

"It wasn't a date." She waved her hand as if dismissing the idea. "It was a thing set up by the studio."

"I see." Rusty'd suspected as much, but it brightened his spirit to hear her say it. "Tell me about it."

As she described the restaurant's décor, the salmon, and the quality of the dance band, he noticed she mentioned just about everything except Mark. Clearly, the good-looking actor hadn't been one of the highlights of her evening.

His spirit brightened even more.

"...and then cherries jubilee. But enough of all that," she said at last. "How goes it with the script?"

"It's going pretty well," he said, pulling out his copy. "I'm just having a little trouble with this one line of Debbie's in the sailboat scene." He read aloud the line in question, then looked at Helen. "What do you think?"

She thought for a moment. "I think it depends on the way she says it. If she says it one way, it sounds sweet. But if she gives it a different inflection, it could sound sarcastic. So it depends on which meaning you intend."

Rusty looked back at the script. "You're right." He made a notation to give a suggestion to Julian about the way the line should be delivered. When he looked back up, she was grinning at him.

"What?"

"Nothing. Only that I'm flattered you asked for my opinion."

"Of course I want your opinion. You have good ideas."

"Some scriptwriters don't care to hear what actresses think."

"I don't want to hear from *all* actresses," he said, thinking of Cynthia Starling, "but you have good instincts. You're worth listening to."

Mortified, he watched a glimmer of moisture gather in her blue eyes.

"Did I say something wrong?"

Quickly she picked up her fork and attacked her salad.

"Oh, no. You're very sweet. I'm just not used to people caring about my opinion. That's all."

He sensed there was something more behind her simple statement.

Turned out he was right.

Helen stirred her tea with a straw, wondering how much of her story was safe to share. Rusty seemed so kind, so easy to talk to. But if she told him about her foolishness over the Chet situation, would he lose respect for her?

She decided it was a chance she was willing to take.

"Chester Scarborough was his name. Chet. He directed a play I was in back home. I sort of fell for him."

Fell for him. Ha! Understatement of the year.

"It wasn't a romance, really," she continued. "I had a gigantic crush on him. An infatuation, if you will. Entirely one-sided."

Rusty gave her a sympathetic look. "What happened?"

"He turned out to be married." She said it in a light tone, but her heart felt heavy with the shame of it. She pushed aside her half-finished salad, her appetite gone.

"Ouch." Rusty winced. "That must have hurt."

"It did, at the time. But leaving Kerryville behind, and all those memories, has helped."

She let out a quick breath and shuddered, shaking off the emotions rising up inside her. Throat tight with unshed tears, she poked her straw up and down in her tea to distract herself.

"He sounds like a real jerk," Rusty said, his voice gentle. "I hope you won't let the experience turn you off from giving a nice guy a chance."

She looked at him and smiled.

"I know there's at least one great guy out there," she said, "because God put the two of us on a train and brought him to me."

His gaze softened. "Do you mean that?"

She nodded.

"He's a good God, isn't he?" he murmured. She nodded again, not trusting her voice.

Neither of them said anything further for a few moments. Then, out of nowhere, Rusty said brightly, "Say, we've been talking about heavy things. Let's do something fun. Would you like to go roller-skating?"

Helen jerked her head up. "What? Now?"

"Yeah. Come on."

He put some bills on the table to cover their meals. Then he slid out of the booth and held his hand out to help her. Then they went out to the sidewalk where he whistled for a cab, and before she knew it, she found herself standing outside a roller rink.

They stood in line talking for almost half an hour before reaching the ticket window. They talked some more as they rented skates. He helped her tie hers on, then they held hands and launched into the sea of skaters.

It took Helen a moment to find her "skate legs," but before long she was flying around the rink, glad that Rusty could keep up. She felt like a kid again. She practiced a few of the tricky turns she'd learned on girlhood afternoons at the Kerryville Roll-A-Rama. He, in turn, impressed her with a few clever moves of his own.

But the thing she liked the very best was skating around and around the rink, side by side, simply holding his hand.

She enjoyed working in Hollywood, but she didn't need Tinseltown's glitz and glamour to feel special and cared for.

Whenever she was with Rusty, she knew that she was.

CHAPTER THIRTY-ONE

On the set of *Stormy River Serenade*, Julian DeJong announced they'd be filming a pivotal scene between Helen and the young lead actress, Debbie Fagan. The production had fallen behind schedule, so they were working late into the night in an attempt to catch up.

"All right, people," DeJong bellowed into the megaphone. "Let's try to get this right the first time so we're not here until morning."

"He makes me so nervous," Debbie whispered to Helen. "I hate it when he yells."

"You're doing great," Helen assured her. "He yells at everyone. Just keep your eye on the ball, do your best to follow his instructions, and everything will be rosy."

But everything wasn't rosy. When they came to a certain line and Debbie said it the way it was written, DeJong interrupted her.

"Cut! You said it all wrong," he shouted. "What's the matter with you?"

"Did I?" Debbie's voice shook. She looked as if she were about to cry.

Helen glanced around the set for Rusty to champion his script, but didn't find him. She stepped forward. "Sorry, Mr. DeJong. Debbie said it right. Rusty rewrote that line a few days ago. I guess he forgot to give you the update."

"I don't want it rewritten," DeJong barked. "I want to keep it the way it was."

Helen didn't know if it was because, in that moment, DeJong reminded her so much of Chet, or because she was genuinely invested in preserving the line the way Rusty wanted it, or because she was just plain exhausted, but she heard herself say in a strong voice, "I disagree, Julian. The line is better the way Rusty wrote it."

The company held its collective breath—nobody argued with DeJong.

The director glowered. His intense gaze penetrated through her.

Helen's heart plummeted. *Crud*. She'd probably gone and gotten herself fired. Worse than fired.

But to her amazement, along with everyone else's, his expression shifted. He shrugged. "Okay." Then he turned to Debbie. "Say the line the way Noble wants you to."

Helen nearly collapsed with relief. The filming proceeded on course. And she felt pretty proud of herself for sticking up for Debbie, and for Rusty, in a way she'd been unable to stand up to Chet.

As the day's work wrapped up, she was approached by Donna's agent, Phil Fairmont. She hadn't realized Phil was even in the studio, but evidently he'd seen the whole exchange.

"You got guts, kid," he said in a tone of grudging admiration. "I like to see that in an actress. Keep it up."

It wasn't an offer of representation. Yet. Nonetheless, Helen took his words to heart and floated on them for the rest of the night.

Across town, Rusty and his coworkers, Smitty and Jim, hunched around the table in Rusty's cramped apartment, dark circles ringing their eyes. Before each of them lay papers and pencils as they each scratched out their vision of how their imaginary movie studio would operate, would make its mark on the motion picture industry.

"We'll produce clean movies," Jim said. "Good, wholesome movies that the whole family can watch together."

"More than just clean," Rusty said. "We want to promote all good things. Decency. Love for fellow human beings. Fair play. We want our movies to be wholesome, warm-hearted, and entertaining."

"It sounds good, but all of that takes quite a bit of cash," Smitty reminded them.

"Money doesn't interest me," Rusty said. "Our ideas are what interests me."

"Well, I hate to be the bearer of bad news, but money interests the actors and the cameramen and the sound people and everyone else who works on a production."

"I know that," Rusty snapped.

He hadn't known where he'd find the time to work on the new studio, but he'd begun waking up exceedingly early each morning to get some planning in before his day job got in the way. And now that Smitty and Jim were fully committed, too, they were meeting at night as well.

"It'll obviously have to stay a side project for now. We have to keep it quiet," he warned them. "If Cooperman gets wind of what we're doing, we'll be out on our ears. And we still need the salaries he pays us. We need to give Cooperman Studios one hundred percent of our efforts as long as we're employed there. But we won't be employed there forever. Not if our studio takes off."

"*When* it takes off," Jim said. Rusty appreciated his confidence. "What about Leroy Cooperman? Has he gotten in touch with you yet?"

"Not yet," Rusty admitted. "Not since our conversation last Christmas."

"That was months ago," Smitty said. "Maybe you'd better contact him and ask him what's up."

"Nah," Rusty said. "He'll come around when he's ready. Maybe he's changed his mind."

In his heart, Rusty knew Smitty was right, but was on the fence about Leroy Cooperman. On the one hand, the studio needed the money. On the other hand, he wasn't sure how much he could trust Leroy. Choosing the wrong project to start with could sink the new studio before it even got off the ground.

"Now, to tally our assets, we've got Helen Corrigan on board." Rusty leaned forward. "She's a peach. She's gorgeous and talented, and she's committed to our mission. Willing to stick up for herself, too."

"Now you're cooking, Rusty," Jim said. "Good job."

"You're like a mosquito, Noble," Smitty said in a tone of grudging respect. "You never stopped buzzing, and you never give up until you get what you want."

It was well past midnight when the three of them parted ways, heads full of plans, schemes, ideas, and dreams. Their final decision of the evening had been what to call the company. Rusty had suggested White Hat Studios. "Like the good guys in all the Westerns," he explained. "The guys in the white hats are the ones who come riding in to save the day."

Smitty was less enthusiastic. "Nah. Sounds too goody-two-shoes. How about Pristine Productions?"

"Talk about sounding goody-two-shoes." Rusty wrinkled his nose.

"I've got it." Jim snapped his fingers. When he said the name, everyone but Rusty agreed immediately that the name was ideal.

"It captures both the founder's name, and the ideals we want to promote," Jim said.

"I'm not so sure," Rusty said. "I'd planned to keep my name out of it."

But the decision was unanimous. From that night on, the name of the soon-to-be studio was Noble Pictures, Incorporated.

The wrap party for *Stormy River Serenade* was held at the Cocoanut Grove at the Ambassador Hotel. With the recent repeal of Prohibition, the manufacture and sale of alcohol had become legal again in California, so the atmosphere was especially celebratory. When Rusty finally pushed his way through the feverish throng and reached the bar, he ordered his usual orange juice and tonic water, plus a ginger ale for Helen. Even though he wasn't a drinker, he felt the whole Prohibition experiment had been a colossal failure and wasn't sorry to see its demise. It hadn't gotten rid of making and selling alcohol at all, just pushed it underground and gave a tremendous boost to bootleggers and organized crime. There were some things, Rusty concluded, best left to the states and out of the hands of the federal government.

The room was enormous and jam-packed with revelers. Larger-than-life palm trees towered overhead, from which stuffed monkeys surveyed the crowd. The room was dark, yet it glowed with a soft, warm light cast by hundreds of shaded lamps. Laughter filled the air over the sounds of a tinkling piano and a wailing saxophone. People in gowns and tuxedos bumped into each other on the dance floor to the rhythm of the band, or stopped to visit from table to table, while others leaned against the walls, glasses and cigarette holders in hand. Booths upholstered in dark brown leather and crimson cushions lined the walls, and it was in such a booth that Rusty returned to Helen.

"I just heard at the bar that the initial reviews are coming in good," he told her. "We have reason to celebrate."

Stanley Cooperman thought so too. He approached their table.

"Well done, Rusty. I'm very proud to have such a fine screen-writer on our staff. And as for you, young lady." He took Helen's hand in his. "I underestimated you. We'll have to talk very soon about your future here."

Thrilled to the core, but aware of Cooperman's possessiveness, an idea clicked in Helen's head. She waited until she and Rusty were alone, on their way home in a taxicab, to say it out loud.

"So, tell me," she said. "Does your special relationship with Mr. Cooperman have any effect on your decision to go out on your own?"

"What do you mean?"

"I mean, do you think it would be disloyal to leave Mr. Cooper-man, after all he's done for you?"

Rusty's expression was grim. "I've thought about that. A lot. I owe Mr. Cooperman a great deal. He took me in when I was a nobody, taught me everything I know about filmmaking. But if I stay at Cooperman Studios for my whole career, I'll never get the chance to make the kind of movies I want to make."

"That we want to make," she reminded him.

"Yes." He squeezed her shoulder. "And I'm afraid that the longer I stay, the harder it will be to leave."

"You're an adult now. You can make your own decisions about how to live your life."

"But I gotta admit, I feel do feel disloyal to Mr. Cooperman for even thinking about going out on my own. After all, he gave me my start in the industry, and has treated me well."

"So why leave, then?"

"Because liking Mr. Cooperman personally isn't reason enough to stay," he said firmly.

As they said goodnight at her doorway, he said, "Thanks for not mentioning anything about the new studio to anyone. Not even to Flo. The closer we get to making it a reality, the more vital secrecy becomes."

"As I told you, I won't breathe a word," Helen promised. "And I'm every bit as serious about this new venture as you are."

She lifted her face to his and sealed her promise with a kiss.

CHAPTER THIRTY-TWO

To the surprise of virtually everyone connected with the movie industry, *Stormy River Serenade* was a hit.

While Debbie Fagan lit up the screen in the lead role, Helen's performance, in particular, captured the public's attention and catapulted her into the spotlight, practically overnight. No longer was she the "Unknown Blonde" of the gossip columns. Through her collaboration with Rusty as well as the on-screen chemistry between herself and Debbie, she'd taken a relatively minor role and put her own spin on it, causing it to shine. The early reviews were glowing, and even the few that were otherwise critical praised Helen's performance.

"Helen Corrigan's got what it takes."

"Rising starlet Helen Corrigan brought unexpected depth and richness to the role of Virginia."

"Helen Corrigan: A name to watch."

Freed from the grueling schedule of filming, only to be faced with another grueling schedule of publicity, Helen found herself being propelled from luncheons to shopping-center openings. When she had a chance to stay home and rest, she grabbed it.

In the middle of one such hectic day, an underling from the publicity department stopped by the Studio Club with a bag of mail. Helen opened one letter and unfolded it.

Dear Miss Corrigan, it read. *I saw you in* Stormy River Serenade. *Are you in love with Mark St. Ives in real life?*

Another one read, *Dear Miss Corrigan, I saw you in* Stormy River Serenade *and think you look exactly like Cynthia Starling, only prettier. Has anyone ever told you that? P.S. Are those your real eyelashes?*

A few were critical. *Dear Miss Corrigan, You might want to do something different with your hair. It looks like cotton candy on a stick.*

Helen flung the letter aside. Obviously the letter-writer had no idea that Helen had absolutely no say in how her hair was styled. That decision, as so many others, was totally in the hands of the studio's experts.

In general, it pleased her to hear from so many fans. At the same time, a heavy mantle of responsibility settled on her shoulders. She was a role model to these girls and young women. They looked up to her, wanted to copy her. She'd better make doubly sure that the roles she accepted were worthy of such admiration.

When Flo came home from work, Helen let her read the funniest or most poignant letters.

"Won't they let you answer them yourself?" Flo asked.

Helen shook her head. "I wish I could—the nice ones, anyway—but apparently the studio thinks I might say something wrong. They want to control my public image, and that includes answering my fan mail."

Helen spent the evening finishing all the letters, then bagged them back up to return to the publicity department for a response, as she'd been instructed. A few days later she hoisted the bag on the trolley to drop off at the studio, where she was to meet with a photographer. The publicity people wanted new photos that could be signed and mailed out to the fans. They gave her all kinds of outfits to wear in the photographs. Silky gowns, a sporty tennis outfit, an English riding habit, all giving the impression that Helen lived a much more exciting and active life than she did.

She drew the line at posing in a skimpy two-piece bathing suit.

"Mr. Cooperman won't be happy," the black-clad publicity representative warned with a shake of her stiffly coiffed head.

But Helen stuck to her guns. She still cringed when she thought of the bathing scene in *Annabel* and wanted to forestall any misunderstandings about the kind of actress she was.

"Better take these two gowns home with you," the publicist said. "You'll need something to wear to parties, and Mr. Cooperman likes the way these look on you."

"Golly," Helen breathed, touching the luxurious fabric. "I get to keep them?"

"They aren't yours," the woman snapped. "They belong to the studio. Try not to spill anything on them."

When Helen got home, the phone was ringing.

"Phil Fairmont calling," the brisk male voice said. "I see you've been getting some impressive publicity. All the major studios are going to want to talk to you. I think it's time we talked."

By the end of the conversation, he'd agreed to represent her and she'd agreed to consider his proposal.

"I knew from the moment I met you that you had something special, kid," he told her just before they said goodbye. "I just needed to be sure."

It turned out Phil was not the only agent interested in representing Helen. But because he represented Donna Delmonico, who'd spoken highly of him, and even more so because Rusty approved of him, she opted to go with Phil.

One of the first meetings Phil set up for Helen was with, of all people, Mr. Cooperman.

"He's very pleased with your box-office success," Phil told her. "I can't say for sure, of course, but he might want to offer you a multi-year contract worth a great deal of money. This probably goes without saying, but if he does offer such a contract, it would be in your best interest to say yes. When Stanley Cooperman decides to make you a star, you are a star."

When she and Phil arrived at Mr. Cooperman's office, he invited them to sit. Too nervous to look straight at him, Helen fixed her eyes on the animal pelts and taxidermy displayed around the room. The cougar's unblinking stare added to her unease.

"Miss Corrigan, we meet again," Cooperman said. "Phil here has convinced me you've got something special, I'd like to offer you a contract for one hundred and fifty dollars a week."

One hundred and fifty dollars a week! Helen thought she might faint.

There was a lot more talking after that. Not by Helen, who'd been struck dumb by the sheer enormity of the situation. Phil and Mr. Cooperman spoke at length.

At last, sheets of very official-looking papers were produced.

Phil spread the papers on the desk in front of Helen. "Do you understand, Helen, what this contract means? It means Mr. Cooperman is offering to take care of you for as long as you're under contract, which will be for seven years."

Seven years. Helen snapped out of her stupor. Seven years sounded like a lifetime to her. Rusty's long-ago remark about a gift of a tie clip signifying the studio's ownership played across her mind.

"However, by law, the contract could be terminated every six months, at the studio's discretion."

"Wait," Helen said. "So it's a seven-year commitment on my end, but a six-month commitment on the part of the studio?" Helen was no lawyer, but that didn't sound very fair.

"It's a seven-year commitment on their part, too, only in six-month intervals." Phil spoke in a confident voice that implied this deal was indeed fair and square. But it made little sense to Helen. Either a commitment was for seven years, or it was for six months, but it couldn't be both, could it?

There were a great many more words. The studio would control the parts she took. She'd have to report to the studio every day, Monday through Friday, and wait around even when she wasn't needed. The studio would supply acting classes and diction classes and control the way she dressed and wore her hair. They'd control her social life as well, requiring her to appear at parties and publicity events and many more staged "dates" such as the one she'd endured with Mark St. Ives.

"One hundred and fifty dollars a week," Phil repeated, uncapping a fountain pen and holding it in her direction, "and guaranteed work with the prestigious Cooperman Studios. For seven years. This contract is every starlet's dream."

It was too much to take in all at once. Much as she dreamed about being offered a contract such as this one, something about it didn't feel right. Maybe she simply needed more time.

"May I have time to think about it?"

Phil looked at her as if she were crazy to pass up this golden opportunity, but Mr. Cooperman said, "Sure, sure. Take all the time you need."

She left Mr. Cooperman's office feeling happy, confused, and scared, all at the same time.

She needed to talk it over with God. And with Rusty.
In that order.

CHAPTER THIRTY-THREE

That fall ushered in the Exodus of the Roommates. In October, Donna moved out of the Studio Club and into luxurious new digs underwritten by her wealthy and totally inappropriate suitor, Herbert Jones. While Helen had had her differences with Donna, she tried to talk her out of this ill-considered move, to no avail.

"This isn't the Middle West," Donna had sneered. "You can keep your goody-two-shoes morality to yourself. Don't try to impose it on me."

Helen hadn't wanted to impose anything on anybody. She'd simply wanted Donna to understand her worth as a woman loved by God who could turn from the path she was on and find a better one. But Donna refused to hear it. Once again, all Helen could do was pray for her former roommate and hope she'd come to her senses before it was too late.

Scarcely a month later, Flo announced plans to move back to Tulsa and marry her longtime boyfriend,

"I'm so happy for you," Helen assured her friend, speaking past the lump in her throat. "But I'm sad for me. You've been the best roommate a girl could ever have. If it weren't for you showing me the ropes on how to behave at an audition, I probably would never have been hired for my first role."

Flo returned her embrace. "You're flying now, little bird."

After Flo moved out, the once claustrophobic apartment suddenly seemed too big and silent, so Helen invited Debbie Fagan to move in with her. Debbie, who'd recently turned eighteen and thus met the Studio Club's minimum age requirement, was quick to accept. Through working together on *Stormy River Serenade*, she and Helen had developed a warm, sisterly relationship that reminded Helen a little of the closeness she'd once shared with Marjorie. And hopefully would again, someday.

Until Helen signed an exclusive contract with Cooperman Studios, she was free to accept other offers. Phil Fairmont had been sending her some scripts from other motion picture companies. But so far none of the roles were the kind she wanted to accept. And he kept pestering her to sign with Cooperman.

She discussed the situation with Rusty over supper at their favorite diner. "I know I should jump at the opportunity," she said, "but seven years sounds like forever. Cooperman will virtually own me. What I wear, where I live, whom I date, even where I vacation. By the time it elapses, I'll be twenty-eight years old! My best years will already be behind me."

"I hardly think that's true." Rusty consoled her. "I think there'll still be a few years left in the old girl, even after the ripe age of twenty-eight."

"I'm serious," she said.

"I'm serious, too. You're a great actress, not just a flash in the pan. You're the kind of actress who will only get better with age, like a fine wine."

She had to smile at that. "Which neither of us drinks. But thank you anyway." She stirred the soup she had no appetite for. "That would be seven years I couldn't work with you at Noble Pictures."

"What's seven years? Jacob worked for Laban for seven years, in order to win Rachel's hand," Rusty said. "And seven more years on top of that."

Helen failed to see the relevance, but she kept quiet. She'd expected him to protest, to hold her to her commitment to wait and join him at Noble Pictures when it came into existence—whenever that would be—but he didn't.

"I can't offer you anything close to what Cooperman's offering," he admitted. "The last thing I'd ever want to do is hold you back."

His honesty melted her heart. And made her decision that much harder. "Phil keeps telling me Cooperman will make me a star," she said. "His exact words were, 'When Cooperman pulls the strings, actors dance like puppets.' What if I don't want to be a puppet? He'll control every part I'm assigned. What if he pressures me to take the kinds of roles I don't want to take? That *God* doesn't want me to take?"

Rusty set down his fork. "How about this?" he offered. "Why don't you tell him you want certain things written into the contract, like setting limits on the kinds of roles you would play, moral lines you won't cross, and things like that? Isn't that part of what Phil takes a commission for? To negotiate on your behalf?"

She set down her spoon and sighed. "I suppose so. But he seems more interested in pleasing Mr. Cooperman than pleasing me. Which is only natural, I suppose. Cooperman will pay his commission. Not me."

He reached across the table and took her hand in his. "Let's pray about it. Ask the Lord to guide you on what you should do." They bowed their heads and prayed together. Afterward, he smiled at her. "Feel better?"

She nodded, returned his smile, and picked up her spoon.

But deep inside, she felt no more peace about the situation than she had before.

"You keep turning down every picture I send you," Phil Fairmont complained over the telephone, frustration evident in his voice.

"So far the parts you've sent me have been vile," she retorted. "Honestly, Phil. A prostitute? A murderess?" She shifted the receiver to her other ear. "I told you. I only want to play *good* parts. Decent parts. Meaning wholesome stories, no graphic sex or violence. The sorts of pictures that the whole family can watch together. Surely somebody's making decent movies nowadays. Especially with the Hays Code cracking down."

Phil sighed audibly. "The Hays Code," he grumbled. "Don't remind me." She heard him shuffling papers. "Cooperman's people just sent over one role that would be perfect for you, and it's a good, clean picture."

"A Western?" Helen hoped so. Rusty wrote most of the Westerns that Cooperman produced. She'd loved working closely with him on *Stormy River Serenade* and hoped to do so again.

"No, not a Western," Phil said, "but still, it's one of those old-fashioned three-hankie things you seem to like." More shuffling. "Here it is, I found it. It's called *Under the Flaming Oak*."

Helen's heart plummeted to her knees. Memories of the play and of Chet and of what she'd come to think of as her Lost Summer came rushing back, flooding her mind with a monsoon of humiliation and regret.

"Helen? You there?"

"I-I'm here, Phil." She took in a deep breath to steady her nerves. *Focus, Helen.*

Phil was continuing to talk. She forced herself to concentrate on his words. "DeJong is set to direct. He likes you—says you've got spunk—so we're all set there. What do you think?"

"I know that play very well." *Alas, not so the playwright.* "In fact, I performed the leading role in summer stock back in Illinois." As her initial shock subsided, she warmed to the idea. "I loved both the play and the role, and it was very well received. I can send you the reviews if you like."

"I believe you. Are you talking about the role of Susannah?"

"Yes."

"Well, okay." Phil sounded more cheerful. "I'll set up a screen test."

After ending the call, Helen collapsed onto the sofa and stared into space.

Under the Flaming Oak.

Written by Chester Scarborough, distinguished Chicago impresario.

Distinguished. Ha!

She didn't know if she could stand so many memories of Chet that making the movie was sure to evoke.

But even so, Susannah was *her* role. She owned it. Everybody back home said so.

It would be different this time. Mr. DeJong would be the director. Maybe with his force of personality, he'd overlay her memories of Chet, erasing them the way an exorcism was supposed to rid a house of ghosts.

She sat up and straightened her spine. One thing was for sure. She wasn't going to let a weasel like Chet Scarborough stop her from pursuing a challenging role in an excellent story—the kind of movie she'd dreamed of making.

Rusty sat alone at his desk in the writers' bungalow, reading through his most recent writing assignment, a screen adaptation of a stage play called *Under the Flaming Oak*. It was a pretty good story, filled with intrigue and bravery and just enough romance to keep it enticing without going over the top. It was the kind of story he'd like to produce at his own studio someday, a story that would make the average viewer leave the theater wanting to be a better person.

For the time being, though, his plans for opening his own studio had been put on hold. Ever since Helen had told him about the juicy contract she'd been offered by Cooperman, he'd been keeping his distance. His struggling studio couldn't compete with an offer like that. It'd be years before he could offer her a similar deal. Maybe never. And he wasn't about to hold her back.

Even though she'd said she wanted to work with him, she was probably only being polite. Without decent financial backing, he couldn't pay her what she was worth. He could hardly expect her to work for free, like he was some charitable cause. But the hard truth was, the studio had no money. And without a talent like hers to attract investors, they had little chance of making any.

He was unwilling to clip her wings or to hold her to a promise to struggle alongside him. Not when she was on the brink of becoming perhaps the biggest star in Cooperman's galaxy. He was elated for her.

But depressed for himself.

He hadn't heard anything more from Leroy Cooperman about his secretive film project. Maybe he'd abandoned the idea. Or maybe he was waiting for Rusty to follow up with him. That was probably the correct thing to do. But Rusty was leery enough of Leroy and his sketchy past to be wary of working with him. Not to mention he was Stanley's brother. How good would he be at keeping secrets?

Meanwhile, Stanley Cooperman was waiting for this screenplay. Rusty stood up from his desk, poured himself a cup of strong coffee, and sat back down, determined to focus all his attention on *Under the Flaming Oak*. As long as he still worked for Cooperman, he owed the company his best effort. And with Jim and Smitty gone for the afternoon, there was nobody around to distract him.

The door to the writers' bungalow swung open and a stranger walked in, a tall man with dark hair slightly graying around the temples. A lost and wandering extra, perhaps.

"You looking for Soundstage C?" Rusty asked. "It's just to the west of this building, two doors thataway." He gestured with his thumb.

"I was told to find the place where the writers work," the man said.

"Oh. You've found it." Rusty stood and extended his hand. "I'm Zachary Noble, but everyone calls me Rusty."

"Zachary Noble," the man said with an unpleasant smirk. "Say, that's a mouthful, isn't it?"

Rusty disliked him immediately.

"I'm here on a temporary assignment," the stranger continued.

"Oh." Confusion muddled Rusty's brain. "I'm sorry, nobody told me you were coming." He looked around, then started to clear stacks of paper off an unoccupied desk. "I guess you can sit here."

The man offered a pleasant smile. "I'm sorry for the disruption. I believe it all came together at the last minute. I've been hired to write the screenplay for *Under the Flaming Oak.*"

Rusty stopped and stared at him. "You're what?" *Under the Flaming Oak* was Rusty's project. Or so he thought.

"You see, I wrote the original stage play, so Stanley has brought me out here to write the screenplay as well. Stanley Cooperman," the fellow added, as if Rusty might not know who Stanley was.

"I see." Rusty scrambled to adjust to this new information. "What did you say your name was?"

"I don't believe I have yet. It's Chester Scarborough, but I prefer to go by Chet."

CHAPTER THIRTY-FOUR

Helen completed a screen test for the role of Susannah, but Phil assured her it was really just a formality.

"Cooperman wanted you for the part as soon as he heard you'd already made a triumph of it back in Illinois. You're a shoe-in," he told her over the telephone when he called her at home with the news that she'd gotten the part.

Helen could hardly wait to get started. Despite the play's deeply unpleasant associations with Chet, she'd relished playing Susannah and knew she would do well at it.

"Who else has been cast?" she asked Phil.

"They're still working on filling the smaller roles, but so far, they've got Loretta Young for Alice, Simon Jarrow for the father, and they're negotiating with Leslie Howard to play Will."

"Leslie Howard!" The ground shifted under her feet. Will was Susannah's love interest in the story, and the very thought of doing romantic scenes with Leslie Howard was enough to make her toes curl.

"I thought you'd be pleased," Phil said.

"Who's been assigned to write the screenplay?"

"Rusty Noble, as far as I know. That's who we asked for, anyway. Out of all of Cooperman's writing staff, he does the best job on these old-timey weepers."

A thrill ran up Helen's spine at the prospect of another opportunity to work closely with Rusty. She'd sensed a subtle cooling-off on his part—nothing she could put her finger on—and she relished the idea of restoring their previous easygoing intimacy.

"The read-through will happen next week," Phil continued, "provided the adaptation is finished by then."

"I'll be ready." She couldn't stop herself from grinning into the phone. "You can count on that."

"One more thing," Phil said. "You've got the part, but Cooperman's still waiting on that long-term contract. Can you sign it and bring it with you to the read-through?"

Helen made a noncommittal reply, but as she hung up the phone, a dull ache wrapped around her belly, an ache she'd begun to experience whenever she thought about the contract. She knew she should be thrilled to the marrow of her bones that a major studio like Cooperman wanted her to work for them long-term. Her money worries would be solved. She could give up her job at Bullock's. Not incidentally, Phil couldn't receive his generous commission until she signed it, which accounted for his impatience. She'd been carrying it around in her handbag for weeks, always intending to sign it.

But seven years. Seven years sounded like a jail sentence.

After hanging up with Phil, Helen's next call was to Rusty's office. She was dying to share the good news that she'd gotten the part and that they'd be working together. And frankly, she just wanted to talk to him. Ever since their conversation about the pending contract with Cooperman, he'd seemed distant and preoccupied. A good conversation might clear the air.

But the secretary said that he'd gone into a meeting and should be done within the hour.

Helen didn't want to wait that long. She grabbed her hat and purse and headed out the door to surprise him at the office. It was almost the end of the workday, anyway. Perhaps they could celebrate her good news over dinner at Sardi's. It'd be a splurge, but worth every penny. Her treat. After all, she may not yet have an exclusive contract, but she'd soon have one for *Under the Flaming Oak* that would cover more than a steak dinner. Maybe a steak dinner plus dessert.

She hopped off the streetcar at Cooperman Studios, flashed her badge to the guard, and made a beeline for the writers' building. She burst in the door and headed for Rusty's desk.

"There you are," she panted. "I've been trying to call you."

He stood when she entered. "I've been in a meeting," he said, "about a new hire." His normally pale skin looked even paler, his eyes huge.

"Oh, no. Bad news?"

He swallowed. "Not for me. But it might be for you."

She frowned. "What do you mean?"

But before he could answer, a familiar voice behind her said "Hello, honey. It's great to see you again."

She whirled. The tall, lanky form of Chet Scarborough occupied another desk. He swept her with his cool gray eyes.

She thought she might be sick.

CHAPTER THIRTY-FIVE

D izzy, Helen placed a hand on Rusty's desktop and leaned on it for support. He looked at her with concern.

"Hey, are you okay?"

"I just... I just need some air." She stumbled from the building and onto the sidewalk. Chet followed closely behind.

"Honey, let me explain."

"Don't 'honey' me."

They were drawing the attention of curious people passing by. She grabbed his sleeve and jerked him around to the side of the building, where they could speak in relative privacy behind some eucalyptus trees. When they were sheltered from prying eyes, she wheeled on him.

"Chet, what are you doing here? You hate Hollywood!"

He shrugged. "It's simple. When Cooperman bought the rights to *Under the Flaming Oak*, he invited me out to adapt it for the screen. It's not unheard of, you know. Plenty of novelists and playwrights have gone on to write screenplays of their work. Hemingway, for example. And F. Scott Fitzgerald."

Helen planted her hands on her hips. "And I suppose you count yourself among these literary luminaries."

Chet spread his hands. "Hey, it wasn't my idea. Cooperman asked for me specifically, and I thought the experience would be interesting."

Helen couldn't believe what she was hearing. "But what about all your high-minded ideals? Your lofty speeches about the superiority of live theater and the cheap tawdriness of the silver screen? Won't you sully yourself by condescending to work in Hollywood?" Sarcasm laced her words.

"Perhaps I was too hasty in my estimation of the medium," he said. "The paycheck's attractive. Besides, this seemed an appropriate time for me to get away from Chicago for a while. Take a break. Get some sunshine."

Sunshine? She didn't think so. She looked at him with suspicion. "Why? You've been doing so well in Chicago. *Under the Flaming Oak* was a hit at the Goodman. Or so I heard."

He began to pace, as if gathering his thoughts. "The play did do well. But behind the scenes, things have gotten a bit... shall we say, uncomfortable for me. Personnel issues, backstabbing, smear campaigns. All completely unfair, of course." He stopped pacing and looked at Helen. "Also, Denise has filed for divorce."

No surprise there. Nonetheless, Helen said, "I'm sorry to hear that." Sorry for Denise, she meant.

Chet's face brightened. "When Cooperman asked me to come out here, he mentioned that he had you in mind to play Susannah. That clinched the deal for me. You *made* that part back in Kerryville. You owned it. And I thought, wouldn't that be great, you and I working together again? We were such a good team, weren't we?"

"Except for the little fact that you didn't tell me you were married," she accused.

"Oh, come on, honey. That was just a little misunderstanding. If you'd asked, I would have told you. The subject never came up."

She exploded. "Never came up? You asked me to come to Chicago with you! My bags were packed."

He winced and rubbed the back of his neck. "I'm afraid you had the wrong idea about us, honey. You heard me promise things I didn't actually promise."

She held her tongue. He had a point. Perhaps she *had* let her imagination get carried away, imagining a romance where none existed. Even so, she couldn't help but feel he had led her on with his pretty words and his kisses.

He stepped closer to her. Lifted her chin so she'd look straight into his gray eyes. "But I'm a free man now, honey. Can't we start over? See where things take us this time?"

Revulsion gripped her stomach. She jerked away from him.

"No. We cannot start over." She took a deep breath, reminded herself she was a professional actress, a grown woman making her mark on Hollywood, not a heartsick schoolgirl. "Look. If Cooperman's hired you, he's hired you. If we must work together on *Under the Flaming Oak*, our collaboration will be strictly professional."

"Oh, strictly." Amusement played around the corners of his mouth.

"I mean it, Chet. Outside of working on the set, stay away from me."

Rusty paced up and down the length of the restaurant's foyer, waiting for Leroy Cooperman to arrive. Did he want an association with Leroy or didn't he? He was still unsure. The man's criminal past was never far from Rusty's mind. But when Leroy finally called, months after stating his initial interest in working on a project together, Rusty's prospects had dwindled to the point that he had no choice but to set his worries aside and hear the man out. Not if Noble Pictures was to have any chance of getting off the ground.

He'd arrived early for their meeting, out of sheer nervousness. When Leroy had called, he'd mentioned bringing along a couple of friends of his to listen to Rusty's pitch. Potential investors.

Rusty had stayed up half the night crafting his "pitch." Now he rehearsed it in his head, wanting to sound polished and assured when he spoke to Leroy and his associates.

Leroy had suggested they meet for lunch at The Trocadero, an expensive restaurant built to impress. But now Rusty wished they'd chosen someplace farther away from the studio. He didn't want to be observed by anyone he knew. If word got back to Stanley Cooperman that Rusty was having lunch with his brother, it might raise suspicion.

Speaking of expensive... Rusty stopped his pacing to ask the host to make sure the bill came to him at the end of the meal. Not that he could afford it, but that's the way things were done in Hollywood. The person asking for the favor bought the meal.

He'd just finished making this arrangement when Leroy entered the restaurant...

Accompanied by two goons.

At least they looked like goons to Rusty. Like Central Casting's interpretation of Al Capone's gang members, all fancy suits, fedoras, and glowering expressions on their lantern-jawed faces. All they lacked were violin cases housing tommy guns.

"Hello," Rusty squeaked, extending his hand. He tried to quell his nervousness as Leroy made the introductions. The friends' names were Sam and Rocco—gangster names, Rusty was sure of it. He'd seen plenty of gangster movies in his time. In fact, he was a huge Jimmy Cagney fan.

But gangsters on the silver screen were one thing. Gangsters sitting across the lunch table were quite another.

It made perfect sense. Leroy had spent time in prison, and these were likely men he'd become acquainted with during that time. Why wouldn't an ex-con have friends who were also ex-cons?

Rusty tried to cast the situation in the best light. Perhaps by investing in a wholesome venture like Noble Pictures, they were hoping to make a fresh start on the outside. Even so, his gut was too knotted to even think of eating.

The host showed them to their table. The Trocadero "cellar" was a large room lined with pine walls and red leather seats. It was less fancy than the Cocoanut Grove, but just as popular a place. Rusty hoped for a quiet table near the back, but Leroy chose a ringside booth where they could watch the lunchtime entertainment, a pianist playing popular tunes.

"I need to say this up front," Rusty said once they were seated. "You can't say anything to your brother about this conversation. If he gets a whiff that I'm considering projects outside of Cooperman Studios, I'll be fired."

"Understood," Leroy assured him. He glanced at his two friends. "We're experienced at keeping secrets. Right, fellas?"

Somehow this proclamation didn't give Rusty the sense of reassurance he'd hoped for. Nonetheless, over lunch he described his vision for Noble Pictures. But the entire time, in the back of his mind, he wrestled with the morality of accepting money from mobsters. Was it wrong to use ill-gotten money for good? Would he be throwing in his lot with a criminal element and regret it later?

He needn't have worried.

While the men listened with patience to his vision for Noble Pictures, their stony expressions never changed. Lunch ended on a cordial note with handshakes all around, but without any offer of investment. Rusty didn't know whether to feel disappointed or relieved.

He said goodbye to Leroy and his friends. On his way to settle the bill with the host, he caught a glimpse of the couple seated in a neighboring booth. He recognized the man as Chet Scarborough, engaged in deep conversation with a blond woman. He was holding her hands across the table and speaking softly to her.

A jolt of jealousy ran through Rusty like a sword. Was it Helen? But no. When the woman turned her head, Rusty saw she was not Helen. But it was almost as bad.

It was young Debbie Fagan.

Helen sat cross-legged on the sofa in her apartment, holding her old dog-eared script for *Under the Flaming Oak* in her lap. Why she'd brought it with her from Illinois, she didn't know, but now she was glad she had. While Chet hadn't yet finished writing the screenplay, she wanted to re-familiarize herself with the story and specifically the role of Susannah.

Since their terrible meeting in Rusty's office, she'd managed to steer clear of Chet so far, but the initial read-through of the screenplay was scheduled for the following week. Chet would be there, and Helen hoped to be able to steel herself to remain polite and professional in his presence.

As she read through the notes and directions she'd penciled in the margins, memories came flooding back of that happy summer in Kerryville. Chet's flattering words about her acting ability. His gray eyes gazing deeply into hers as he complimented her face, her hair, her legs. His gentle touch when he wanted to direct her movements on stage, to have her turn this way or that.

What a ninny she'd been! She tossed the script aside in disgust. Well, he wouldn't get away with it this time. She was on to his tricks.

The door to the apartment opened and Debbie came in.

Helen greeted her. "How was your lunch date?" Debbie had told her she was going to have lunch with someone she'd met at the studio.

"Hellooo!" Debbie waved, then gave a little glassy-eyed wobble.

Helen shot to her feet. "Have you been drinking?"

Debbie held up a finger and thumb and pressed them together. "Jussht a little." She wobbled again and leaned against a chair. "Whassa matter? There's no more Prohibi-Prohip-Prohibisssh-"

"Oh, my goodness. You'd better sit down." Helen guided Debbie to the sofa. "Did anyone see you come in like this? Not only are you underage, but the Studio Club strictly forbids alcohol. You could be tossed out onto the street for getting drunk. What were you thinking?"

"Issh okay."

"It's not okay, Debbie. It's very, very not okay. You didn't ride the trolley like this, did you?"

"N-No. No trolley. My boyfrien' put me in a tassicab. He paid for it an' everything."

"A taxicab!" Fury mixed with concern made Helen's heart pound. "Oh, that's just great. He sounds like a real prince. A guy who takes an underage girl out drinking, then doesn't even make sure she gets home safely. Tell me, what's this new boyfriend's name?"

But by the time she'd paused in her tirade, the only response emanating from Debbie was a gentle snore.

CHAPTER THIRTY-SIX

The next morning, having wormed a confession out of a very nauseated Debbie, Helen stormed into the writers' bungalow and pointed a manicured finger in Chet's face.

"You stay away from Debbie."

Sitting before his typewriter, Chet seemed unfazed. "Good morning to you, too."

"I mean it, Chet. She's just a child."

"She's eighteen," he said in a calm voice. "That's only a few years younger than you were when you and I... " He let his suggestive words dangle in the air.

"Shut up. There is no 'you and I.' There never was."

"Relax. We were merely enjoying each other's company."

"You can do that without giving her any alcohol," Helen said. "Not only is she too young to drink legally, but judging by the state she came home in yesterday, she doesn't know her own limits. Just stay away from her. Pick on somebody your own age, for once."

"Now, Helen," he said. "Do I detect a note of jealousy?"

"Jealousy?" she screeched. "You're crazy if you think that I—" She closed her eyes and tried to collect her wits before she lost it completely. Thankfully, no other writers, especially Rusty, were present to witness her outburst. "No. I'm not jealous. I'm concerned for Debbie's welfare. That's all."

He held up his hands, as if in surrender. "All right, all right. I'll back off. But I have to warn you... she's a pretty persistent little thing."

"You're vile." She drew a deep breath. "Where's Rusty?"

"I believe he went over to see Stanley Cooperman. He was summoned a little while ago."

Rusty stood in Cooperman's office, defenseless against the chief's red-faced rage.

"So, Noble, you don't deny that you're planning to open your own movie studio?"

"No, sir."

"After all I've done for you?"

Rusty swallowed. "You've done a great deal for me, sir. I'm truly grateful."

"And this is how you show your gratitude—by making plans to start a competing studio."

"Not competing, sir. We'd be making very different kinds of movies."

"And who's in on it with you? Who's been helping you plot this treachery?"

"Nobody, sir."

"Smith? Ingersoll?"

"No, sir." Rusty balked at the lie, but he didn't want to get Smitty or Jim in trouble. No sense in all three of them losing their jobs on the same day.

"Get out of my sight, Noble," Cooperman thundered. "I want you gone and your desk cleared out by the end of the day. You're fired."

"Yes, sir."

On shaking legs, Rusty left the office for the final time. Midge mouthed a silent "I'm so sorry" as he passed her desk. If he wasn't mistaken, Rusty saw a single tear slide down her cheek.

"'Bye, Midge."

He'd gotten what he deserved. Cooperman was within his rights to fire him. He knew the rules and he'd broken them.

But how did Cooperman find out about Noble Pictures? Who could have told him?

Cooperman couldn't have known about Jim's or Smitty's involvement, or he would have fired them too. So it couldn't have been one of them who told.

It had to have been Leroy.

Because if it wasn't Leroy who squealed on him, the only possibility left would be Helen.

And he couldn't stomach the thought of that.

Unable to find Rusty, and still furious with Chet, Helen needed to burn off steam before returning home. She walked miles without a particular destination in mind, thinking things through and praying about how she should handle the situation.

One fact kept nagging at her mind. In addition to his pending divorce, Chet had mentioned some trouble in connection with his play at the Goodman. Maybe writing the screenplay of *Under the Flaming Oak* wasn't the only reason he'd abandoned Chicago for Hollywood.

It was only a hunch, but it was worth checking out.

She wasn't far from the Los Angeles Public Library when she had a sudden flash of inspiration. She hurried up the library steps and asked the clerk at the information desk to direct her to the newspaper collection. There she found daily newspapers from major cities all over the world. She sifted through the collection until she found the back issues of the *Chicago Tribune*. Then she found a table in a quiet corner and set the newspapers in a stack.

It didn't take long for her to find what she was looking for. She carried the newspaper to the front desk.

"May newspapers be checked out of the library?" she asked the librarian.

The woman nodded. "Back issues can be, as long as one has a library card."

"How does one get a library card?"

When she left the library a little while later, Helen's purse contained both a library card and a piece of incriminating evidence.

"I should have known better than to trust that shady ex-con," Rusty muttered to himself as he emptied a sturdy carton of typing paper and filled it with the contents of his desk. Personal copies of his screenplays. A framed photo of himself shaking hands with Ronald Colman. A pretty rock he'd picked up in the desert near Tucson. His favorite much-chewed pencil.

For six years he'd poured his heart and soul into Cooperman Studios. Now everything he had to show for his dedication fit into a single carton, with room to spare.

Yesterday he'd been the star racehorse in the writing stable. Today he was just another out-of-work screenwriter.

Good thing he didn't have a wife and family to support.

He was both glad and sorry Smitty and Jim were out of the office. Glad they weren't forced to witness his humiliation as he cleaned out his desk, but sorry not to have the opportunity to say goodbye. Maybe he'd call them later from home, after he'd had time to cool off. Or maybe he wouldn't. Hearing their expressions of sympathy and disbelief would be hard to take.

Riding home on the trolley, balancing the carton on his knees, he sorted through his options. He had some solid writing credentials to his name. Chances were another studio would take him on, but he'd likely have to start at the bottom again and work his way up. And if word got around that Stanley Cooperman had fired him, and why, it could be a black mark on his reputation.

He could try freelancing. But that was too precarious an existence for his liking. He enjoyed eating too much.

Or he could go after his dream. Stop waffling and go for broke on launching Noble Pictures. He might even have his first project soon, if Leroy and his friends came through and inked the deal.

But Leroy had betrayed Rusty's plans to his brother, Stanley—probably. Could Rusty really afford to enter a business deal with a fellow who couldn't be trusted?

On the other hand, could he afford *not* to work with him, if the opportunity arose? He had no other fish on the line.

Furthermore, he'd lost their best acting talent to an attractive offer from the all-powerful Goliath that was Cooperman Studios. What chance did the little guy have, lacking even a slingshot?

As the trolley jerked along the boulevard, Rusty closed his eyes and prayed for guidance on what to do next.

When he got home, he dumped the carton on the sofa and slumped down next to it. There he sat for a seeming eternity, staring into space, thinking. Then he did what he had to do.

He picked up the phone and dialed Leroy Cooperman's number.

"Why'd you go telling your brother about our plans?" he blurted when Leroy answered.

"What are you talking about?" Leroy sounded genuinely shocked. "I didn't say anything to him."

"Well, you must have, because he called me into his office and read me the riot act. I told you he'd fire me if he found out, and he did."

"I'm sorry that happened, Rusty. I really am. But you gotta believe me. I didn't breathe a word."

"Maybe it was Sam or Rocco then."

"Sam and Rocco have never even met Stanley," Leroy said. "They wouldn't know him if they passed him on the street, much less hold a conversation with him."

"Then it had to be you. I thought I could trust you," Rusty barreled on, Leroy's lame protests barely registering in his brain.

"You *can* trust me." Leroy's voice chilled. "What are you saying? You think you can't?"

Rusty released his breath in a huff. "I don't know what to think. All I know is, somebody blabbed to Stanley, and I'm out on the street."

"Maybe that's not such a bad thing," Leroy reasoned. "Maybe it's the kick in the pants you need to get your studio off the ground."

"A studio without any projects," Rusty blurted.

"You've got a project. Our movie, the one we talked about. The fellas and I, we just need a little more time to—"

"A little more time," Rusty shouted, no longer able to hold back his frustration. "It's always 'a little more time' with you people."

"What do you mean, 'you people'?" Leroy's voice dripped ice. "You mean guys like us who've done time? Once a criminal, always a criminal?"

"That's not what I said." Rusty gripped the receiver. "You know what? Forget it. Forget everything. If I can't even trust you to keep our work confidential, we'll never work well together over the long haul."

He slammed down the phone. And slammed the door on his dream.

Later that night, when he couldn't sleep, he sat on his apartment's miniscule balcony, looking out over the twinkling lights of the city, his thoughts churning. What if he couldn't find another job right away? How far would his savings stretch? What if he started his own studio and nobody wanted to work with him?

And the most disturbing thought of all. What if Leroy Cooperman was telling the truth? That he hadn't told Stanley about Noble Pictures, and neither had Sam or Rocco?

If that were true, Rusty had treated him horribly. Said terrible things. Once again, he'd let his fiery temper get the better of him.

Worse, if Leroy was telling the truth, that left just one person who could have been the culprit. Only one other person both knew about Noble Pictures and had access to Stanley Cooperman.

Helen.

The thought was too distressing to contemplate. Helen wouldn't ever betray Rusty's trust. Would she?

He wished he knew for sure.

CHAPTER THIRTY-SEVEN

First thing the next morning, Helen headed for the headquarters building. When she saw Midge wasn't at her desk, she stormed straight into Mr. Cooperman's office.

"What the devil do you think you're doing?" Mr. Cooperman thundered, looking up from his paperwork.

"You need to fire Chet Scarborough."

Mr. Cooperman stood. "What? Why?"

Helen slapped a copy of the *Tribune* on the desk and stabbed her finger at an article. The headline read "Theater Director Resigns Amid Scandal."

Mr. Cooperman took a moment to scan the article. Helen waited, fully expecting him to explode in outrage. Instead, he laughed.

"Is that all?" he said.

Helen put her hands on her hips. "What do you mean, 'is that all?'"

"I mean, these things happen. It's nothing to get upset about."

"How can you say that, Mr. Cooperman? It says it right there. *Scandal.* Involving *a woman not his wife.*"

"I understand Mr. and Mrs. Scarborough are divorcing," Cooperman said mildly. "It wouldn't be unusual for her to try to hunt up some scandal in an attempt to sway the judge to her side." He walked around the desk, placed a soothing hand on Helen's shoulder and gently guided her toward the door. "It doesn't sound like any crime was committed. No charges were filed."

Helen was not soothed, and she refused to be guided. She stood her ground.

"Do you really want a man like that working here at Cooperman Studios?"

Mr. Cooperman sighed. "If I hired only morally upright people in this business, I'd have no employees left."

"You need to give the project back to Rusty Noble," she insisted. "He's the man for the job."

"Mr. Noble no longer works here."

"What?"

"I found out about his little scheme to start his own studio."

"But... who told you?"

He folded his arms. "So you're in on it too, eh?"

She lifted her chin. "Well, what if I am?"

"I like you, Miss Corrigan. And I'm not in the mood to fire two employees in one day. I want to keep you on. I'll give you one last chance to sign that contract."

"I won't do it."

"That's not the way the world works, Miss Corrigan."

"Well, it's the way my world works." She reached into her purse for the contract and tore it in half. "I won't be working for you anymore," she told him bluntly. "I work for Noble Pictures now."

Unfortunately, working for Noble Pictures turned out not to be as easy as she hoped.

"I'd love to give you work, Helen," Rusty said when she called him at home to commiserate over his firing and tell him what she'd done. "But the studio has no funding. We can't afford paper and ink, much less acting talent." His voice sounded oddly distant. Distracted.

"But I can get my job at Bullock's back," she said, trying to inject some cheer into the conversation. "I can manage without a studio salary for a while."

"I wish it were that simple," he lamented. "We were very close to getting our first picture, but it turns out, that's how I lost my job."

"What happened, exactly?" She only knew a few sketchy details surrounding his firing.

"You remember I was talking to Leroy Cooperman about doing a picture."

"Yes, but what kind of picture is it?"

"I don't know exactly, but it would have been Noble Pictures' first project. It could have lifted our sails, gotten us out of port. But before we could ink the deal, Leroy must have blabbed our plans to Stanley, because the next thing I knew, I was being shown the door."

"Oh, Rusty," she cried in dismay. "Are you sure it was Leroy who told?"

"It wasn't Jim or Smitty." He paused. "And it wasn't you."

It was that hesitation that bothered her.

"Of course it wasn't me." Her tone came out more defensive than she'd intended. "Anyway, I'm so sorry that happened."

"Yeah, well, easy come, easy go."

Even over the phone she could tell he was trying to be brave. Probably for her sake. "Would you like to get together for dinner? Maybe talk about it?"

"Not tonight. I have some thinking to do. And some praying."

"All right. I'm here if you need me."

As she hung up the phone, her heart was breaking right along with his.

CHAPTER THIRTY-EIGHT

Freed from the shackles of any commitment to work with Cooperman Studios, and with Noble Pictures still stuck at the castle-in-the-sky stage with no promise of coming to fruition anytime soon, Helen launched her freelance acting career with optimism. But a few weeks later, Phil Fairmont had still not been able to get her a single appointment with a studio. Not even one of the smaller, less prestigious ones.

Twice he'd sent over scripts for her to review, and she perused them, but didn't have to read further than a few pages to know she wouldn't want her name associated with the projects, the kind of low-quality material she'd turned down in the past. In one, she'd play the victim of a mad fiend and her lines would consist mainly of screaming in what was sure to be a skimpy nightgown. In the other, she'd play an evil, seductive sorceress. Neither part would do anything to further her goal of morally uplifting cinema.

After multiple failed attempts, she got through to Phil on the telephone.

"Have you even read these scripts you've sent me? They're not worth the paper they're printed on. You know I won't portray those kinds of characters."

He didn't apologize. In fact, he didn't even sound particularly concerned on her behalf. "Something better is bound to turn up, sooner or later."

She knew he resented her decision to turn down Cooperman's offer, especially in such a dramatic fashion. She could hardly blame him. In losing her temper, she'd also lost not only her own income, but Phil's generous commission as well.

"But there must be something else, isn't there?" She hated the pleading note of desperation that weaseled its way into her voice.

Silence hung heavy before Phil spoke. "I'm sorry, Helen. Cooperman is a powerful man in the industry, as you well know. He's spreading the word around town that you're difficult to work with. We just have to be patient."

Easy for him to say. It was like being back at Kerryville High, waiting for the phone to ring, for some boy to invite her to a dance. To be chosen.

"Listen, I was just going into a meeting," Phil said. "Can I call you back?"

But she knew he wouldn't. She knew a brush-off when she heard one.

She tried praying, but felt no comfort or peace. She waited for her usual can-do spirit to return, to give her the strength to pick herself up and start again. That's what Hollywood was all about, after all—a place of reinvention, of second chances. There must be somebody, somewhere, willing to give her a chance.

But her can-do spirit had disappeared, crushed under the weight of disappointment and regret.

A few nights later, Rusty sat across the table from Helen in a Chinese restaurant, toying with his chopsticks. He had little appetite. Yet Helen had insisted they go out for the evening. Her treat.

"I can't let you pay for dinner," he'd protested.

"Why not? I'm back working at Bullock's, so I can afford chop suey. Besides, we could both do with some cheering up."

The cheering-up portion of the evening was lacking. Helen made a valiant effort to keep a conversation going. Rusty had given up.

Finally she blurted in apparent frustration, "Come on, Rusty. Tell me what's going on with you? What's on your mind?"

He looked up from his uneaten egg roll. "What do you mean?"

"You've been acting awfully strange for the last few days. Getting fired was a blow, but it's not the end of the world. You're a brilliant writer. You'll get through this and likely end up with something even better."

"It's not the getting fired that's bothering me," he said. "I mean, sure, that's part of it. But the betrayal bothers me more."

"You mean the fact that Leroy spilled the beans? Maybe he didn't do it on purpose."

"Or maybe it wasn't him. He swears it wasn't."

"Then who?"

Rusty looked at her, miserable. Her curious expression shifted to one of disbelief, then outrage.

"Me?" She pointed to her chest. "You think *I* told Mr. Cooperman?"

"No. I'm sure you didn't tell Cooperman." He chose his words carefully. "But maybe you let it slip to someone else. Accidentally, of course. And word somehow got back to him." He needed to know. "Did you say anything about it to Flo or Debbie?"

Her eyes flashed. "Of course not."

"Because it can't have been *nobody*. Obviously somebody said something to somebody."

Her chopsticks clattered to the table. "I promised I'd keep it a secret, and I have."

"Of course. But even if you hadn't..." He groped for words. "I mean, I'm not saying you did it on purpose."

"But you are saying I did it." Frost tinged her words.

"Not necessarily. But, well, *somebody* did." Rusty deeply regretted bringing it up. But she'd asked what was bothering him, and she deserved an honest answer. "It could have been Leroy. But I just have this... this feeling that it wasn't."

"But you do have a feeling that it was me."

"I didn't say that."

"You didn't have to." She picked up her purse and stood, her face flushed, her eyes glistening. "If that's what you think of me, Rusty Noble, then perhaps it's best we part ways here and now."

She turned and began walking away.

"Don't go," Rusty called after her. "Please, can't we discuss this?"

She stopped, turned, and walked toward him. Hope flickered in his heart. She wasn't giving up on him. On them.

She opened her purse, pulled out a few bills, and let them flutter to the table. "I told you dinner was on me," she said, "And I always keep my promises." With that, she turned and walked away. For real this time.

Rusty fought the urge to run after her. What good would it do? She was mad as fire at him. With good reason.

He should be mad at her, too, if indeed she had betrayed his trust.

But what if she hadn't? He just wanted to know for certain. Even if she had, he'd forgive her. Let bygones be bygones.

That was the thing he'd most wanted to tell her. To reassure her of his love for her, no matter what she'd done or not done. But they'd not gotten that far.

And now he'd gone and ruined everything.

Helen sat on the sofa in her darkened apartment, drenching one handkerchief after another with her tears. Thankfully, Debbie was out for the evening. Probably in the dubious company of that no-good character, Chet Scarborough. But there was nothing Helen could do about that. She was Debbie's friend and coworker, not her guardian. All she could do was pray about the situation.

In the meantime, she had her own problems to deal with. Her misery over Rusty's firing was intensified tenfold by his accusation that she'd spilled the beans about Noble Pictures. She wracked her brain to think of some occasion when she might have inadvertently said the wrong thing to the wrong person, but could think of nothing.

It didn't matter. Nothing mattered anymore.

She'd ruined her chances for a career at Cooperman Studios and seemingly every other studio in town, including Noble Pictures.

She'd burned a bridge with her agent.

And now she'd lost Rusty. If he thought he couldn't trust her, if he questioned her integrity, then they had no business working together, much less anything else.

Besides, hadn't he said he wanted no encumbrances to hold him back? Perhaps his accusation was his way of getting rid of an encumbrance. Her.

Her dream of making movies filled with truth, beauty, and goodness, of having a positive impact on the world of cinema, lay in tatters all around her.

Along with her dream of a future with Rusty.

Maybe it was time to admit defeat, call it quits, and go home.

CHAPTER THIRTY-NINE

Early on a Monday morning, in the old, dusty warehouse that served as Noble Pictures' headquarters, Rusty labored alone at a rickety table, punching numbers into an adding machine and trying not to tear his hair out at the results. He didn't see how he was going to build the studio into a viable business. And it didn't help his concentration that he couldn't get Helen off his mind. How many times had he picked up the phone at home, intending to call her? The same number of times he'd chickened out, unsure of what he'd say, only that he wanted to start again, to be given another chance to make things right.

The newly installed telephone rang, and as soon as Rusty remembered where it plugged into the wall, he dug it out from a pile of papers and answered it.

"Noble Pictures. Zachary Noble speaking."

"Hi, Rusty. Smitty here. Say, I'm over here with the Monday morning prayer group. Say hello, everybody."

A general cacophony ensued as a chorus of voices greeted Rusty.

He laughed in spite of his dour mood. "That's great. Thanks, buddy. Tell everyone hello back."

"The thing is, we realized you haven't been back to prayer group. And it took us a while, but we figured out it's because you can't get back onto Cooperman property. And neither can Helen."

"That's right," Rusty said. "I had to forfeit my entry badge when I got fired. And I suppose Helen did, too, when she quit."

"So we figure, what's the big deal about meeting at Cooperman? We can meet anywhere, right? So we're wondering if we can start meeting at Noble Pictures instead. Since it's just a short walk down the street from Cooperman. And there's a doughnut shop right next door."

"Here?" Rusty glanced around in dismay. "Gosh, it's in awful shape."

"I know. I helped you find the place, remember? We don't mind a little mess. Do we, gang?"

In the background, the crowd shouted "No!"

"Okay then," Rusty said, bemused. "Feel free to come on over."

He hung up the phone. A rush of enthusiasm energized him.

A little while later, nine people trooped through the rickety doorway of Noble Pictures, doughnuts in hand. The single-story building, a former produce warehouse, had seen better days, but it was sturdy and had "good bones," the rental agent had said. Rusty couldn't help but feel a puff of pride as he gave his friends the grand tour.

"This will be the soundstage," he explained as they looked around the large, high-ceilinged space that took up the majority of the building. Three smaller rooms toward the back would eventually house props and costumes, a construction workshop, a writers' room, and an office for Rusty.

After the tour, everyone returned to the main space, where Rusty had set several folding chairs in a circle, with a pot of coffee percolating nearby.

"I really appreciate you all coming here," he said after they'd taken their seats. "We really need prayer. The studio is struggling to get off the ground. We have a couple of projects in the wings, but need help. And financing."

After all the prayer requests had been collected, they bowed their heads and asked for God's sanctification of this place. Rusty could scarcely hold back the tears. The only thing better would be if Helen had come. The prayer group had been her idea, after all. But maybe it was better for all concerned if she stayed away for now. Just for a while. Just until he got used to the idea that they were no longer a couple. Maybe no longer even friends.

When they finished praying, the group got up to leave.

"Thanks for coming," Rusty said. "See you again next Monday?"

"Actually, we'll see you tonight." Simon Jarrow's eyes twinkled.

"Why? What's tonight?" Rusty's mind launched a frantic search for the commitment he must have forgotten in the chaos of starting up Noble Pictures.

"We all talked it over, see, and we're going to take turns coming here to help you after work and on weekends," Smitty said. "We'll help you clean up, paint, plaster... whatever you need us to do."

Rusty was deeply touched. "Gosh, everyone. You'd really do that for me?"

Simon clapped him on the shoulder. "We're doing it for us. We all want to work for Noble Pictures. Every one of us. We're hoping that if we put in sweat equity now, you'll give us jobs later, as you get work."

"I'd hire you all today, if I could," Rusty said. "But I don't have the funding and I don't have the work."

"You will," Simon assured him.

"We don't know that for sure," Rusty said.

"Sure, we do. We just asked the Lord, didn't we?" Simon winked at Rusty. "Have a little faith."

The group trooped out. Soon it was just Jim, Smitty and Rusty sitting on the folding chairs.

"Has anyone heard from Helen?" Rusty asked, trying to sound casual.

"She's had a rough go of it," Jim said. "After she gave Cooperman the heave-ho over refusing to get rid of Chet, she started getting blackballed around Hollywood, and her agent dropped her."

"I knew about Cooperman," Rusty said. "She told me about that. But I didn't know the other stuff."

"We tried to encourage her to come with us today, but she seemed reluctant. What happened?" Smitty asked. "I thought you two were close."

Rusty looked down at the dusty floor. "We were. But then I guess I got pretty sore, thinking that she blabbed about Noble Pictures, and Cooperman found out and fired me before I was ready to go."

"What?" Jim looked at him.

"I mean, maybe it wasn't her," Rusty said quickly. "It could have been Leroy. And even if it was Helen, I know she didn't mean to. She's not the kind of person to do that sort of thing on purpose. But somebody told somebody who told somebody, and it got back to Cooperman. I know it wasn't either of you, and Leroy and

Helen were the only other people who knew about it. So it's gotta be one of them."

Jim and Smitty exchanged a glance.

"Uh, Rusty..." Jim began.

"What?"

"Helen didn't tell anyone, and neither did Leroy. Chet Scarborough did."

Rusty's mind whirled. "Chet? But that doesn't make any sense. I barely know Chet. Why would I confide in him about our plans?"

"You didn't need to," Smitty said. "He overheard you talking to the investors at the Trocadero."

Rusty recalled seeing Chet and Debbie at the restaurant, and a light began to dawn in his head. "How do you know that, though? You weren't there."

"Later Chet was asking Smitty and me questions about it," Jim said. "We played dumb, of course. But he must have taken the information to Cooperman anyway. He's always trying to get in the chief's good graces, hoping to be kept on permanently."

"In any case," Smitty said, "it wasn't Leroy, and it sure as heck wasn't Helen."

Rusty's stomach roiled. He owed Leroy a huge apology. And Helen. How could he have accused her?

He had to try to call her and explain. But he wouldn't blame her if she never wanted to speak to him again.

In spite of a lack of funding, Noble Pictures soon became a buzzing hive of activity. Spurred by Rusty's dedication, both Jim and Smitty quit their jobs at Cooperman and threw their lot in with Rusty, the three of them laboring full-time on the new business.

Rusty was toiling away at an ad to place in *Variety* when Smitty's head appeared in the doorway.

"Mr. Cooperman's here to see you."

Mr. Cooperman? Rusty sat up straight. Maybe he'd come to apologize? Try to hire Rusty back? Well, just let him try.

"Send him in, I guess."

But it wasn't Stanley Cooperman who walked through the door. It was Leroy.

"Hope I'm not bothering you," he said.

"Not at all, Leroy. Come on in." Rusty found him a chair that wasn't covered in papers and boxes. "In fact, I've been wanting to speak to you. I owe you a big apology for accusing you of telling Stanley about our studio. I found out who the culprit was, and I'm deeply sorry for accusing you."

"Thank you for that, Rusty. I knew you were a man of integrity. That's why I've come here. To talk about our project."

"We still have a project?" Rusty'd thought that possibility had ended with their argument.

"The boys and I talked it over, and we decided that, in spite of everything, you're the right man to make our movie. All our movies."

Rusty thought he'd misheard. Movies, plural? "I'm sorry. What?"

"My partners and I. We want to invest in your studio. So you can make the kinds of movies that matter."

"I'm—I'm ecstatic. But I don't understand. Why are you so interested?"

"We've got a special project for you."

Here it comes, thought Rusty. *The other shoe's about to drop.*

Much as he wanted, needed, pined away for financing, he was prepared to turn Leroy down politely but firmly if asked to do something illegal.

"As you know, I've recently been released from prison. I'm sure that's common knowledge around the studio."

Rusty acknowledged that yes, he may have heard something about that.

"So did Sam and Rocco. We're all trying to go straight."

"I see," Rusty said cautiously. Wanting to go straight was a good sign.

"We've been watching you, Rusty. You and Helen and your friends in that there prayer group. You have the kind of good, wholesome values that we want to instill in kids that are growing up today, so they don't make the same mistakes we did."

"You knew about the prayer group?"

"Like I said, we've been watching. Anyway, we have a vision for a screenplay aimed at a teenage and young adult audience, to warn them of the dangers of narcotics abuse and falling in with the wrong crowd. That's what happened to me, and it's what happened to Sam and Rocco, and we all ended up doing time in prison for it. If I hadn't gotten involved with drinking and drugs, I wouldn't have landed in the slammer."

A little flame of excitement ignited in Rusty's gut. This type of picture, one that promoted good values, especially for young people, was exactly the sort of project he imagined producing at Noble Pictures.

"I considered making it a documentary, but I thought it might have a stronger impact on young people if it were told in the form of a story. That's where you come in. I'm not good at writing stories, but I hear you're the best."

"I don't know about the best, but—"

"So are you interested or not?"

"It sounds like a great project," Rusty said. "But why not go to Mr. Cooperman with it? Why do you feel you need to take it outside the studio?"

Leroy paused as if choosing his words. "My brother has been gracious enough to give me work at the studio, but he's balking at letting me create this film. He says it lacks commercial potential. And maybe he's right." Leroy shrugged. "But I still want to produce it. The idea's been gnawing at me and won't let go. I'm looking for people willing to work on the project. And I want one of those people to be you."

Rusty's heart went out to the man, who'd made serious mistakes and had served his time. He felt sorry he'd gossiped about him with Midge, and accused him of betraying his trust.

"It's a very important message to put out to teenagers," Rusty acknowledged. "I'd love to help. Unfortunately we don't have the budget."

Leroy looked perplexed. "No budget? Didn't Sam get in touch with you?"

"No. I haven't heard from Sam or Rocco since the day we had lunch."

Leroy shook his head. "Man. If you want something done right, you gotta do it yourself." He looked Rusty square in the eye. "He was supposed to tell you that we're committed to investing in Noble Pictures." He named a figure that made Rusty's eyes water.

Rusty was speechless for a moment. Then he vowed, "I'll do my best to help you."

They talked some more about the particulars, then Leroy stood to leave. Rusty shook his hand.

"I can't thank you enough, Leroy. And one more thing."

"Yeah?"

"The prayer group is meeting here now, every Monday morning. You're welcome to join us. You and your friends."

Leroy said he would. After he'd gone, Rusty picked up the phone, dying to share his good news with Helen. He gave her number to the operator.

"Hey, Helen," he said when she answered. "This is Rusty calling. Say, I just wanted to tell you that... "

"Oh, Rusty!" she wailed. "Come quickly. Meet me at Hollywood Presbyterian Hospital. Something's happened to Debbie."

CHAPTER FORTY

Rusty rushed into the hospital and found Helen sitting alone in a waiting room. She rose when she saw him, and he put his arms around her and pulled her close. She melted against him.

"Oh, Rusty. It's so awful."

"What happened?"

"The doctor says it's alcohol poisoning," Helen said. "Apparently she'd gone to a party with Chet and got so drunk she passed out and fell down a flight of stairs. Someone called an ambulance."

"Thank God," Rusty breathed. "Not that she got alcohol poisoning, but that she didn't—you know." He shifted the subject. "How did you find out? Did Chet call you?"

"Nobody's seen Chet," she said. "One of the party guests happened to have worked as an extra on *Serenade*. He knows Debbie and knew she'd moved in with me and so he called me."

"Did the doctor give a prognosis?"

Helen dabbed at her eyes with a white handkerchief. "He said she'll pull through. But she has a long road of recovery ahead of her. One of her ankles broke in the fall, and she's pretty bruised and banged up. But it's her spirit—" She choked a little on the words. "It's her spirit that needs healing the most."

Rusty guided her to a chair. "Let's pray right now." They put their heads together, and Rusty prayed out loud for Debbie. When he'd finished and Helen lifted her head, her eyes were glistening, but she looked less distressed.

"Thank you."

Rusty continued to hold her hands. "Smitty and Jim told me that it was Chet who blabbed to Cooperman. Not Leroy, and certainly not you." He related the circumstances. "I'm so sorry I even thought of blaming you, Helen."

She squeezed his hand. "That's all right. You couldn't have known. I would have drawn the same conclusion, given the evidence."

"Still, I'm sorry I doubted you. That was wrong of me."

"Let's not talk about it anymore," she said. "Tell me what you've been up to at Noble Pictures."

"I have some good news on that front," Rusty said. "But maybe this isn't the time."

"Please tell me," Helen begged. "I could use all the good news I can get right now."

He told her about his conversation with Leroy Cooperman and his friends, and about their investment in the studio.

"Oh, Rusty. That's wonderful! I'm thrilled for you."

"For *us*," he blurted. "Don't you see? Now we can make the movies we've always wanted to make, and you'll have the starring role, just like we'd dreamed of."

Helen looked away. "You'll have to make it without me, I'm afraid."

Rusty's heart sank. "What do you mean?"

Her gaze connected with his. "I've decided to go back to Kerryville. This life isn't for me."

He couldn't believe what he was hearing. "But I need you here."

She turned to him. "Need me for what, Rusty? To act in your pictures? To help write your scripts?" She looked down at her hands folded in her lap. "I need something else. Something more solid, more tangible. I want a home. A family. With you. But you can't give me that. Can you?"

He sat silent, dumbfounded. Home? Family? He could scarcely afford to support himself, much less a family. Every spare penny and then some went into Noble Pictures. Maybe in a few years... but who knew? He needed time. And yet, here she was, right in front of him. The woman he'd prayed for, the kind he never thought he'd meet in Hollywood. How could he let her slip away?

He tried to articulate his thoughts, but they wouldn't obey. Helpless, he watched as they changed shape and slipped from his grasp like demented sea creatures escaping capture.

His silence extended long enough that she nodded sadly and turned away, taking it for an answer.

CHAPTER FORTY-ONE

R usty tried to talk her out of leaving. He used every argument he could think of to get her to stay and give Tinseltown—and him—another chance. But as long as Chet Scarborough was in Hollywood, she would not stay. *This town isn't big enough for the both of us*, she might have said if she'd been a character in one of Rusty's Westerns. But she wasn't.

She was the light of his life.

He stayed at the hospital with her until the doctor declared Debbie out of danger, then he drove her home. He caught a few hours' sleep, then put in a full day at Noble Pictures. His heart wasn't in it, though. So much of the joy of starting his own studio depended on her.

When Rusty arrived back at his apartment, he was starving. But the stack of scripts to be reviewed loomed large, and going out to dinner would take too much time. So he padded around, making himself a fried bologna sandwich so he could eat supper with one hand while holding a script in the other.

He'd just set the frying pan on the stove when the telephone jangled. "Get dressed," Smitty told him when he answered. "St. Ives's people are willing to meet with us, but it has to be tonight 'cause he's leaving for New York in the morning. At the Brown Derby in an hour."

Energized with hope and gusto, Rusty turned off the burner under the frying pan and jumped into the shower. He had just emerged, vigorously toweling his hair, when the phone rang again.

As he crossed the room wrapped only in a towel, he sent up a prayer that it wouldn't be Smitty calling the meeting off.

He lifted the receiver. "Yes?"

"Sorry to bother you, Mr. Noble," the doorman said. "Miss Corrigan is in the lobby. Shall I send her up?"

Rusty checked his watch and almost instructed the doorman to tell her to come see him at the studio in the morning, but something nagged at him. Helen never just turned up out of the blue. She might have something urgent to tell him that couldn't wait until morning. He didn't want to just turn her away.

"Let her come up, by all means," he told the doorman, then hurried to the bedroom to throw on some clothes. He wished he'd chosen something other than fried bologna for his sandwich, as the smell lingered in the warm air.

Helen entered the apartment carrying a large, beautifully wrapped package in her hands. She handed it to Rusty.

"What's this? It's not my birthday," Rusty quipped, staring at the silky bow on top.

"I know. It's just a little something. Something silly. Open it later."

Rusty invited her in. "I've only got a few minutes. Smitty managed to score a meeting with St. Ives's people."

"He did? That's great news. You've been wanting that meeting for a long time." She sounded genuinely happy for him. He remembered his manners. "I'm afraid I don't have time to sit and eat, but if you're hungry, there's bologna. I could make you a sandwich real quick."

"Just a glass of water, thanks. I'm parched."

"Have a seat." Rusty went into the kitchen, set the gift on the table, and filled two glasses at the tap. When he returned, she was still standing. He realized that instead of taking the proffered seat, she'd retrieved a suitcase that now sat at her feet.

"You were serious about leaving." He handed her a glass and she took a long sip of the cool beverage.

"Yes. I'm going home." Her voice cracked a little. "Home to Kerryville." She took another long sip, as though she'd been thirsty for a very long time.

A rock dropped in his stomach. "For a visit to the folks?" He hoped she'd say yes, that she'd be returning to L. A. in a week or two and they could pick up where they'd left off.

But to his dismay, she shook her head. "For good. That's where I belong."

"You can't go," he said, setting his glass on an end table.

She looked surprised. "Of course I can. Cooperman doesn't own me anymore. Hollywood holds too much heartache, too much pressure to compromise. I need to face the fact that Kerryville is where I belong. Where I've always belonged."

He felt a rising sense of panic, but fought to conceal it. "What happened to all that stuff you told me about your childhood, about never feeling like you fit in back there?"

"I was a kid then. I'm older now, and I have a different perspective. Anyway, I just came to say a final good-bye."

He couldn't let things end like this. He groped for words. He pointed to her suitcase. "That all you got? Or is your other luggage waiting at the station?"

"This is all I have. You know me. I always travel light."

"But what about all your gowns? All those pretty dresses and things?"

"Those belong to Cooperman Studios. Not to me." She swallowed. "They were never really mine. None of it was. It was all just make-believe."

"I see." Had her feelings for Rusty been make-believe too?

Neither of them spoke for a long moment. Then Rusty said, "Well, then. Best of luck to you. You'll be missed." Not *I miss you*. Not *Don't go*. Words he was aching to say. But the words wouldn't form, crumbling to dust somewhere between his heart and his mouth.

She looked at him for a long moment, her eyes round as full moons. Had she expected him to protest? Well, he wouldn't. Wouldn't give her the satisfaction. If she wanted to leave, then it was best that she leave. In his experience no one ever stayed around for long. He was a fool for imagining that she would, that his love would be enough to hold her. A fool.

"Thank you for the drink," she said, her tone as cool as if he were a waiter in a restaurant. "I should be going if I'm going to catch my train."

"Yes, I suppose you should." He accepted the glass from her hand.

She took a step toward him and gave him a sisterly peck on the cheek. The familiar scent of lilacs wafted from her hair. He felt frozen, as though if he made one tiny move, he might shatter to pieces. She kept her head close to his for an extra beat, as if waiting for something. But he'd used up all his words. That night in the hospital waiting room, he'd told her all the reasons she should stay. He could think of nothing more to add to what he'd already said, nothing more to do, that would make her change her mind.

She backed away and picked up the suitcase. "I'll always remember you, Rusty. Thanks for everything." Her eyes grew bright with a watery sheen. "Thank you for believing in me. I'm sorry I let you down."

His heart lurched. "You didn't let me down, kid. I let myself down."

He watched her go, a strange mix of regret and resignation roiling in his middle. That's what happened when you let a woman get hold of your heart.

After she'd gone, he checked his watch. Time to leave for the Brown Derby. He stared at the closed door for a moment, then returned to the kitchen. As he put the glasses in the sink, he noticed hers bore a trace of her rose-colored lipstick. For one insane moment, he thought of keeping the glass forever unwashed, a silent testament to the lips that had once touched his. Then a wave of anger washed over him. Furious with himself, with her, he took her glass and smashed it in the sink.

Immediately he felt foolish. *A lot of good that did.* He'd have to clean up the pieces later, after his meeting with St. Ives.

As he turned, something bright and shiny caught his peripheral vision. The cheerfully wrapped package Helen had given him still sat on the table, next to the tall stack of unread scripts. He sighed. In his current mood and rush to leave for the meeting, he was tempted to ignore it, but curiosity propelled him toward the table. What sort of thing would she have left him as a parting gift? A cake? A box of macaroons? A coconut cream pie to remember him by?

He untied the ribbon and ripped away the colorful paper. His breath caught in his throat.

It was a box of Lincoln Logs.

He stared at it for a moment. Then he noticed a small white envelope taped to the wrapping paper. He picked it up and read it. It contained two lines.

Now you have what you've always wanted.

Build your dreams.

He felt for a moment as if all the air was sucked out of the room. The only dream he wanted was wrapped up in her. He'd never have what he'd always wanted. Not if he didn't have her.

He dropped the box on the table, found his shoes, grabbed his hat from the peg by the door, and raced downstairs, not waiting for the elevator. The Brown Derby and St. Ives's people would have to wait. Smitty would be furious with him, but it couldn't be helped.

As he hurtled through the lobby, the doorman lifted his receiver. "Call a cab for you, Mr. Noble?"

"No time, Herb. Thanks."

He hurried to the curb and flagged down a cab himself. He climbed in the back seat. "Central Station, please. And step on it."

Helen sat in her seat on the train and gazed out the window at the platform, waiting for the train to leave the station. Her heart hitched at the memory of her arrival in Los Angeles. Had it only been a couple of years ago? It felt like forever. Her mind sifted through memories of the kindness of Henrietta Mears, of life in front of the cameras, of her own youthful optimism, of friends like Flo and Debbie. And of Rusty. Always of Rusty.

She hoped he liked the present she'd given him. Lincoln Logs were so versatile. They could be used to build a fortress, like he wanted. Or a home, like she wanted. But apparently not both.

She had tried. They both had. But they wanted different things. He wanted success, Hollywood style. And she, having tasted that kind of success, wanted something more. Something he was unable or unwilling to give. A home. A family. Roots.

A sudden banging on her window startled her out of her reverie. To her shock, there on the platform stood Rusty.

"Don't go," he shouted through the glass. Hurriedly she lowered the pane. "Please don't go. I can't live without you."

"Rusty, stop making a scene," she hissed. "I want to go home. Hollywood isn't home."

"All aboard," called the conductor.

"Of course it is. You're made for Hollywood. You're made to be with me."

The engine puffed. The bell clanged.

"Helen, please! I love you. You're my best friend in the whole world. We'll make it work."

She hesitated. Then she grabbed her purse and her suitcase off the rack and stumbled toward the exit. Over the conductor's protests, she jumped off the train just moments before it began to move, landing in Rusty's arms. They clung to each other for a long moment as the train began its slow chug out of the station.

"Welcome home," he said, his voice husky against her hair.

"Will you just kiss me already?"

He lifted her face, lowered his head, and gave her a kiss that left no doubt in her mind that he meant it.

When she'd caught her breath, together they turned toward the station, arm in arm. He hoisted her lone suitcase.

"This all you got?"

She beamed up at him. "That's all I need, now that I have you."

CHAPTER FORTY-TWO

"*Stormy River Serenade* is a masterpiece, and Helen Corrigan in the role of Virginia is box office gold!"

At the moment when Helen read these glowing words of praise in the morning newspaper, she was seated on a hot, crowded bus on her way to work. Once so important, they meant little to her now. She had other fish to fry.

In a crazy twist, she'd recently received word that Cynthia Starling had returned to the Cooperman fold and been given the role of Susannah in *Under the Flaming Oak*. Knowing that Cynthia would appear in the role that originally had been hers stung Helen's heart, but only momentarily. As much as she loved that play, it was too saturated with unpleasant memories, too soured by its close association with all things Chet. In some ways, when she thought about that long, hot summer at the Orpheum, it seemed as if it had happened to someone else, someone she'd known long ago and had lost touch with along the way.

The bus screeched to a halt at her stop. She stepped off, then tripped lightly up the stairs of Noble Pictures. Rusty, Smitty, and Jim were already there, hard at work, getting ready for the first day of filming *A Vicious Circle*, the anti-narcotics screenplay Rusty had written on behalf of Leroy Cooperman. It was Noble Pictures' very first film. The lead character, a high school girl named Vivian, would be played by Debbie Fagan, who'd lost her contract with Cooperman Studios for showing up to work intoxicated. As a condition of her employment at Noble Pictures, she had joined a rehabilitation program, paid for by Leroy Cooperman. She'd be joining the rest of them as soon as her daily meeting with the program had adjourned.

"We should have named it the Studio of Second Chances," Jim remarked. "It seems like everyone on Noble Pictures' payroll gets a fresh start."

"Noble Pictures is like a family," Helen told him. "Everyone on the set is on the same page. We have the same values. We know what we're trying to accomplish, and we're invested in the outcome."

"People say careers and marriage don't mix here in Hollywood," Rusty added. "Yet several couples working in the industry have managed it. We think we'll be among those rare few who succeed."

He grinned at Helen. She grinned back.

"Ready?"

"Ready."

She took her position. He lifted the clapperboard and let it fall with a snap.

"The Vicious Circle, Scene One, Take One."

EPILOGUE

Seated at the dinner table in the Corrigan house in Kerryville amid rollicking laughter from her family ringed around it, Helen glowed with the satisfaction of being surrounded by everyone she loved.

Everyone, all in one place. It was a wonder to behold.

And in less than one week, she and Rusty would be married at the Kerryville church where she'd grown up. They'd thought of having a sophisticated Hollywood wedding, but Helen wanted to be married here in Kerryville before she moved back to California for good.

Rusty set down his coffee cup with a satisfied *thunk*. "And that, my friends, is when I first knew Helen was the girl for me," he declared, drawing to a close his mildly embellished account of the day he and Helen met.

Helen's nephew Bobby, sitting on Rusty's knee, laughed along with everyone else, even though he was too young to understand what was so funny. From a nearby booster seat, Barbara concentrated on finishing her apple pie, at least some of which made it into her mouth.

"That's not exactly how I remember it," Helen chimed in, giving Rusty's shoulder a playful nudge. "As I recall, you didn't know I was 'the girl for you' until quite some time later. And I definitely didn't know that you were the fellow for me. I thought you were a lunatic, yelling at me on a public conveyance that way."

Rusty shrugged and took Helen's hand in his. "Well, it *seems* as if I've loved you from the very moment we first met."

"And that's what matters." Marjorie wiped her eyes with a napkin. "Mercy. I haven't laughed that hard in a long time." She stood and began clearing plates from the table. "We'd better get a move-on if we're going to get to the movie on time."

"They wouldn't dare start without us," Charlie said.

With a great clattering of dishes and scraping of chairs, the family pushed themselves away from the table and scattered in search of coats, hats, and boots. Helen and Dot stacked the dishes on the counter while Marjorie filled the sink with hot water.

"We'll tackle these later," she said. "I'll just let them soak for now." She called to Peter, "Do you think we should take the car? It's cold out."

"Won't all fit." He pulled his cap over his ears. "Besides, it's a short walk, and the snow's stopped. We'll give the walk a quick shovel before we head out. Come on, fellas." Charlie and Rusty followed him out the back door. After they'd gone, Dot turned to Helen, her dark eyes shimmering.

"Rusty is positively the bee's knees," she gushed. "Charlie and I are so glad you brought him home to meet all of us."

"I'm glad, too," Marjorie added. "I think you two are perfect together, and so does Peter. But aren't his own family missing him? After all, it's Christmas."

Helen basked in the glow of their praise. "We're his family now. All of us."

After they'd donned their coats and Dot and Helen had bundled the twins into snowsuits and boots, everyone headed out the door. The whole family trouped en masse toward Main Street, chattering and laughing under the clear, starry sky.

The white chaser bulbs of the Orpheum's marquee cast a brilliant glow over Main Street. On the sign the words "Welcome Home, Helen C." sat directly below the title of the picture, *Stormy River Serenade*.

Excitement thrummed in Helen's belly. Even though she and Rusty had parted ways with Cooperman Studios, they'd been invited, along with the rest of the cast and crew, to attend the premiere. But they'd chosen not to go. Their status as defectors from the Cooperman fiefdom might have made such an event awkward for both of them. And for Helen, even the experience of a Hollywood premiere paled in comparison to watching the movie in the company of her own dear family. Even though *Stormy River Serenade* was no longer a brand-new release, whispers of a potential Academy Award nomination had stirred fresh interest in it. And because of the glacial pace at which new movies reached Kerryville, the timing was perfect.

When they reached the ticket window, Peter and Charlie reached into their coats to pull out their wallets, but Gloria Farnham, the gray-haired clerk seated inside the booth, grinned and waved them away.

"Your tickets have already been paid for."

Peter's eyebrows rose. "For all of us?"

Gloria nodded. "All of you." She pointed at Rusty. "That young fellow over there came by earlier and bought up a whole row. Row E is all yours."

Everyone turned and looked at Rusty's flushed face.

"You didn't have to do that, Rusty," Marjorie chided. "You're supposed to be our guest."

He shrugged and gave a sheepish grin. "You've all been so kind to me on this visit. It's my way of saying thanks for making me feel welcome."

Charlie clapped him on the back. "You *are* welcome, bud. On New Year's Eve, you're marrying my little sister. You're one of us now."

"Yeah," Peter seconded. "Thanks a bunch, and merry Christmas."

As the family rushed ahead through the glass-paned double doors, Helen grabbed Rusty's elbow and gave it a squeeze. "You told me you went for a walk," she murmured in mock accusation.

His eyes widened. "I *did* take a walk. I walked right over here and had a little conversation with Gloria Farnham."

They all trooped into the theater and found their seats just as the music swelled and the opening credits began to roll. When the name *Helen Corrigan* flickered across the screen, Row E erupted into cheers and whistles.

Several minutes into the picture, when she made her first appearance in the horse-stable scene, more excited twittering arose from the audience. The imposing figure of Simon Jarrow, playing the role of the father, strode onto the screen. To Helen's relief, his breeches looked a lot less ridiculous in black-and-white than they had in reality. As Rusty had promised.

Helen reached across the armrest and sought out Rusty's hand in the darkness. His strong fingers closed around hers.

"What say you, daughter?" thundered her on-screen father.

Seated in the Orpheum, where all her dreams had taken shape, surrounded by her family and Rusty, Helen's eyes filled with unexpected tears.

"Oh, Father, this moment could not be more perfect," she murmured in tandem with her counterpart on the screen. "I don't think I've ever been so happy."

The End

AUTHOR'S NOTE

On childhood Saturday mornings, while other kids were watching Scooby-Doo on TV, I liked to tune in to a local station that broadcast classic black-and-white films from Hollywood's "golden era." To me there was something magnetic about those movies. Shirley Temple and her dimples and tap shoes. Mickey Rooney and Judy Garland and their solution to every problem, "Let's put on a show!" Fred Astaire and Ginger Rodgers cutting a rug with a certain style and grace. The old Hollywood movies seemed a world apart, a sort of escape from reality, a different planet from the real world.

The escapist quality of these movies was there by design. In the depths of the Great Depression, a nickel spent at the movies was a cheap way to forget one's troubles and lift one's spirits, at least for an afternoon. And the strict standards of the Hays Code kept things comparatively clean and wholesome on the silver screen.

Off screen, of course, was a different story. Then as now, Hollywood rewarded bad behavior, even as the studio system sought to maintain stars' public images. Today, with both the studio system and the Hays Code a distant memory, bad behavior is celebrated both onscreen and off.

Call me a dreamer, but it doesn't have to be this way. I believe film is a neutral medium, like books and song lyrics, that can be used for evil or for good. "The good person out of the good treasure of his heart produces good, and the evil person out of his evil treasure produces evil, for out of the abundance of the heart his mouth speaks." (Luke 6:45). Back in the Golden Age of

Hollywood, stars like Jimmy Stewart and Loretta Young sought to create movies with a Christian message. My hat goes off to those men and women of faith who continue the struggle to uphold God-honoring values in hostile territory.

In *Wrap Your Troubles in Dreams*, the majority of characters and situations are entirely fictional, products of my imagination, with one exception. Henrietta Mears was a real-life person, a former public school teacher who became a highly respected Bible teacher, evangelist, author, and founder of Gospel Light Publications and the Forest Home Conference Center. Although in the story Helen's encounter with Miss Mears is brief, the results of their conversation illustrate the Bible teacher's heart for addressing the spiritual needs of young adults.

IN GRATITUDE

To God be the glory.

I offer my deepest thanks to:

Pegg Thomas, storytelling ninja. What would I do without you?

Anita Aurit, Melissa Bilyeu, Cassandra Cridland, Terese Luikens, and Grace Robinson, cherished writer friends and all-around smart cookies;

Linda Nelson and Diedre Osman, first readers, who navigated the almost-but-not-quite-a-book stage with style and grace;

My late parents, Donald and Patricia Lamont, who knew I had a writer inside me, and told me so.

And especially my husband, Thomas Leo. You are my sunshine.

And thanks to you, dear reader, for taking a chance on my book. Please visit my website at http://jenniferlamontleo.com to sign up for my newsletter or drop me a line. I'd love to hear from you.

MOONDROP MIRACLE

WINDY CITY HEARTS - BOOK ONE

If you enjoyed the Corrigan Sisters series, you'll also love Windy City Hearts, stories of courageous women surviving and thriving through tough times. Here's a sample of the first book, *Moondrop Miracle*. Enjoy!

MOONDROP MIRACLE, CHAPTER ONE

S leet slashed against the tall damask-draped windows of the Gold Coast apartment, casting gloomy shadows over Constance Sutherland's face as she sat at her dressing table. Already she regretted her decision to speak at the Young Entrepreneurs of Tomorrow banquet. The miserable evening would be much better spent in the coziness of her own firelit library than shivering in some drafty banquet hall. Now, making matters worse was a notice in the newspaper that a local TV station would be featuring, on this very evening, a retrospective of the films of the late Gilda Miller, Connie's favorite actress. She'd have to miss it. *Hell's bells.*

When her dear friend Sonja Atwater had called and asked Constance to speak, whatever had possessed her to say yes? What nugget of wisdom could she possibly offer these vibrant young women about to sail forth with their freshly minted degrees, ready to conquer the world? The very vitality of today's young women made Constance feel old and well past her prime.

Or perhaps it was just the incessant rain that was making her feel like a bowl of yesterday's oatmeal. The pounding of it against the windows carried her mind back to a similar storm, nearly seventy years earlier, on a dark Tuesday that had changed her life forever.

She turned away from the window. Mustn't dwell on the past. Mustn't let her mind slip away. Mustn't give in.

In any case, she'd given her word. And even though one would hardly blame an octogenarian for declining to go out on such a blustery evening, Constance was not one to shirk a commitment.

With a sigh, she lifted her tortoiseshell comb as if it were a weapon and gave a few firm strokes to her silvery hair, still shiny and falling into the soft chin-length waves that had been her signature style for years.

A gentle rap sounded at the door, and the housemaid carried a tray into the bedroom and set it on the dressing table. "I thought you might appreciate a hot cup of tea, ma'am, before you head out."

"Thank you, Elsa. That's very thoughtful."

"Are you sure you ought to go?" Elsa frowned at the dripping windows. "Looks right nasty out there."

"Of course I'll go," Constance said with a note of mild disapproval, as if she hadn't just been entertaining those exact thoughts herself.

"You look lovely. I remember how much your husband liked you to wear blue."

"Yes, he did." A bittersweet pang tweaked Constance's heart. She handed Elsa the newspaper. "If you're staying in, you might want to catch this Gilda Miller film festival on television. I'm sick about missing it."

Elsa took the paper and glanced at it. "You don't have to miss it. Just record it to watch later. That's why your son gave you that VCR last Christmas."

Constance waved her hand impatiently. "I can't ever get that darned gizmo to work right. Too many buttons."

"Don't worry. I'll set it up for you," Elsa promised. "You can watch it later when you get home, or tomorrow. I know how much you liked Gilda Miller."

"Thank you." As Connie took a grateful sip of the steaming tea, a buzzer sounded from the front hall. The cup clinked as she set it in the saucer.

"That will be the doorman to tell us the car is here. Please call down and have him signal the driver I'll be ready momentarily." Under her breath she added, "I do hope the Young Entrepreneurs haven't sent along a chatterbox this time."

"Yes, ma'am."

After Elsa left the room, Constance took another sip of tea, checked her evening bag for the index cards on which she'd jotted some notes for her speech, and glanced once more at the mirror. At eighty-one, she was still blessed with the graceful, almost regal bearing of her youth. Above a long pale blue silk shantung skirt, her silver-and-blue beaded top shimmered in the lamplight and nicely complemented her coloring.

Before leaving the bedroom, she applied one final swipe of lipstick and slipped the tube into her bag.

"Remember to sparkle, old girl," she told her reflection and smiled in spite of herself.

Within moments of pulling away from the curb, it became apparent that the Young Entrepreneurs had indeed sent a chatterbox.

"Oh, Mrs. Sutherland, I can't even tell you what an honor it is to meet you in person." The red-haired, alabaster-skinned driver blurted the words as she weaved the Volvo in and out of city traffic on rain-slick streets.

Constance clung to the armrest and tried not to flinch visibly as the side-view mirror of a cab passed within a hair's breadth of her window.

"When Mrs. Atwater asked for a volunteer to pick you up for the dinner, I begged and begged and begged to be chosen."

"How kind," Constance said, wishing she'd do a little less begging and a little more steering.

"I can't wait to hear what you have to say. Why, you're simply a legend."

What should have been a fifteen-minute drive took no more than ten, thanks to the woman behind the wheel, who drove as fast as she talked. Constance could hardly keep up with the woman's plans to start some sort of a computer technology business. Fortunately, the girl accepted her noncommittal responses without question, hardly stopping to breathe. The car lurched to a stop at the curb in front of the elegant Palmer House Hotel. The legend emerged shakily and gratefully accepted the capable arm of a uniformed doorman, who escorted her into the lobby while the driver handed the keys to a parking valet. In the light and warmth of the gilded lobby, she regained her bearings, glad to be back on *terra firma*.

"This way, Mrs. Sutherland." The redhead caught up to her and gestured toward an escalator rising to a crimson-carpeted mezzanine. Together they rode the escalator, Constance stepping careful to keep the hem of her long skirt from catching in the machine's gnashing teeth. It would never do to fall and break a hip in front of all these people.

The mezzanine was crowded with women milling around outside the ballroom. Some of them gathered in small whispering clumps, sliding glances her way, and she looked down at her outfit to make sure nothing was askew. Several ladies murmured greetings as she passed. Some of their faces looked familiar, but her escort hustled her along before she could place any of them.

"They're waiting for us."

Constance halted. "Miss—MacDonald, did you say? Before we go in, I'd like to stop and powder my nose."

"Oh, um, sure. The restroom is right down that hallway." The girl hesitated. "Do you want me to go with you?"

"I'm not *that* elderly, dear." Constance added a smile to soften the words and headed toward the ladies' lounge.

Satisfied that her appearance was in order, she let Miss Mac-Donald guide her through the ballroom to the speakers' table. In the low light of the room, she made out her place card. She'd only been seated a moment when a shrill voice pierced through the dusky gloom.

"Connie, darling! I'm so glad you've come, and on this beastly night, too."

"Sonja." Constance's heart lightened at the sound of a familiar voice. An elegantly dressed woman not much younger than herself, but apparently a good deal more spry, slid into the empty chair next to her and the friends embraced. "Thank you for inviting me, although, truth be told, I don't know what I have to say to these young women that they haven't heard a thousand times before."

"You're too modest." Sonja grasped Constance's hand and squeezed it. "Why, the girls insisted I invite you. You're a legend in your own time."

There was that word again. *Legend.*

Introductions were made around the table. The other speakers for the evening, both decades younger than herself, included a prominent neurosurgeon who'd founded a medical technology company and a banking executive whose name Constance had seen on the business pages of the *Tribune*. Four bright-eyed members of the Young Entrepreneurs' board, including Miss Mac-Donald, filled out the table of eight.

Over shrimp cocktail and French onion soup, Constance and Sonja got caught up. Sonja explained her mentoring role with the Young Entrepreneurs of Tomorrow, a position she'd taken on after retiring as professor *emeritus* at a local university.

"Goodness, you're as busy in retirement as you ever were," Constance remarked.

"Oh, I love working with the young women." Sonja's eyes sparkled. "They have the whole future ahead of them. Kind of makes me feel young again. And what about you? I'm *dying* to hear about the new Pearlcon facility that just opened in Hong Kong."

Connie started to explain, but just as the entrée was served, Sonja was called away to look after some detail of the production. Connie turned her attention to the conversation elsewhere at the table, which had turned to higher education.

"More women should be encouraged to major in STEM fields," the banker said.

"STEM?" Constance tested the unfamiliar acronym on her tongue.

"Science, Technology, Engineering, and Math," the neurosurgeon explained. "It's a new acronym gaining traction in the universities. Too many women today are opting for the liberal arts, taking the easy way out. How can we ever make headway in a man's world if we don't tackle the same hard subjects they do?"

"Women are trapping themselves in a pink-collar ghetto," the banker asserted. "This alarming situation needs to change. What do you think, Ms. Sutherland? It is Ms. Sutherland, isn't it?"

"*Mrs.* Yes, that's the name I use professionally." It was simpler that way.

"Well, what do you think? Do you agree that women are trapping themselves in a pink-collar ghetto?"

"*Ghetto* seems a strong word, don't you think?" Constance said. "Not all women are cut out for science and math. Not everyone wants to compete toe-to-toe with men."

"Women who shirk doing a man's work are letting down the sisterhood," the neurosurgeon declared. "Of course, you made your fortune in a pink-collar field," she added with a nod toward

Constance. "But times have changed. STEM is the wave of the future."

Feeling a bit pounced upon, Constance straightened and addressed the woman directly. "While it's true that few fields are more 'pink-collar' than the cosmetics industry, there are of course a great many women scientists working in Pearlcon laboratories around the world. We wouldn't have much of a company without them, would we?" She dabbed her lips with a white linen napkin, taking a moment to plan her next words. "Many women can and do excel in science and math. But a woman shouldn't feel she has to become like a man to achieve success."

"We don't need to become *like* them. We need to become *better* than them," said the banker with what sounded like a sneer.

"What field did you take your degree in, Mrs. Sutherland?" asked the neurosurgeon.

"Oh, I never went to college," Constance said. "After high school, I attended a year of finishing school. Then I married and had a child. I didn't start my career until later."

"Finishing school?" The neurosurgeon could not have looked more astonished if Constance had claimed Stateville Prison as her alma mater. The doctor and the banker exchanged a glance, clearly wondering why such an undereducated woman was speaking at an event aimed at soon-to-be college graduates. Constance wondered herself. "It's a wonder your business succeeded as it has," the neurosurgeon concluded.

"I didn't know it would succeed at the time. All I knew was that I had to do it. And eventually, I became most interested in offering women opportunities that didn't seem to exist anywhere else."

All at once, the face of an old classmate flitted across Constance's memory. *Julia Harper. That's who these women remind me of. Good old Julia with her no-nonsense leather brogues, mannish hats, and leaflets proclaiming the rights of women and whatnot.* The memory amused Constance so much, she almost missed what the banker was saying. A few minutes later, she wished that she had.

"Thank goodness times have changed," the banker said. "Maybe foregoing a proper education was acceptable back then, but it certainly isn't a viable option these days. After all, very few people have a rich daddy to bankroll their business. Most of the young people here tonight are not women of privilege, such as yourself."

The woman had hurled the word "privilege" as if it were an accusation. *Rich daddy, indeed.* Heat rose in Constance's chest and spread to her face. Why were these rude women attacking her? Where was Sonja? Whatever was keeping her? Constance felt her sparkle melting faster than the ice cream served for dessert. It took everything she had not to snap back some witty barb and put the women in their place. In her mind she heard Aunt Pearl's voice say, *Don't stoop to their level, Connie. A gentle answer turns away wrath.* So she said simply,

"Apparently, you haven't heard my story. Perhaps my speech will fill in some of the gaps for you. I suggest you listen carefully."

Before her tablemates could respond, the lights dimmed. Sonja stepped behind the podium and introduced the neurosurgeon as the first speaker.

The room grew warm. Constance slipped out of her wrap and folded it over the back of her chair. It was too dark to read the index cards in her bag, so mentally she reviewed her speech, noting portions she could skip if the hour grew late but reminding herself of the one point she absolutely had to make to these impressionable young females.

For heaven's sake, be glad that God made you a woman.

As the neurosurgeon droned on about entrepreneurial opportunities around today's highly specialized wellness environments—apparently no one called them "hospitals" anymore—Constance let her mind drift back to her own youth.

She had not cared about college. At twenty-one, she'd had no greater purpose in mind than marrying Winston Sutherland III and having fun. Lots and lots of fun. Aunt Pearl had been the one who had longed to go to college—and been denied the opportunity.

But God had other plans for both of them.

Like it so far? Keep reading! Pick up your copy of Moondrop Miracle today.

WHAT'S THE BUZZ?

R eviews are pure gold to an author! If you enjoyed this book and want to help spread the word, post reviews on book-oriented websites like Amazon, Goodreads, and BookBub. Reviews can be short or as long as you like. And please talk about the book, in person and on social media. Word-of-mouth is still the best way to promote just about anything!

Let's stay in touch. Please stop by and say hello.

JenniferLamontLeo.com (Join my Reader Community for book news, exclusive content, and more)
Facebook
Goodreads
BookBub
Amazon
A Sparkling Vintage Life (My podcast! Listen online at JenniferLamontLeo.com or subscribe in your favorite podcast app)

9 781737 874164